"Would you b‥ moved here I ‥ anyone?"

Probably… Maybe…

No, not really. "It seems as if you've had a lot of opportunity."

His grin made her cringe. She was sounding jealous again. Because she *was*, darn it. It was totally irrational, not to mention impossible to control.

"I did have a lot of opportunity, and a lot of offers." His eyes locked on hers. "I wasn't interested."

Was he implying what she thought he was implying? She hadn't planned to respond, but without her permission her lips formed the question. "Why?"

"You know why."

He moved closer, looking like a tiger on the prowl, his eyes shining with male heat. If this were the wild, he would take her in an instant. And because it was the wild, she would be helpless to stop him.

He looked like he was going to kiss her, and she wanted him to.

* * *

The Doctor's Baby Dare

i‥

THE DOCTOR'S BABY DARE

BY
MICHELLE CELMER

MILLS & BOON

First Published in Great Britain 2016
By Mills & Boon, an imprint of HarperCollins*Publishers*
1 London Bridge Street, London, SE1 9GF

© 2016 Harlequin Books S.A.

Special thanks and acknowledgement are given to Michelle Celmer for her contribution to the Texas Cattleman's Club: Lies and Lullabies series.

ISBN: 978-0-263-91848-9

51-0216

Our policy is to use papers that are natural, renewable and recyclable products and made from wood grown in sustainable forests.The logging and manufacturing processes conform to the legal environmental regulations of the country of origin.

Printed and bound in Spain
by CPI, Barcelona

Michelle Celmer is a bestselling author of more than thirty books. When she's not writing, she likes to spend time with her family and their menagerie of animals.

Michelle loves to hear from readers. Like her on Facebook or write her at PO Box 300, Clawson, MI 48017, USA.

One

Dr. Parker Reese considered himself an all-around great guy.

He was affable and easygoing and had a great sense of humor. He was also honest and respectful and always willing to lend a hand. He was a rock in a crisis and a natural born leader. And despite the fact that he'd lived in Texas for only three months and knew nothing about cows, he had just been accepted into the prestigious Texas Cattleman's Club. And they didn't let just anybody in.

Parker was one of those rare individuals who got along with everyone. Everyone who knew him liked and respected him.

Well, almost everyone.

Parker glanced across the hospital cafeteria to the table where the object of his recent fascination sat eating her lunch, phone in hand, earbuds in place to deflect any unwanted attention. Head nurse of the new pediatric ward at Royal Memorial Hospital, Clare Connelly was smart and competent, by far one of the best nurses he'd ever worked with. She ran a tight ship on her ward, and was highly regarded by her coworkers.

And for reasons that escaped Parker, she refused to like him.

Lucas Wakefield, chief of surgery and fellow Texas Cattleman's Club member, set his tray down on the table and dropped into the seat across from Parker. "Mind if I join you?"

Parker grinned. "I think you just did."

If it wasn't for Luc, Parker wouldn't even be in Texas. The two had met at a conference when they were both medical students. At the time, Parker had been working toward a career in cosmetic plastic surgery for the rich and famous, the only medical field his father considered lucrative enough for a tycoon's son, and one that Parker knew would never elicit any real sense of pride. As was often the case, his father's own selfish demands and archaic values trumped Parker's happiness.

Luc had told him to screw the old man and convinced Parker to follow his true passion. Pediatrics. And for the first time in his life Parker stood up to his father. There had been a fair amount of shouting, and threats to cut Parker off financially. His father had even threatened to disown him, but Parker told him that was a chance he was willing to take. His father finally, though reluctantly, conceded. That put an end to the threats and manipulations his father had always used to control him, and for the first time in his life, Parker felt truly independent. But the event had caused a fissure in their relationship, one that took many years to heal. Even so, by the time his father had passed away last year, they'd managed to resolve most of their differences.

After a lifetime of coveting his father's approval, he'd earned it. And now, with his inheritance, Parker had the means to do anything he wanted, wherever he wanted. He knew that he needed a change, that the only reason he'd stayed in New York was to be near his ailing father. Aside from his practice, and a few good friends, there was nothing tying him there. He knew it was time to move on. But where?

Enter Luc. He'd called out of the blue to offer Parker a job in the town of Royal, Texas. Dr. Mann, Royal Hospital's neonatal specialist, was retiring and they were looking for a replacement. The salary wasn't all that impressive, but Parker's inheritance left him set for life. So he sold his practice and relocated to Texas.

Best move he ever made.

"So, did you ever call that girl you met in the gift shop?" Luc asked, dumping a packet of sugar in his coffee.

"We had dinner," Parker told him.

"And..."

"Then I took her home."

"Your home or hers?"

"Hers."

"Did she invite you in?"

They always did. And he didn't doubt that the next stop would have been her bedroom, and a couple of months ago he wouldn't have hesitated. But something about it, about all of his romantic relationships lately, felt hollow. "She invited, I declined."

Luc made a noise like he'd been punched in the gut.

"Dude, you're killing me. I'm married and I'm having more sex than you are."

At thirty-eight, the ever-widening age span between Parker and the twentysomethings he'd been dating was losing its luster. What he was looking for now was an equal. Someone to challenge him. He glanced over at Clare again. Someone capable of stimulating his intelligence as well as his libido.

Luc followed Parker's line of sight and rolled his eyes. "Dude, let it go already. How many times have you asked her out?"

Parker shrugged. He'd honestly lost track. A couple dozen at least. At first her rejection was firm, but polite—for the most part. Not so much anymore. Lately he could feel the tension when they were forced to work together. Which was often. But that was okay. It would just be that much more satisfying when she gave into him. And she would. They always did.

"What do you think it is about me that she finds so offensive?" he asked Luc.

"Could it be your inability to accept *no* as an answer?"

Parker shot him a look. "She wants me. I guarantee it."

He glanced over at her again. Her eyes were lowered, but she knew he was looking. He wasn't sure how he knew, he just did. He could feel her from across the cafeteria. In her early thirties, she was nearly a decade older than the women he typically dated, but he liked that.

"You really can't stand it can you?" Luc said and Parker turned to him.

"Can't stand what?"

"That she won't bend to your will."

It would irritate him a lot more if he didn't know that it was temporary. But yes, he was used to women falling at his feet. And honestly, it wasn't as great as it sounded. "Clare will change her mind. I just have to catch her at the right time."

"When the chloroform kicks in?"

Parker laughed in spite of himself and said, "Let me tell you a story. When I was a kid, there was a girl at my school named Ruth Flanigan. And for reasons unknown to me, Ruth relentlessly picked on me."

"You were bullied by a girl?" Luc laughed. "Is that some sort of ass-backward karma?"

"It's funny now, but at the time it was traumatic. She would shove me in the lunch line or kick my shins on the playground. She pulled my hair and knocked me off the swings. For years I was afraid of girls."

"Clearly you got over that."

Had he? Sometimes he wondered. When it came to relationships, he was always the one calling the shots, the one in control. He only dated women who were substantially younger and intellectually inferior. That had to mean something.

"So, what happened?" Luc asked him.

"At some point in the second grade she either moved or switched to a different school. I don't remember exactly. I just remember coming back to school in the fall, and being relieved that she was no longer there. I didn't have any contact with her again until college. I was home for the holidays and I ran into her at the party of a mutual friend."

"Did she kick your shins?"

"No. She confessed that she'd had a huge crush on me, and torturing me was just her way of showing it."

"Don't tell me you're going to kick Clare in the shins and pull her hair."

"Of course not." Though he was sure the hair-pulling part would come later, if she was into that sort of thing. "My point is, just because someone acts as if they don't like you, it doesn't mean it's true."

"Are you seriously suggesting that Clare is only *pretending* not to like you?"

Parker shrugged. "It's not impossible."

"You clearly have your pick of female companions. Why this infatuation with Clare?"

Because she fascinated him, and not just because she was the only woman he'd ever met who was seemingly immune to his charms. Weird as it sounded, he just felt drawn to her. He wanted to crack her open, peek inside and see what made her tick. Metaphorically speaking of course.

Clare had been on the hospital staff for almost a decade, but Parker had yet to find a single person who knew her on a deeply personal level. Which he thought was weird. He spent far more time with his coworkers than anyone. He liked to think of them as extended family. But then, he had always been a very social person. Clare was not. She always sat alone in the cafeteria, and kept to herself on the ward. He'd heard that she had never been married or had kids, and had lived with her old-maid aunt since college. But like the librarian who wore sexy lingerie under a conservative and drab suit, Clare had layers, and boy would he love to be the one to peel them back. He was sure he would find sexy underthings in there somewhere. He was betting that if she wanted to, Clare could teach him a thing or two about having fun.

"I'd just like to get to know her."

"I've never known you to fixate on a woman this

way," Luc said. "I have to say it's a little disconcerting. It's like you're obsessed."

He had no explanation for why he felt such a deep connection to Clare. In the past he'd avoided deep connections like the plague. Why this time did it feel so…natural?

He knew her work routine like the back of his hand. Knew exactly when she started her rounds, when she ate her lunch, when she worked on charts. He knew her smile, and the melody of her voice, though when she used it to address him it was always filled with irritation. But he was getting close, he could feel it.

Okay, maybe he was a *little* obsessed.

"Even if you're right," Luc said, "and she doesn't hate you as much as she lets on, everyone knows that Clare doesn't date coworkers."

"There's a first time for everything," Parker told him. "And I never say never."

"I think that's your biggest problem."

Luc could poke fun all he wanted—Parker was confident he would wear her down. "I give it a month, probably less."

With a sly grin that said he was up to something, Luc asked, "Are you willing to bet on that?"

"You'll lose," Parker told him.

"If you're so sure, put your money where your mouth is."

It wouldn't be the first time they had entered into a friendly wager. "The usual amount?"

"You've got a deal," Luc said and they fist-bumped on it.

Parker's phone rumbled and he pulled it from the pocket of his lab coat. It was Vanessa, a nursing assistant from the NICU.

"I'm sorry to bother you, Doctor, but we need you up here. Janey's vitals are erratic again."

He cursed under his breath. Born premature and abandoned on the floor of a truck stop, Baby Janey Doe had been brought into Emergency last month and had instantly captured the heart of everyone on the ward. And though she was getting the best medical care available, her little body just wasn't ready to heal.

"Be right there," he told her, then rose, telling Luc, "Gotta go."

"Janey?" Luc asked, and when Parker nodded Luc shook his head grimly. "No improvement?"

"It doesn't make sense," he said, gathering up what was left of his lunch. "I've run every test I could think of, scoured the internet and medical journals for similar cases, but nothing fits. I'm at a loss. In the meantime her little body is shutting down. I'm worried we might lose her."

"It sucks, but you can't save them all."

He knew that, and he'd lost patients before. "Maybe I can't save them all," he told Luc, "but I'll never stop trying."

Clare Connelly sat in the hospital cafeteria, headphones in, wishing this day would hurry up and be over. This morning when she'd gotten into her car, it had stalled several times before she finally got it running. Then it had stalled again at a red light when she was halfway there, and she'd wound up with a line of angry drivers behind her. As she'd pulled into the hospital lot the skies had opened up and dumped a deluge of rain on her as she walked to the building.

Yesterday had been their monthly family dinner at

her parents' horse farm an hour away, and though she had warned them that she might have to work, apparently Clare's absence had caused a stir again. Her phone had been blowing up all morning with calls from her seven siblings. When her brothers or sisters missed dinner no one freaked out. Of course, they all saw each other on a regular basis.

Her three brothers and two of her sisters worked on the farm, and her other two sisters were stay-at-home mothers with four children each. In total Clare had twenty-two nieces and nephews ranging in age from newborn to twenty-six. It seemed as if every time she turned around one of her siblings was expecting another child, and her oldest niece and nephew were both newly married with first children on the way. An entirely new generation to remind Clare how much of a black sheep she really was.

Being single and childless in such a traditional family made her a target for well-meaning and sometimes not-so-well-meaning relatives. No one could grasp the concept that she actually enjoyed being single, and that she wasn't deliberately going against the grain. She was just trying to be happy on her own terms. Refusing to join the family business after high school had sent relations into a tizzy; they'd tagged her as the rebel. If they had bothered to pay attention they would have known she had always dreamed of being a nurse. But from the day she graduated from nursing school they had teased her relentlessly, saying that she'd only entered the profession to snag a rich doctor and live in a mansion.

Her gaze automatically sought out her new boss.

An attractive, smooth-talking multimillionaire well-known for his philanthropy, Parker was every woman's dream. With his *GQ* model physique, rich brown hair always in need of a trim and eyes that looked green one minute and brown the next, he was way above average on the looks scale. Way, *way* above. At the sight of him on his first day at the hospital, her female staff had been reduced to giggling, blushing, hormonally driven adolescent girls.

He was hands down one of the finest physicians she'd ever worked for. He was trustworthy, honest, reliable, and she had never once seen him in a foul mood. He was as charming as he was funny, and his often rumpled, shabby-chic appearance only added to his appeal. And despite being an East Coaster, he had exceptionally good manners. But most important, his rapport with children made him an outstanding pediatrician.

He was also a shameless, womanizing serial dater. Or so she had heard. One who had apparently set his sights on her.

As if.

She'd learned the hard way that emotional entanglements with a coworker, especially one in a position of power, were a prescription for disaster. It was how her no-dating-coworkers rule had come to be. And though she'd made every effort possible to ignore him, he made that nearly impossible with his relentless teasing and barely veiled innuendo. All of that unwanted attention had resulted in a mild crush.

Mild crush? She nearly laughed out loud at the understatement. She could fool her family and her coworkers, but she couldn't fool her own heart. And though she would die before admitting it to another human being, she wanted him. Badly.

Getting that first guilty glimpse of him every morning, with his slightly rumpled hair and lopsided tie, was by far the highlight of her day. She would imagine brushing back that single soft curl that fell across his forehead and straightening that tie and then she would push herself up on her toes…

And that was where it always ended because if she let herself go any further, she would forget all of the reasons she needed to keep him at arm's length. But even if he wasn't her boss, he was off-limits. If her family got wind that she was dating a doctor, especially a rich one, they would never let her live it down.

She just wished he would stop *watching* her. He had her so tied in knots she could barely eat her lunch. She supposed that was one of the advantages of a crush, or lust, or whatever this thing was. Inevitable weight loss. Since Dr. Reese had moved there, Clare had dropped a total of eighteen pounds. She hadn't been this skinny since her first year of college. She felt so good without the extra weight that she'd begun jogging again. Though she did realize she would have never put on those eighteen pounds in the first place if she hadn't gotten lax with her exercise regimen. Then again, she'd had no one to look good naked for. Nor the time or even the desire to go out and find someone.

In her peripheral vision she saw Dr. Reese rise from the table where he'd been sitting with Dr. Wakefield, and her stomach did a flip-flop. He would have to walk past her to leave the cafeteria. Keeping her eyes on her phone, she watched in her peripheral vision as Parker neared her table, and when he walked past she could feel the air shift.

Would he stop and give her a hard time? He was always making excuses to talk to her about things that weren't work related. Probably because he knew it annoyed her. That's what she wanted him to think anyway.

Parker must have been in a hurry because he didn't stop this time. She should have been relieved, so why the feeling of disappointment? She couldn't go on this way, harboring an irrational lust for a man who was completely wrong for her, walking around in a state of constant confusion.

Her phone rang and she answered, instantly back in work mode when Vanessa, one of her nurses, told her Janey's vitals were no longer stable and getting worse by the minute.

Clare jumped up, leaving her tray on the table and shoving her phone in her cardigan pocket as she headed for the closest elevator. Since she'd been discovered in the truck stop, just minutes after her birth and barely clinging to life, Janey's condition had been touch and go. Being in the medical field, Clare had been trained to put her personal feelings aside and remain objective, but Janey was like no other patient she'd ever had. She had no one, and despite efforts to find her family, or anyone who may have known who her family was, the police had come up empty, so Janey had become a ward of the state. Clare couldn't imagine being so helpless and alone, nor could she understand how a woman could abandon her child that way. Though she had no children of her own, or plans to have a baby anytime soon, Clare could see how fiercely protective her sisters were of their children. What could have happened to Janey's mom to make her think that her baby would be better off without her? Or maybe she hadn't been given a choice.

The idea gave Clare a cold chill.

She rounded the corner to see the elevator doors sliding closed and broke into a run, calling, "Hold the elevator!"

A hand emerged to stop the door, a hand that she realized, as she slipped inside, was attached to the very person she was trying to avoid. And now she was the last place she wanted to be.

Stuck alone with him.

He hit the button for the fourth floor, wearing a look that made her knees weak, and as the doors slid shut said, "Hey there, sunshine."

Two

Clare shot Parker one of those looks. This one seemed to say, *Seriously, did you really just call me that?*

But a month ago she would have completely ignored him, so that was progress. Right?

"They called you about Janey?" he asked her.

"Erratic vitals," Clare said, her concern for the infant clear on her face. Janey had made an emotional impact on everyone in the NICU, but Clare seemed more attached to her than anyone. He couldn't deny that Janey's case had tested his objectivity from the minute she was admitted to the hospital, barely clinging to life. And now, with treatment options diminishing, he was feeling the pressure.

There had to be something he was missing…

"She's not getting better," Clare said as if she were reading his mind.

"No," he agreed. "She isn't."

A code blue was called over the PA for the fourth floor. Parker looked at Clare, and she looked at him, and they cursed in unison. Their fragile patient had gone from unstable to arrest.

Knowing it wouldn't do a bit of good, he stabbed the button for the fourth floor again. Janey could be dying and the two people responsible for her care were stuck on a damned elevator.

"If this thing moves any slower I'll have to get out and push," he told Clare.

It felt like an eternity before the elevator dinged for their floor. They stood side by side, like sprinters at the starting line. The instant the doors slid open they broke into a run. By the time he reached her, Janey was in full cardiac arrest. Nurses stood around watching anxiously as a pediatrics resident performed manual CPR on her pale and limp little body. The sight of it was so heartbreaking Parker had to dig down extra deep for the focus to perform his duties.

"Let me through," he barked, and a group of startled staff instantly cleared the way. He never raised his voice to his team, or anyone for that matter, but this was bad.

"She's not responding," the resident said as Parker took over the heart compressions.

"Call her cardiologist," he barked to no one in particular, knowing someone would do it.

He tried to find a pulse, and couldn't. "Come on, little one. Fight for me."

He continued the compressions to no avail.

Damn it, he had hoped it wouldn't come to this. "Paddles," he said, turning to his left where Clare always stood, surprised to find a different nurse there.

He glanced around and found Clare standing *way* over by the door. Her face looked pale and her eyes wide, and for an instant he was sure she was about to either be sick or lose consciousness. Unfortunately he had a sick infant who took priority.

Even using the paddles it took almost thirty minutes to get Janey stable, and afterward everyone breathed a huge sigh of relief, including him. She was okay for now, but that had been a really close call. He turned to find Clare, who he had assumed wouldn't leave Janey's side for the reminder of her shift, but she was gone.

He texted her, checking the hallway as he waited for an answer, but after several minutes the message was still tagged as unread. Clare always read and answered her messages.

He frowned. Something was definitely up.

Assuming she'd gone back to the nurses' station, he headed that way. "Have you seen Nurse Connelly?" he asked Rebecca, the nursing assistant sitting there.

"She walked by a second ago." She looked up at him through a veil of what he was sure were fake lashes. "So, I was thinking we could get together again this weekend."

Oh, no, that was not a good idea. He liked Rebecca, but she was a party girl and these days he could barely stay awake past eleven thirty. His father used to tell him, *You're only as old as you feel.* After a night of partying with Rebecca and her friends, he felt about eighty. She was fun and sexy, but the inevitable hangover wasn't worth it. He could no longer stay out till 3:00 a.m. then make it to work by seven and still function. He was pushing forty. His party days were over.

He checked his phone but still no text.

"Did you see where Nurse Connelly went?" he asked Rebecca, ignoring her suggestion completely, which she didn't seem to like very much.

"Sorry, no," she said tartly.

He doubted he would be getting any more help from her. Ironically, this very situation was probably why Clare didn't date people from work. A lesson he clearly hadn't learned yet.

So, where the hell had she disappeared to? Did she go back down to the cafeteria? Had she slipped past Rebecca and gone to the elevator? No, he thought with a shake of his head. Knowing Clare, she wouldn't want anyone to see her lose her cool, so where would she go for guaranteed privacy? At the end of this hall there was a family waiting room—the last place she would go—and the door to the stairs…

Of course! That had to be it. He'd taken a breather or two in the stairwell himself. Or used it to sneak a kiss with a pretty young nurse. She had to be there.

He found Clare sitting on a step halfway between the fourth and fifth floor, arms roped around her legs, head on her knees so her face was hidden.

"Here to harass me in my moment of weakness?" she asked without looking up.

"How did you know it was me?"

"Because that's the kind of day I've been having." She lifted her head, sniffling and wiping tears from her cheeks with the heel of her palms.

Tears?

Clare was *crying*?

Just when he thought she couldn't be more interesting, or perplexing, she threw him a curveball.

"And I know how your shoes sound," she added. "From hearing you walk up and down the halls."

He would be flattered that she paid attention, but she paid attention to everything on the ward.

"Are you all right?" He offered her one of the tissues he kept in his lab coat pocket. He dealt with parents of sick children on a daily basis. Tissues were a part of the uniform.

She took it and wiped her nose. "I'm okay. Just really embarrassed. I don't know what happened in there."

"You choked," he said, knowing Clare would want an honest answer. "It happens to the best of us."

She lifted her chin stubbornly. "Not to me it doesn't."

If she had been standing, and was a foot taller, he was sure she would be looking down her nose at him. "At the risk of sounding like a tool, all evidence is to the contrary, cupcake."

Outraged, she opened her mouth, probably to say something mean, or respond to the *cupcake* remark, then something inside her seemed to give. Her face went slack and her body sort of sank in on itself. She dropped her head to her knees again, groaning, "You're right."

He was? She really *must* have been out of sorts because she never thought he was right about anything.

"Are you okay?" he asked.

"You know those days when you feel like you could take on the world? When everything goes exactly the way you want it to?"

"Sure."

She looked up at him with red-rimmed, bloodshot eyes. "This is not one of those days."

He cringed. "That bad, huh?"

She dropped her head back down to her knees. "Choking on the job is just the icing on the cake."

Clearly. "So you really never choked?"

She shook her head, making her messy bun flop from side to side, and said, "Not even in nursing school."

He took a chance and sat down beside her. She didn't snarl or hiss, or unsheathe her talons, so that was good. "Is there anything I can do?"

"Shoot me and put me out of my misery."

"I think you're being a little hard on yourself," he told her. He had heard of surgeons who choked during surgery and never got their confidence back, but this was different. This wasn't a matter of confidence, this was pure human emotion.

"What if it happens again, when she *needs* me?" Clare said, looking up at him. She had the prettiest eyes, and she smelled amazing. It would barely take anything to lean in and kiss her. Her lips looked plump and delicious. It might even be worth the concussion afterward, when Clare clocked him.

"If there hadn't been fifteen other people in the room to compensate, if it had been just you and me, or even just you, I have no doubt that you would have performed admirably," he said.

"It's getting more difficult to be objective with her," Clare said, looking genuinely distraught. "When they called the code I thought for sure that this was it, that this time she wouldn't snap back. It made me sick inside, like she was my own flesh and blood."

"Your compassion is what makes you such a good nurse."

"Yeah, I'm awesome," she said. "I was so limp with fear I barely made it out of the elevator. I was sweating and my heart was pounding and I felt like I couldn't breathe, and all the way down the hall it was like I was walking through quicksand."

It sounded like a panic attack, but to suggest it would probably only make her feel worse. "These are special circumstances."

"How do you figure?"

"Until they find Janey's mother, or get her into foster care, you and I are the only 'parents' she has. She may be a ward of the state, but it's up to us to see that she gets the best care. That's a huge responsibility."

"You're right," she said, sounding cautiously optimistic. "Maybe that's why I have this deep need to protect her."

"Right now, she needs protecting."

She looked up at him and there were those lips again. Plump and juicy and pink. She had pale, flawless skin and the brightest, clearest green eyes that he had ever seen.

He would never forget the day he'd met her, when she'd walked into the staff meeting and the administrator had introduced them. He had been totally blown away. He'd probably held her hand a little too long when he shook it, and all through the meeting he hadn't been able to stop staring at her. Which, in retrospect, might have seemed a little creepy. Maybe they'd just gotten off on the wrong foot.

"I'm not sure if I've ever said it, but you're a really good doctor," she said.

He wiggled his brows and said, "Flattery will get you everywhere."

"Now if we could just do something about your personality," she grumbled with an exasperated shake of her head, but there was the hint of a smile, and a twinkle of something sly and impish in her eyes. She was teasing him.

"Admit it," he said, teasing her right back. "I'm starting to grow on you."

"I admit nothing," she said, nose in the air, trying not to smile, but he could see that she was having as much fun as he was. "Though I will say that after this, it might be a little more difficult to dislike you."

He grinned and wiggled his brows. "Then my evil plan is working."

Clare laughed. She couldn't help it. Because it was just so *Parker*. And boy did it irritate her that she knew him well enough to say that. Five minutes ago she'd felt lower than low; now he had her laughing. How did he do that?

Try as she might to push him away, he always pushed back a little harder. Was this campaign to keep him at arm's length a futile waste of time? Was falling for him an inevitability?

She refused to believe that. She would just dig extra deep for the will to resist him.

No meant no, not maybe.

"You know that I don't date people from work," she said. "Especially doctors."

He grinned. "Who said anything about dating?"

The way he was looking at her mouth… If only he knew how tempting that really was.

On second thought, it was probably good that he didn't know. "I don't sleep with people at work either," she said.

"We definitely won't be sleeping. And we won't be

doing it at work." His grin was teasing, but there was a fire in his eyes, and it was one hell of a blaze. He was so damned sexy and he smelled so good. He'd missed a small strip of stubble on the underside of his chin. Any other man would look sloppy or unkempt. On Parker it looked sexy and charming. And she wanted to kiss him there. And pretty much anywhere else.

Okay, *why* was she saying no? He had a body to die for; he was beyond gorgeous. Not to mention nice, with a really good sense of humor, and she had the feeling that he would not disappoint in the bedroom. Maybe, if they could keep it a secret…

No, no, no!

What was wrong with her? She was a strong, independent woman. When she made up her mind about something, there was no changing it. So why this sudden ambivalence? What was it about being around this man that made her go all gooey?

The dynamics were fairly simple: rich doctor, bad.

Parker was watching her, looking amused. "Penny for your thoughts."

Considering the semismug grin he wore, her inner struggle must have been pretty obvious.

Swell.

"Tell you what," he said. "Since you seem to be having a rough time with this, I'm going to give you an easy out."

Why would he do that?

Suspicious, she asked, "What's the catch?"

"No catch. If you can *honestly* tell me that you aren't attracted to me, and that you want me to leave you alone, I promise I'll back off."

Really? After all this time he would really just give up? "I'm not attracted to you," she said.

His smile was smug. "That was great. Now tell it to *me*, cupcake, not your shoes."

Darn, she was hoping he wouldn't notice the lack of eye contact. The truth was, she was a terrible liar. As a child she could never get away with anything.

There was no avoiding it—she had to look at him, and the instant their eyes met, she was totally tongue-tied. He seemed to know every button to push and he pushed them liberally. But that was what womanizers did, right?

"You *are* evil," she said.

"Nah, just irresistible." He stood and held his hand out to give her a boost. "We'd better get back on the floor before someone misses us."

Without thinking, she took his hand, realizing as he pulled her up how insanely stupid it had been. Though they bumped elbows and shoulders occasionally, other than a handshake when she met him, they had never deliberately touched each other. And while she didn't actually see any sparks arcing between them as his hand wrapped around hers, boy did she feel them. And so did he.

"Interesting," he said, with a slight arch of his brow. "*Very* interesting."

That single word spoke volumes. But mostly it just told her that she was in *big* trouble.

Three

Her arms loaded with bags of donated clothes, Clare trudged through the brisk February wind to her car in the staff lot. It had gotten so cold the puddles of rain from earlier that day had turned to patches of ice. All she wanted now was to go home, take a long hot shower, crawl into bed and forget today ever happened. Although mostly she just wanted to forget the part with Parker.

Janey had begun to show very slight signs of improvement over the course of the day, but she was nowhere close to being out of the woods. Fragile as she was, her condition could turn on a dime. Until they could figure out what was wrong, they were treating the symptoms, not the cause.

Clare left the night staff very strict instructions to contact her if Janey went into distress again. She wasn't obligated to come in on her off hours, but this wasn't about obligation. And hopefully it wouldn't come to that.

Shivering, Clare popped the trunk, dropped the bags inside and then unlocked her car with the key fob and slid onto the icy-cold seat. Shivering, she stuck the key into the ignition and turned…

Nothing happened.

"Are you kidding me?" she grumbled.

She tried again, and again, but the engine was dead.

She got out, pulling her collar up to shield her face from the icy wind. She popped the hood and looked at the engine for anything obvious, like a loose battery wire. She'd watched her brothers work on cars her entire childhood and she had learned a thing or two. Her car was almost fifteen years old and malfunctioned from regular wear and tear. She had been planning to look for a new one next month when the weather was better, but it looked as if she might have to do it sooner.

With her aunt away for a week she really had no one to pick her up. She would just have to call a tow truck and wait around. Hopefully it wouldn't take long.

She dialed the garage and was informed that they would be there ASAP. Which meant no more than an hour.

"I'm supposed to wait in the freezing cold for an hour?"

"Just leave your keys in the glove box."

Grumbling to herself, she hung up. Now she would have to call a cab to get home. But she would do it inside the hospital where it was warm.

She put her keys in the glove box and shut the door. She was getting ready to close the hood when she heard a vehicle pull up behind her car. She knew before she even heard him call out to her who it was. Because that was the kind of day she was having.

"Looks like you could use some help, angel face."

There he was, in his sporty import, grinning at her. She wanted to be exasperated but she couldn't work up the will.

"Car's dead. I called for a tow."

"Need a lift?"

It sure beat waiting for a cab, though she knew she was asking for trouble. But she was exhausted and frustrated and she just wanted to get home. "If it's no trouble."

Oh, that smile. "Hop in."

"Can I put something in your trunk?"

"Is it a dead body?"

She opened her trunk. "Well, not the whole thing."

He grinned and popped his trunk. "In that case, absolutely."

She tossed the bags inside, closed the trunk and climbed in the passenger's side. The interior was soft black leather and her seat was toasty warm.

She took off her gloves and held her hands in front of the heat vent.

"Where to?"

She told him her address, and how to get there, but as he pulled out of the lot he went in the opposite direction. "Hey, genius, my house is the other way."

"I know. But dinner is this way."

She blinked. "Who said anything about dinner?"

"I just did. If I don't eat something soon I'll go into hypoglycemic shock."

"You really think I'm going to fall for that?"

His grin said that she didn't have a whole lot of choice.

Damn it. She should have known better than to get in his car. But she was too exhausted to argue. She let her head fall back against the seat rest.

"You can't tell me that you're not hungry. I know for a fact that you didn't get to eat your lunch."

Of course she was hungry. She was starving, but he was the last person she wanted to be seen with in a social setting. The way gossip traveled in the town of Royal, people would have them engaged by the end of the week.

"No offense, but I really prefer that we not be seen together outside of work."

"So, not only do you not date coworkers, but you don't dine with them either? Is that why you always eat lunch alone?"

"That's not why I eat alone, and no, I have nothing against dining with coworkers. It's just something I don't do often."

"So then having a meal with me shouldn't be a big deal, right?"

She was pretty sure he already knew the answer to that question. And as he pulled into the parking lot of the Royal Diner, the number one worst place to go when trying to avoid the prying eyes of the town gossips, she found herself wishing that she'd called a cab instead.

"I can't risk someone seeing us and getting the wrong idea."

"We're just two colleagues sharing a meal while you wait for a tow. Not to mention that I'd like to talk about Janey. Bounce a few ideas off of you. Think of it as an offsite work meeting."

Well, if it was a work meeting…

"Just this one time," she said. "And I mean that."

He grinned, shut the engine off and said, "Let's go."

Since he was the type of guy who would insist on opening a car door for a woman, she hopped out before he could get the chance. And when he reached past her to open the diner door, she grabbed it first. She didn't want anyone getting even the slightest impression that this was a date.

The hostess showed them to a booth near the back. It was after eight so most of the dinner rush had already cleared out. Which could only be a good thing. "What would you two like to drink?"

"Decaf coffee," Clare said.

"Make that two," Parker told her.

"Enjoy your meal," the hostess said, laying their menus on the table.

As they sat down Parker said, "See, it's not so bad. There's hardly anyone here."

He was right. The subfreezing temperatures must have kept people inside tonight. But it would take only one nosy person to see them together and draw the wrong conclusion.

Their waitress, Emily, was someone Clare knew well. She often brought her autistic daughter to the free clinic on the weekends when Clare was volunteering, and her husband worked at the auto-repair shop. She set their coffees down and Clare didn't miss the curious look as she said, "Hey, Clare, Dr. Reese. Looks cold out there."

"So cold Clare's car wouldn't start," Parker told her.

"Are you still driving that old thing?" Emily asked her.

"I know I need to get a new one," she said, warming her hands with her coffee cup. "I just haven't had time."

"Do you know what you'd like to order or would you need a minute to look at the menu?"

"I know what I want," Parker said, eyes on Clare. From his mischievous grin, Clare knew he wasn't talking about the food.

"Caesar salad with the dressing on the side," she told Emily.

"Would you like chicken on that?"

Would she ever, but she was only five pounds away from her high school weight and she wanted to hit that number by swimsuit season. "No chicken."

"My usual," Parker told Emily.

"One Caesar, one bacon cheeseburger and fries, comin' right up."

When she was gone Parker said, "She knows what car you drive?"

"Everyone around here knows what everyone drives."

His brows knit together. "That's weird."

Not for Royal it wasn't. "You've never lived in a small town, have you?"

"Nope. I've always lived in the city, but I like the slower pace. Though it has taken some getting used to."

"You must eat here often if you have a usual," Clare said.

"Several times a week at least, and sometimes I come in for breakfast."

"You eat a burger and fries several times a *week*?"

"I'm a carnivore. I eat meat."

"There's this thing called vegetables…"

He shrugged, sipping his coffee. "Sometimes I order a side salad."

He was a doctor, for God's sake. He should have known better. "What do you have the other four days?"

"That depends on who I'm with," he said, and his cheeky smile said that once again they were no longer talking about food. But she'd sort of walked into that one, hadn't she?

Why did he have to be so damned adorable, with his stubbled chin and dark, rumpled hair? The soft waves begged to be combed back by her willing fingers and his hazel eyes smoldered, though they looked more whiskey-colored in this light. He'd loosened his lop-sided tie and opened the top button on his dress shirt…

"Have you lived in Royal your whole life?" he asked her.

Jarred by the sudden change of subject, she realized she was staring at his chest and lifted her gaze to his handsome face instead. Which was just as bad, if not worse. Sometimes when she was sitting at the nurses' station and he was nearby she would watch him in her peripheral vision. He had such a nice face to look at.

"I moved here to live with my aunt about a year after nursing school," she told him.

"Where are you from originally?"

"My parents own a horse farm about an hour from here. Five of my siblings work there."

He blinked. "*Five?* How many siblings do you have?"

"Seven. All older. Three boys, four girls."

"Wow." He shook his head in disbelief. "That's a lot of kids."

"Tell me about it."

"Catholic?"

"No, just very traditional. My mom has six siblings and my dad has four. They both grew up on farms."

"What about your siblings. Do they have kids?"

"As of last month I have twenty-two nieces and nephews, and two great-nieces on the way."

"Wow. That is a *big* family. And you're the baby?"

There was nothing more annoying than being referred to as *the baby* by her family. It was their way of pushing her down and keeping her in her place. But when Parker said it, with that teasing smile, it wasn't demeaning at all.

"I'm the youngest, yes."

"Were you spoiled?"

As if. "My parents were pretty burned out by the time I came along. As long as I did my chores and kept my grades up they pretty much left me alone. I would rather be invisible than get sucked into all the family drama."

"I used to wish that I had a big family."

"Do you have siblings?" she asked him.

"Only child."

"I had a friend in school who was an only child and I was always so envious."

Emily returned to the table with their food and Clare's stomach howled. Though getting a salad had been the responsible thing to do, Parker's juicy burger and greasy fries beckoned her.

"Well, it's not all it's cracked up to be," he said, popping a fry in his mouth, and when he offered her one, she couldn't resist. Her mouth watered as the greasy, salty goodness sent her taste buds into overload.

She looked at her plate, then his, and thought, *Man, I should have ordered a burger.*

"Growing up I always wanted siblings," Parker said, pushing his plate toward her, gesturing to her to take more.

"I had to share a room with three of my sisters. I had no privacy whatsoever." There hadn't even been anyone who'd keep things in confidence. If one sibling knew, they all knew. Because of that it had always been difficult for her to trust people to keep her secrets. Her aunt was the only person in her life she could be totally honest with.

"For what it's worth, I didn't either," he said, and she watched his lips move. She loved looking at his lips. It was always the first place her eyes landed.

"My father was very strict throughout my entire childhood," Parker said. "He controlled pretty much every aspect of my life, like which friends I was allowed to have, what books I was allowed to read. He even chose the classes I took in high school. He was grooming me to take over his business. I always thought that if he had another child he might not be so focused on my every move."

"What does he do?"

"He was a financial tycoon. He passed away last year."

"I'm so sorry."

"We had a very tenuous relationship. I had no interest in finance, and he considered practicing medicine beneath me. He agreed to pay for medical school, but only if I studied to be a cosmetic surgeon. He even set up a job for me with his own cosmetic surgeon when I graduated."

As amazing as he was with children, that would have been a terrible waste. "Clearly you changed his mind."

"It was Luc Wakefield who talked me into standing up to my father."

"How did that go over?"

"There was a lot of shouting and threats. He said

he would disown and disinherit me. I said go for it. At that point I was so sick of being controlled I honestly didn't care."

Her family may have been a ginormous pain, but his father sounded a million times worse. "What did your mom have to say about it?"

"Not much," he said, and his casual reply belied the flash of something dark and sad in his eyes. But as soon as it was there, it was gone again. "She wasn't around."

For whatever reason, she had just assumed that someone as successful as Parker would come from a well-adjusted and happy home. She imagined him as the golden child, probably captain of the football team, valedictorian and loved by all.

It would appear that she was wrong. Again. That's what she got for drawing conclusions without facts.

"Have I got something between my teeth?" Parker asked suddenly.

She blinked. "No. Why?"

"Are you sure? Because you haven't stopped staring at my mouth."

Her cheeks went hot with embarrassment. Was she really doing that?

"It's either that, or you're thinking about kissing me."

She was almost always thinking about kissing him. She really had to be more careful in the future where she let her eyes wander. And her thoughts.

"I don't suppose you played football in high school?" Clare asked, and Parker laughed.

"No, I didn't. But if I had, boy, my father would have loved that." The only thing that would have pleased his dad more than Parker taking over the family business was if he'd become a professional athlete. But it had been obvious from a very early age that Parker had no interest, and more important, no natural talent.

He was barely out of diapers when his father began pushing him into various sports. First soccer, then T-ball, but he'd sucked at them both. He'd been more interested in sitting on the sidelines, searching the grass for bugs and snakes.

His dad had enrolled him in tag football when Parker was six, and had forced him to stay for the entire season. Luckily Parker had had a sympathetic coach who'd let him spend most of his time on the bench. Because as fanatical as his father had been about his son's physical abilities, he'd never once made it to a practice or even a game.

Swimming lessons had come next, but Parker got so many ear infections as a result that the doctor told his father the lessons had to stop. Parker's equestrian training was probably the least horrible thing he'd been forced into, and though being so high up on the horse's back had always made him nervous, he loved animals. Until his horse was spooked and threw him, and nearly trampled him to death. That was the last time he'd ever gone near a horse.

"My father played ball in college," Parker told her. "I guess he just assumed that I would want to play, too. He was real big on me following in his footsteps. He wanted a mini me, and I seriously didn't fit the bill. I was skinny and scrawny and kind of a geek."

"You were not," she said, taking another fry, eyeing his burger with a look of longing. She had barely touched her salad, but she'd already eaten half his fries.

"I'm serious. I was a total nerd. Remind me and

I'll dig out some old pictures." He slid his plate closer. "Take a bite."

She blinked. "Of what?"

"My burger. You haven't taken your eyes off of it, and I think I see a little drool in the corner of your mouth."

She hesitated, looking a little embarrassed, but her stomach won the battle. "Well, maybe a little bite…"

There was nothing little about the bite she took.

"I didn't start to really fill out until my third year of college," he said. "When I started weight training."

"So you were what, like, twenty-one?"

"Eighteen. I graduated high school when I was fifteen."

"Wow, you really were a geek. But your dad must have been happy about that."

"My dad was never happy about anything. He was a tyrant. Thankfully I saw more of the nanny and the house staff than him."

"I went through sort of the same thing when I was a kid. Although not the tyrant part. Everyone assumed I would work on the ranch after high school, but I wanted to be a nurse. I knew from the time I got my first play doctor kit as a kid that I wanted to work in medicine. I wanted to help people."

"Did you ever tell your family that?"

"Probably a million times, but I was more or less invisible. No one ever listened to what I had to say. Hell, they still don't. If it isn't ranch business, or my various nieces' and nephews' academic accomplishments, they don't discuss it. So I worked my butt off in school and got a scholarship to a college far away from home and haven't looked back since. My parents were not very happy with me."

In what universe did that make even a lick of sense? "Aren't most parents proud when their kids go to college?"

"Like I said, they're very traditional. Nothing was more important to them than their children 'paying their debt to the family,'" she said, making air quotes with her fingers. "Whatever the hell that meant. I didn't ask to be born. I never felt as if I owed my family anything."

It amazed him that despite their very different upbringings, their childhoods weren't really all that different. "I felt the same way about my father. He had my entire life planned out before I was out of diapers. With no regard whatsoever to what I might want. But that was just who he was. People were terrified of him and he used that to manipulate. No one dared deny him anything."

"Stubborn as I am, my parents' archaic thinking probably only pushed me further from the fold. The thought of staying on the farm and working with my family for the rest of my life gives me hives. And they have no respect for what I do. To this day I still hear snide remarks about going into medicine just to snag—" She stopped abruptly, but it was already too late. He knew exactly what she'd been about to say.

"A wealthy doctor?" he said.

Her cheeks flushed a deep red and she lowered her eyes to her salad, her juicy bottom lip wedged adorably between her perfect teeth. He'd never seen her blush, but damn, she sure was pretty when she did. But then, she always looked good to him. And suddenly her attitude toward him made a whole lot more sense.

"I didn't mean to tell you that," she said, looking mortified.

"At least now I know why you spend so much time pretending you don't like me."

She lifted her chin, getting all indignant on him. "Who says I was pretending?"

He laughed. "Sweetheart, I've dated a lot of women. I know the signals."

She opened her mouth to argue—because she always argued when he was trying to make a point—then must have had a change of heart and closed it again. "Okay, yes, that is *part* of the reason I can't see you. But there are other factors, as well, things I'm not comfortable getting into right now."

"So you do like me," he said.

"I respect you as a physician and peer, and you seem like a good person. I could even see us eventually becoming friends, but it can never be more than that."

Four

"Do you want to be friends?" Parker asked her.

She wanted that and so much more, and it wasn't fair that she couldn't have it. But she of all people knew that life was not often fair. She also realized that neither of them had said a word about Janey. Not that it surprised her. It was all just a ruse to get her alone. And she'd fallen for it. Willingly. She looked at her phone to check the time. "It's late. I should go home. I want to get up early tomorrow and go jogging."

Her very obvious brush-off didn't seem to faze him. "You don't strike me as the jogging type."

"I like it. There's a cute little park behind my house."

"Are you one of those die-hard joggers who's on the road before the sun's up?"

"God, no. If I'm on the track at seven thirty it's a good day."

He just grinned and said, "Could you be more intriguing?"

She didn't even know how to respond to that. She led a pretty unexciting life. What did he see that was so special? So interesting? If he was just looking to get laid, he was seriously overplaying his hand.

Parker motioned Emily for the check, and refused to let Clare pay her portion.

"You can buy next time," he said, but she didn't think there was going to be a next time. It was stupid to think that she could ever be friends with Parker without wanting more. *So. Much. More.* So she figured, why tempt herself? Out of sight, out of mind. Wasn't that the way it was supposed to work?

"Where to?" he asked when they got into the car. He blasted the heat and switched the seat warmers on.

"We're just outside of town. Turn left." Thankfully this time he followed her directions.

"Didn't that area get hit pretty hard by the tornado?" he asked as he pulled out of the parking lot.

"Our house was leveled," she said, realizing that she could look at his mouth all she wanted now; he was focused on the road.

"Tell me you and your aunt weren't in the house," he said.

"My aunt was away on a trip and I was at the hospital."

"Were you able to salvage anything?"

"We lost everything. Clothes, furniture, keepsakes. My aunt travels extensively and she had things from all over the world. Things she'd been collecting for decades. By the time it was over, they were scattered all over the city. Wet and broken. My aunt's file cabinet, with the papers still in it, was found over a mile away. The tornado picked her car up and launched it through the house across the street. It was utter devastation."

"I can't even imagine," he said. "I've seen some major hurricane damage on the East Coast, but nothing that bad. And you saw it? The tornado, I mean."

She nodded. "It was surreal at first. I kept thinking that it couldn't happen to Royal, that at the last second it would change course or blow itself out, then the debris started to hit things. Windows started breaking and cars in the hospital lot were getting pummeled with softball-sized hail and we knew we were going to be right in the middle of it. You feel like a sitting duck. All you can do is take shelter, hang on tight and hope for the best."

"The hospital has a shelter, right?"

"Yes, but I wasn't in it. It happened so fast, there was no time to move the patients, so, along with the rest of the staff I stayed on the ward."

"That was very brave."

"No." She shook her head. "I was terrified. It was the longest five minutes of my life."

"You were terrified but you did it anyway. You put the lives of those kids before your own. That's the definition of bravery."

The compliment, coming from him, made her heart go pitter-pat. Why did he have to be so nice? And so ridiculously handsome? Did the man have a single negative attribute? Other than being extremely stubborn. But to be fair she was guilty of that, too. He turned into her subdivision and took a right onto her street.

"It's the third house on the left."

"You know, I've learned more about you tonight than in the past three months," Parker said.

"There isn't much to know. The tornado aside, I don't lead a very exciting life."

"Excitement is highly overrated. And believe me, I'm speaking from experience. I love the slower pace here. The people are so different, so much more laid-back. For the most part. It's exactly what I needed."

It was all about perception, she supposed, because for her this was just normal. But she was sure that moving from Royal to somewhere like Dallas, or even New York City, would be a jarring change of pace. But she never would. She was a country girl at heart and that would never change.

He pulled into the driveway and the automatic outdoor lights switched on, illuminating the exterior of her aunt's sprawling colonial. "This is nice."

"Thanks. It's pretty much identical to the old one, just a little more modern."

"It's a lot of house for two people."

"My aunt has out-of-town guests frequently, so she likes the extra space." She gathered her purse and gloves and said, "Thanks for the ride. And dinner."

"I'll help you with your body," he said, shutting off the car.

She blinked. Oh, man, if he only knew the things she wanted him to do to her body. Sexy, tantalizing things…

Uh-oh, was she drooling a little again…?

She must have looked confused, because he said, "In the trunk. The body bags."

Oh, right, she would have completely forgotten and left them there. "I can get them," she said.

"Nonsense, I'll help." He popped the trunk open and got out of the car. She met him around back.

"Did you really just say *nonsense*?"

"Isn't that how people talk in Texas?"

"If you're eighty. And a woman."

"My bad," he said, but he was grinning. Did the man ever stop smiling? No one should be that happy that much of the time.

She reached for the bags but he snatched them up first. Darn it, the last thing she wanted was to let him into her house. She had the feeling that once she did, it would be near impossible to get him back out the door.

"I've got it," she said, but he was already heading up the walk. Her exasperated breath crystalized in the air as she jogged to catch up. She had no choice but to go along with it. And of course there was a small part of her that wanted him in her house. Or maybe not so small.

"I think you have a hearing problem," she told him as they walked up the porch steps.

"No, I hear you just fine," he said, waiting for her to unlock the front door. "I think what you mean is that I have a *listening* problem."

She laughed; she couldn't help it. "If I say I've got it from here, and it's been a long day and I'm tired, is there *any* way I'm going to stop you from coming in?"

He considered that for several seconds then shook his head. "Probably not. I'll just make up some lame excuse like needing to use the bathroom and we both know that you're too polite to say no."

He was right. Damn those pesky Southern manners her parents had drilled into her. She couldn't decide if it was more disturbing or pathetic that she had little to no ability to deny him anything. Like the tornado, he'd blown into her life and had the potential to make a huge mess of things.

"You could have the decency to look a little less smug," she said, pushing the door open and letting him inside.

"Kidding aside, I really would like to discuss Janey's case," he said, stepping into the foyer, which led into the open-concept great room and kitchen. "We didn't get a chance at dinner."

As if she would say no to that. Besides, this time he sounded sincere, and less like he was trying to get into her pants.

She wondered what he would do if she invited him up to her bedroom. There was no point pondering the possibility, as it would never happen. Not in this lifetime anyway. But it was the kind of thing that she liked to think about. When she was alone. Usually in bed. If he was as good as her fantasies…

No man was as good as the fantasy. She had pretty high standards when it came to casual sex. Her philosophy was simple. Why did she need a man around when she could do it better herself?

"I have to make an early start in the morning, so you've got thirty minutes," she said, shrugging out of her coat and hanging it on the coat tree by the door. He did the same, looking even more rumpled than he had at dinner. Since it would be rude not to offer him a beverage—there were those pesky manners again—she said, "I'm going to make myself a cup of tea. Would you like one?"

"I'd love one," he said.

She gestured to the couch, probably the safest place to confine him. "Make yourself comfortable."

She stepped into the kitchen and filled the kettle, then set the burner on high. The stove, like the rest of the kitchen, was a chef's dream. Major overkill considering neither she nor her aunt liked to cook, but her aunt only bought top-of-the line appliances. She bought top-of-the-line everything.

Clare grabbed two cups from the cupboard and set them by the stove, then pulled out a box of chamomile tea. "Do you take sugar or honey?" she asked him, bracing herself for some sort of suggestive innuendo, but he didn't say a word. She turned to him, and realized that he hadn't answered because he was *gone*.

"Where the heck did you go?" she called, and heard him answer from the second floor.

"Up here."

She was fairly sure that his voice was coming from her bedroom. So much for having to actually invite him to her bedroom. He'd found it all on his own.

Did the man have no boundaries? No shame?

She should have known. She never should have turned her back on him. Hell, she never should have let him into her house.

She charged up the stairs to her bedroom. She found him *sitting* at the foot of her bed, looking around the room. It had been a really long time since she'd had a man under, or even on top of, her covers and he looked damn good there.

"What the hell, Parker?" she said, realizing, as his name rolled off her tongue, that as long as she had known him she had referred to him as Dr. Reese. This was her first time addressing him by his first name. It felt a little odd, but also kind of natural.

He flashed her a toothy smile. "Hey there, short stuff."

At five-five she was hardly short, but she let it slide. "What do you think you're doing?"

"You said to make myself comfortable."

"I meant on the couch."

"But you didn't *say* the couch."

"I pointed to it!"

"Clearly I don't take direction well. You're going to have to be a little more specific next time."

Next time? After this did he seriously think she would let him back in?

Who was she kidding? Of course she would.

She folded her arms. "Get off my bed."

He grinned. "You didn't say please."

"*Please* get off my bed," she said, feeling a little desperate. The urge to jump in there with him was almost too strong to fight. She felt a little winded and tingly all over, as if her libido had just awakened from a long hibernation.

"No need to shout," he said, pulling himself to his feet and walking to the door.

"I don't like having people in my bedroom. I like my privacy." She straightened the covers where he'd been sitting. They were still warm from his body heat, and the slightest hint of his aftershave lingered in the air.

She turned to him to say that it was time for him to go, but he wasn't there!

"Are you kidding me?" she mumbled. "Parker!"

She found him in her craft room next door. He'd switched the light on and was examining the quilt samplers she had sewn and tacked to the wall. "Oh, my God, are you for real? Did I not just say that I like my privacy. You have the attention span of a *three-year-old*!"

"You said you don't like having people in your bedroom. This isn't your bedroom, is it?"

She didn't justify that one with a response. And her thin-lipped glare only seemed to amuse him further. "The truth is, I just wanted to hear you say my name again. Or shriek it, as the case may be."

She ignored the warm shiver that whispered across the surface of her skin and raised the fine hairs on her arms. Or tried to at least. He wasn't making it easy. "I'll say it a thousand times if it will make you go downstairs."

"These are fantastic," he said, gesturing to the wall. She wasn't buying it. He was the kind of guy who knew quality when he saw it and this was definitely not quality sewing.

"Compliments won't get you anywhere," she told him.

"I'm actually serious," he said, leaning in closer. "Where did you get them?"

"I made them, and for the record, they suck. The fabric is puckered and the rows are crooked. My stitching is totally uneven. Which is why I keep them in here. Where no one will see them."

"But the colors are striking," he said, and she realized that he really wasn't bullshitting her. He was genuinely impressed.

Weird.

"You have a gift," he said.

"It's just a hobby. It relaxes me."

"Did you do these drawings, too?"

He was looking at the pages she'd laid out on her craft table.

"I couldn't draw my way out of a paper bag. I just

colored them in. It's the new big thing in stress relief for adults."

"Coloring?"

"Absolutely. There are like a million adult coloring books to choose from."

"No kidding. It seems a little…pointless."

"That's the whole point." She gestured to a pile of coloring books on the shelf beside her craft table. "I've finished all of those. I did a lot of coloring in the park last summer. And look how calm I am."

"Yeah," he said with a wry smile. "You looked pretty calm in the stairwell today."

Of course he would point that out. But it was hard to get angry when he was flashing her that adorable grin.

"May I?" he asked, nodding to the pile.

No one had looked at her coloring books before. It had never even occurred to her to show them to anyone. "Go ahead, but they're nothing special."

He took the top book, a panoramic foldout of a magical fairyland. "Wow, you sure do have a way with color."

The compliment made her feel all warm and squishy inside. "I just pick what looks right."

"That's the weird thing. Normally these colors don't even go together, but you make it seem like they do."

She shrugged, thinking he was making a way bigger deal about this than he should be. "Maybe I wasn't clear. You can rave all you want and I'm still not going to sleep with you."

"You should frame some of these," he said, looking through a book of flowers, ignoring her completely. Or, knowing him, he was only pretending to. She had the feeling that he didn't miss much.

"Why?" she asked him. "They're not art."

"No, this is definitely art."

"Okay, but it's someone *else's* art."

"Yes, the shapes are already there, but the color adds dimension. It brings it to life. That's the hardest part."

Maybe, maybe not. Either way, his enthusiasm was giving her warm fuzzies all over the place. Her inability to resist his charms bordered on the absurd.

"How many finished books do you have?" he asked her, flipping through a collection of mandalas.

She didn't even want to go there. "Too many. I don't get out much."

"Me neither," he said, and she gave him a dubious look. "I'm serious."

"That's not how I hear it."

"Keeping tabs on me?"

She was making it sound that way, wasn't she? "Word gets around. You're reputed to have a very busy social calendar."

"When I first got here I was going out pretty frequently. But I was in a new place and meeting lots of new people."

"New women, you mean."

He shot her a sideways glance through the curtain of his unfairly thick lashes, then winked. He actually *winked*. "Be careful, Clare, you almost sound jealous."

Probably because she was. A little.

He moved closer, looking like a tiger on the prowl, his eyes shining with male heat. If this were the wild, he would take her in an instant. And because it was the wild she would be helpless to stop him. He looked as if he was going to kiss her, and she wanted him to.

His eyes locked on hers, he started to lean in, slowly,

cautiously, as if he was expecting her to hit him over the head with something.

Up until today he had been subtle but consistent. He had never pushed, exactly, but he'd made sure that she knew he was around. Something told her now that all bets were off.

Five

Downstairs in the kitchen the kettle whistled but Clare didn't move. She stood totally still, her eyes locked on Parker's, the energy whirling between them electrically charged. Parker knew that he could have her right now if he wanted to. This was the moment he'd been waiting for, but half the fun of a relationship was the chase. No matter who was doing the running. And call him a megalomaniac, but it would be much more fun if she made the first move. If she came to him.

Just for fun, he dropped his gaze to her mouth. Her chin lifted a fraction and her tongue darted out to wet her lips.

Oh, yeah, she wanted it bad.

"Your water is boiling," he said.

Clare blinked several times, as if waking from a daydream. "Huh?"

"The kettle, it's boiling."

"Oh. I should probably get that," she said, but she didn't move. She was waiting for him to kiss her. He could feel the anticipation, see the throb of her pulse at the base of her throat.

A wisp of dark blond hair had escaped the messy bun she wore, so he reached up and tucked the silky-soft strand back in. Clare's breath caught and her pupils dilated, and as the tips of his fingers brushed the shell of her ear, she leaned into his palm. He realized, with spine-tingling awareness, that this was the first time he'd touched her. They had bumped shoulders or elbows a time or two while treating a patient, and he'd held her hand to pull her up on the steps today. Touching her felt exciting, and a little naughty.

Her skin was just as smooth and soft as he thought it would be, and damn, she smelled good. He knew that if he kept touching her this way the chase would end right here, right now.

He dropped his hand to his side. "You need a push?"

She blinked with confusion. "A push?"

"To get the kettle. I don't think it's going to turn itself off."

"Right, the kettle," she said, peeling her eyes from his, taking a slightly unsteady step back. The truth was, he was feeling a little unsteady himself.

He gestured her through the office doorway, and she shook her head. "Uh-uh. There's no way I'm taking my eyes off you for even a second," she said. "Next thing I know you'll be going through my closet or something. You're too sneaky."

And she was way too much fun.

He went down first, with Clare watching him like a

hawk. When they got to the kitchen, Clare shut off the burner, never once turning her back on him. Not that he blamed her.

"I'm going to head out," he told her.

Her look of disappointment made him smile. "I thought you were staying for tea."

"Watch yourself, Clare, or I might have to assume you like having me around."

"We wouldn't want that," she said, but it was too late. It was written all over her face. "Thanks for the ride home. And dinner."

"My pleasure." And boy, did he mean that. He walked to the door and pulled his wool coat on. Clare met him in the foyer.

"Do you need a ride to work tomorrow?" he asked her.

"I can use my aunt's car until she gets back next week. I don't like relying on other people."

"And you're afraid that someone will see us together and get the wrong idea." Or the right one.

She folded her arms across what he was sure were a perfect pair of breasts. And he would know soon enough. "We never did discuss Janey."

"Good night, Parker."

He winked. "Good night, hot stuff."

Her eye roll was the last thing he saw as she closed the door. Oh, yeah, she was definitely into him. As if there had ever been a question.

Clare lay awake half the night, and the other half she spent dreaming about Parker. It was as if she couldn't escape him, no matter how hard she tried. Not even when she was sleeping. He was starting to get under her skin. And that was a very bad thing.

The absence of any physical contact between them had been her secret weapon, but he'd taken care of that, hadn't he? The warm weight of his palm against her cheek had been unexpected and startling and so erotic that the resulting surge of estrogen had short-circuited the logic pathways in her brain. It was a wonder smoke hadn't billowed out of her ears. She had been positive that he was going to kiss her, then he didn't and she didn't quite understand why.

She got out of bed late, pulling her hair back into a ponytail and dressing in her warmest jogging outfit. According to the weather report she had seen online last night, the daytime high would barely break thirty degrees. She was so ready for spring and warmer weather.

Her breath crystalized and the icy air burned her lungs as she stepped out the back door onto the multilevel deck. She crossed the yard to a gate, which led right to the jogging path.

She was getting warmed up, stretching her hamstrings, when she heard a familiar voice, using a really bad fake Southern accent.

"Fancy meeting you here, ma'am."

Oh, no, not this morning. She turned to see Parker leaning casually against a barren tree in what looked like a brand-new jogging getup.

"God, give me strength," she mumbled, and told Parker, "You *really* need to stop trying to sound Southern. You're not any good at it."

He just grinned that adorable grin, making her a tiny bit weak in the knees.

"What are you doing here?"

"It just so happens that I jog, too, and I'm always looking for a change of scenery. A different path to take. Your description of the park intrigued me so I thought I would check it out."

"I said it was a cute little park. Which word got you? *Cute?* Or *little?*"

Despite her snippy tone he smiled.

"If I asked you to go away, would you?"

Looking apologetic, he shook his head.

Of course not. She sighed and said, "Let's get this over with."

They started down the path toward the pond, Parker huffing along beside her. But gradually he started to fall behind. They were no more than five minutes in, and Parker was gasping for air. She hadn't even broken a sweat.

Then he stopped altogether, and she had to backtrack. He stood hunched over and out of breath, holding his side. "Damn, this is harder than it looks."

Clearly he was not a jogger. And of course she planned to use that to teach him a lesson. "I'll race you to the pond," she said.

"Are you trying to kill me?"

"I'll make you a deal. If you can beat me there, I'll sleep with you."

His stunned expression was the last thing she saw as she took off running, leaving Parker in the dust.

She got to the pond and was using a bench to stretch when Parker finally wheezed his way over. He dropped like a lead weight onto the grass at her feet, red-faced and sucking cold air into his lungs.

She shook her head sadly. "I know eighty-year-olds in better shape than you."

"You really *are* trying to kill me," he gasped.

"You did lie about being a jogger. You sort of asked for it."

"Technically I didn't lie, because starting this morning I plan to be a regular jogger. If I don't die from exhaustion first. Or a heart attack. I don't suppose you have water."

She took the bottle from her jacket pocket and handed it to him.

"Thanks." He sat up, chugging half the bottle.

"Maybe you should head back to the house while I do my laps. When I'm finished I'll make you breakfast. I guess I owe you that much, since I did almost kill you. Not that I was trying or anything."

"Sure you weren't." He pushed himself to his feet. "Can I wait in the house?"

Did he honestly think she would fall for that one again? "Sure. If you can figure out the alarm code."

She took off running again and he shouted after her, "You're really going to make me sit out in the cold? I could freeze to death!"

She waved without turning around, feeling not an ounce of guilt. More than likely he had a still-warm luxury vehicle parked somewhere nearby. There would be no freezing to death for him.

She jogged her usual laps around the park, then just for fun added a few more, pushing herself harder. Maybe if she was gone a really long time, he would get bored and leave.

As if. If it had been possible to shake him off that easily, he would have been long gone by now.

When she stepped through the gate into the backyard,

Parker was sitting on the steps of the upper deck, tapping away on his cell phone. So much for him leaving.

Parker heard the back gate open and looked up from his phone. Clare was cute when she was all sweaty, her hair a mess. "Good run?"

She nodded, only slightly out of breath. "It got better when I ditched you. You were dragging me down."

"Do I still get my breakfast?"

"Yes," she said grudgingly. She opened the back door and disarmed the alarm. "But don't expect anything fancy."

He tugged off his jacket and took a seat at the kitchen island. "Do I at least get coffee?"

She reached over to the coffeemaker and pressed the start button.

She used the term *making breakfast* loosely. What she should have said was that she would warm up breakfast for him. She "made" him one of those individually wrapped breakfast sandwiches out of the freezer.

"Make yourself useful and get the juice out of the fridge," she said, putting the sandwich in the microwave.

He opened the refrigerator. Aside from the juice and various condiments, there were mostly just carryout containers.

He had the distinct feeling that Clare didn't cook, which was fine, as it was one of his favorite things to do. It was a little spooky the way they seemed so perfectly matched. It was like destiny, or fate or some other crap like that.

Serendipity maybe.

She took two glasses down from the cupboard for

him to fill. Then the microwave dinged and she handed him the sandwich. "Bon appétit."

He bit in to find the middle still partially frozen, but the look she was giving him said not to push it. He forced a smile and said, "Delicious."

"As soon as you're finished eating you have to leave," she said.

"Actually, it's my day off. I can stay as long as I want."

She gave him one of those *looks*, and he grinned. Damn, did he love teasing her.

"You look like a grown man," she said. "You even sound like a grown man…"

He grinned. "If it walks like a duck and talks like a duck."

"You're going to make me late for work," she said.

"As your boss, I give you the day off."

"I don't want to take the day off. I actually like going to work."

"That's probably why you're so good at it."

She shrugged. "Well…"

"I'm serious, Clare. I've never seen a more efficiently run children's ward. Your employees respect you. They look up to you. Sometimes they even fear you a little."

She blinked with surprise. "Really?"

"You can be a little intense at times, and intimidating."

She frowned. "I don't want them to be afraid of me."

"They fear your authority, not you personally. You hold everyone to a super high standard. You demand the best performance at all times. They don't like to let you down."

She actually blushed. "I couldn't ask for a better staff."

"They're as good as they are because of you."

"I'm sure you had something to do with it, too. You're incredibly easy to work for. I liked Dr. Mann, but he was incredibly arrogant. He was always right, and God help you if you disagreed with him. Especially in front of a patient. I've seen some really good nurses get fired for challenging his authority. And even if it turned out they were right, he would never admit it."

"Sounds like he had a God complex."

"Don't get me wrong, he was a good doctor. Just not a very good person. I think he got into medicine for all the wrong reasons."

"We all have our reasons," he said.

"What were yours?"

"Mostly to get laid," he said, wiggling his brows. "Chicks love doctors."

"Chicks?"

"That's right, baby. They dig me."

She was trying really hard not to grin. "The 1960s called. They want their slang back."

He laughed and she cracked a smile.

"Your time is up, daddy-o. Make like a tree and leave."

She was funny, too. And really snarky.

Could she be more enchanting?

Figuring he'd hassled her enough for one morning, he slugged back the last of his coffee, and then left.

Parker spent the remainder of the day catching up on his reading. Medical journals mostly. Then he did some online research regarding Janey's case. Once again, he found nothing that fit her symptoms. He finished around nine that evening, more frustrated than ever. Feeling restless and edgy, he headed over to the Texas Cattleman's Club for a drink. Only a few tables in the lounge were occupied; Logan Wade sat at the bar, hunched over a beer. A hockey game played on the television, but he didn't seem to be watching it. He just stared into the beer mug, mesmerized as he swirled the dark lager around and around. Barely a month ago, Logan had taken custody of his twin brother Seth's baby daughter after Margaret, the child's mother, died in a car crash giving birth. Paramedics were able to deliver the baby, who was surprisingly unharmed, but Margaret never regained consciousness. Margaret's mother, in her grief over losing her daughter and believing that Logan was the baby's father, left the child in his care. Logan swore he'd never met Margaret, and a blood test confirmed that he was related to the baby, but not the parent. So it had to be Seth.

Parker took a seat next to him, and Logan greeted him with a very unenthusiastic, "Hey."

The bartender, without prompting, brought Parker his regular, a scotch and soda. "Who's winning?" he asked Logan, but his friend stared at him blankly.

Parker gestured to the television. "The game?"

"Oh, right," Logan said, and then shrugged. "I guess I have no idea. To be honest, I don't even know how long I've been sitting here. Is it possible to sleep with one's eyes open?"

Parker chuckled. "Baby Maggie not letting you get much rest?"

"She's so fussy. Hadley keeps telling me it's normal, but damn…" He shook his head in exasperation. "Don't get me wrong, she's my niece, and I love her, but I really wasn't prepared for this."

"No luck reaching your brother?"

He shook his head. "The navy took the message, but Seth is on a mission. Who knows when he'll get it. If and when he does, there's still no guarantee he'll come back to claim her. I honestly don't know what I would do without Hadley."

Hadley, Logan's new bride, had come to work for him as a nanny, and the two had fallen hard for each other. It seemed as if everyone around Parker was finding their perfect match and settling down. A year ago that would have given him the heebie-jeebies. Now he wanted what they had.

"She's a keeper," Parker said.

The game went to commercial and the station broke in with a special news report. Both men looked up at the wide-screen behind the bar. Janey's picture flashed across the screen with the caption "Abandoned Baby, Mother Found?" Parker sat up straighter, asking the bartender, "Can you turn that up?"

According to the anchor, a truck driver who had been in the lot of the truck stop the night Janey had been found had come forward with a video. While videotaping his rig, he'd caught a glimpse of a woman, now presumed to be Janey's mother, entering the building. They played the clip, which was grainy and difficult to make out clearly.

"Holy shit!" Logan jumped up so fast the bar stool flipped over backward and everyone in the room turned toward the commotion.

"You recognize her?" Parker asked him.

Logan rubbed his tired eyes and squinted at the television. "That looks like Margaret!"

"Margaret? You mean Maggie's mother?"

"Margaret's mother showed me a picture. I'm pretty sure that's her," he said, and asked the bartender for the remote to rewind the clip. He rewound it twice. "Yeah," he told Parker, "I'm positive. That's Margaret."

And just like that Parker knew exactly how to treat his fragile little patient. He laughed and shook his head. Could it really be that simple?

"Call the police," Parker told Logan, pulling on his coat. "I have to get to the hospital."

Stunned, Logan said, "If Margaret is Janey's mother, that means…"

"It means you have *two* nieces."

A look of shock crossed his face. *"Twins?"*

"A simple DNA test will prove it definitively." Honestly, it was a wonder they hadn't put it together before now. "But if I were you I would go home and get some sleep. If they are twins, your life is about to get a bit more complicated."

Six

Clare woke the next morning to her phone ringing.

She sat up and looked at her phone. Of course it was Parker. Who else would call her at *7:00 a.m.*? On her day off?

"Hello," she grumbled.

"You awake?" he asked.

Duh. "I am now!"

"Good. Come down and let me in."

"You're *here*?"

"I have some very good news."

"Fine," she grumbled, tossing the covers off and rolling out of bed. She tugged on her beat-up terry-cloth robe, and still half asleep, trudged down the stairs to the front door.

"Good morning," he said with a smile when she flung open the door.

"It's 7:00 a.m.," she told him.

"I know."

"On my day off."

"I know." He walked right past her without invitation and took his coat off, dropping it over the back of the sofa on the way to the kitchen, acting as if he owned the place.

It took a good minute to notice that he was unshaven and his clothes were a wrinkled mess.

"You look like hell," she said.

He took in her messy ponytail, puffy eyes and ragged old robe. "Look who's talking."

At least she had a good reason. What was *his* excuse? And what man in his right mind would tell the woman he was trying to sleep with that she looked like hell?

She supposed that was what made him so...*Parker.* When he poured on the charm he was tough to resist. But didn't he know that honesty was not always the best policy?

"Did you not go home last night?" she asked, regretting the words the instant she spoke them. She didn't want to know where he'd been. Or whom he had been with.

Grinning from ear to ear he said, "I did not. I spent the night with a beautiful girl."

Because you're not man enough for a real woman? she wanted to say. "And you woke me at 7:00 a.m. on my day off to tell me this? Are you on drugs?"

He shook his head.

"Mentally challenged?"

He just smiled, then he looked toward the coffeepot and sniffed. "What, no coffee?"

Was he kidding? He really *was* mentally challenged.

"*Seven a.m. Day off. Sleeping.* Is any of this ringing a bell?"

"I'll make a pot," he said.

Ooookay. She flopped down on the sofa. "Knock yourself out."

This was her own fault. She never should have let him get in her head. Or her house. But it was too late now. Now that he was here there was no getting rid of him. And she hated that somewhere deep down she didn't *want* to get rid of him.

She let her head fall back, closed her tired eyes and pinched back the migraine building at the bridge of her nose with her thumb and forefinger. She must have dozed off for a minute or two, or maybe ten, because the next thing she knew Parker was waking her, holding a steaming cup of coffee.

"Time to get up," he said, holding it out to her. "Black, one sugar."

She took the cup, grumbling under her breath as she did. It irritated her to no end that after just one shared meal at the diner he already knew exactly how she fixed her coffee.

"Not a morning person?" he asked, sitting down beside her with his own cup.

"Not on my *day off.*" Especially when she'd spent the previous night tossing and turning, and all because of the man sitting next to her.

"So, about that girl…"

"Ugh! Do I really need to hear this?" she said, resisting the urge to stick her fingers in her ears and sing, *Lalalalala.*

"There you go again, thinking the worst of me," he said.

She had to. It was the only way to keep him at arm's length.

"I spent the night at the hospital," he said. "With Janey."

Clare's heart dropped so fast and hard that she felt woozy. She set her coffee on the table for fear of dropping it from her shaking hands. And though she needed to know what happened, she was terrified to ask.

"She's okay," he assured her with a smile, laying a hand on her arm. "She's been improving all night."

Oh, thank God.

The sudden gush of relief had her shaking even harder. "How? What happened?"

"I finally figured out what's wrong. From watching the news, no less."

"So what is it?"

"It's called twin-to-twin transfusion."

She blinked. "But…she's not a twin. And if she is, where is the other baby?"

"Healthy and happy, and living with her uncle Logan."

She gasped. "Baby Maggie? But…"

"Some truck driver filming his rig got a video of Janey's mother at the Lucky Seven truck stop. She was identified as Margaret Garner by several people. Which means that Maggie and Janey are twins—we confirmed it with a blood test. Although she isn't Janey anymore."

"They gave her a new name?"

"Madeline. But they're calling her Maddie."

"Maddie and Maggie. That's cute. But how did we not make the connection?"

"I beat myself up over that all night. They were brought in separately, worked on by two different teams. She was healthy. There was really nothing to connect.

We're thinking that Margaret didn't know she was having twins. I think she had Maddie at the rest stop. She was probably in shock, and losing blood. I'm sure she had no idea she was still in labor when she got back in her car."

Meaning she probably got little to no prenatal care. "If she'd seen an OB-GYN she would have known it was twins and they could have treated their condition in utero."

"But we both know that it doesn't always work that way. And all things considered, Maddie is lucky to be alive. She'll always have issues with her heart, but for the most part she'll lead a normal life."

"Now what? She's still too sick to go home, even if she has one."

"There's a children's center in Plano that specializes in the disorder. She'll be moved there until she's well enough to go home. And even then she'll need special care. She's still a very sick little girl, but at least now there's a light at the end of the tunnel. We have effective treatment options."

It was usually a happy occasion when a patient left the hospital, and while Clare was relieved that Maddie—that name would take some getting used to—was improving, she would miss the baby terribly.

"When are they moving her? I'd like to see her before she goes."

"She's being taken over by ambulance tomorrow morning," he said.

Clare fought the irrational urge to cry. "I want to get over there and spend some time with her."

"Of course. And I know this is difficult because we're all very attached to her. But it's for the best."

Logically, yes.

"Would you mind if I just lie here on the couch and take a catnap?"

"It will have to be a short one," Clare told Parker. "I won't be long."

"Take your time," he said with a huge yawn, putting his head back and closing his eyes. "I'm beat."

He looked beat, and kind of harmless. But she was still a little unsure…

"You're staying right here?" she said.

He looked up at her with bloodshot, sleepy eyes. "I'm not going to move, I promise. And this time I really do promise."

"I'll only be five minutes," she said.

His eyes slipped closed again and he mumbled something incoherent.

Feeling a little on edge, but also fairly certain he was telling the truth, she jogged upstairs to her bedroom. If she gave him too much time alone he might get bored and into trouble.

She picked her clothes out and laid them on the bed then went into the bathroom to brush her teeth and hair. She'd slept like hell last night. Not even a date with the water jets in her spa tub had been enough to soothe the restless, itchy feeling in her soul. She knew of only one person who could throw her into such turmoil, and he was napping on her couch.

She brushed the knots from her waist-length hair, reminding herself that it was time for a trim. She reached for a hair band, still thinking about Parker, wondering what he could be getting into down there. Her hand stopped in midair halfway to the drawer, then fell to her side, and she asked her reflection, "What *could* he be getting into?"

That was a really good question, because knowing Parker the way she did, he was definitely getting into some sort of trouble. He couldn't seem to help himself.

She frowned at her reflection. What the hell was she doing? Instead of making him promise not to snoop, she should have sent him on his way instead. Politely but firmly. It wasn't as if she needed him to drive her to the hospital. She had her aunt's car for that. He literally had no reason to be there. Other than to frustrate and annoy her.

Still in her robe she headed back down the stairs, calling out to her uninvited guest. "Hey, Parker, I was thinking—"

Parker didn't hear her. He was stretched out on her couch, hands tucked behind his head, sound asleep and snoring softly. He was taking a catnap, just as he'd said he would. But that wasn't what had her tripping over her own feet, or whimpering like a wounded animal.

Parker still had his pants on, which was a really good thing. Unfortunately that was *all* he had on. His shirt, undershirt, shoes and socks were on the floor beside the sofa. And oh, did he look good. Better than she had ever imagined he would.

Damn him!

Hard as she'd tried to deny it, there was definitely some sort of connection there. An irrational and scary kind of connection. It didn't make any sense. But lately it seemed that very few things in her life made much sense anymore. So if she just crawled up there with him…

You cannot let that happen, Clare.

No, she could not.

She closed her eyes and shook her head, wishing away the mental picture of him lying there looking all sexy and perfect. Wishing *him* away. But when she peeked through the small slit between her mostly closed lids he was still lying there, still looking amazing with his muscular chest and wide shoulders. And his abs? They were freaking perfect. She could do a million crunches a day and never look that good.

On the bright side, this was without a doubt the least obnoxious she had ever seen him. But now more than ever he really needed to go. And she really needed to stop staring at his chest.

"Parker," she said, keeping a safe distance between them. When he didn't respond she said it louder. "Parker!"

Still nothing.

She clapped her hands hard and loud, thinking it would startle him awake. He didn't even flinch.

This was not working.

She stepped just close enough to the couch so that she could reach him with her foot. She gave him a firm jab in the leg with her toes then stepped back. Parker kept on snoring.

Wow, he was out.

She stepped a little closer and nudged him again, then once more.

Nothing.

This was getting ridiculous.

She laid her foot on his stomach, intending to give him a good hard shake, right up until the second the sensitive bottom of her bare foot touched his warm, smooth skin.

Oh, that was dumb.

He didn't budge, and she realized, as she dropped her leg, that if he had woken he would have opened his eyes to an X-rated, full view of her goods from the waist down.

And why was she more disappointed than relieved that he remained asleep?

Okay, it was time to get serious. He really had to go. She wasn't thinking straight at all.

Using her opposite foot, in case he actually did wake up at some point, she hauled off and kicked his leg.

He mumbled something and shifted onto his side, facing her, and when he did his phone slipped out of his pocket, hit the hardwood floor with a thud and slid under the couch.

Crap.

She would have just left it there, but Parker was on call. If his phone rang he needed to be able to hear it.

Realizing that the odds of him waking at this point were slim to none, she got down on her knees and fished his phone out from under the couch, finding a couple of dust bunnies under there, as well.

Sitting back on her haunches she laid the phone on the arm of the couch next to his ear, then changed her mind and set it down on the cushion next to him. As she did, the backs of her fingers "accidentally" brushed against his stomach. She felt the contact with the intensity of an electric shock and it left her feeling limp and shaky.

This was getting out of hand fast, and she knew she should stop. Problem was, she really, *really* wanted to touch his abs. Not for long. She just wanted to know how it would feel. A few seconds tops. He would never have to know.

The idea of touching him was terrifying. And intoxicating. Her hands shook in anticipation. But did she have the guts to do it?

Her aunt was always telling Clare that she needed more excitement. That she was in the prime of her life, and she needed to take chances every now and then. Kay's life had been one long adventure, and despite what the family may have believed, she had no regrets.

Clare gnawed on her lip, fists balled tight. Should she or shouldn't she? He was sleeping like the dead. So what was the harm? It would quench her curiosity, and he would never have to know about it.

Just do it, Clare.

Her hand trembled as she reached out. She let it hover over his stomach for a second, so close she could feel the heat of his skin, working up the courage to take it one step further.

She was really going to do this. She was going to *touch* him.

Nervous, and excited, she lowered her hand, and the charge she felt as her skin touched his would have buckled her knees if she hadn't already been on the floor. The contrast of her pale skin against his much darker olive complexion was a crazy kind of erotic, and she sat there like that, watching his face for any sign that he was waking. She was playing with fire and it was more exhilarating than she could have ever imagined. It had been so long since she allowed herself to let go and follow her heart, she had forgotten how good it could feel to want someone. And now that she had a small taste of what it felt like to touch him, to be so close to him, she didn't want to stop.

Once she rang that bell, it was impossible to un-ring it.

She let her hand drift upward, toward his pecs, which were as impressive, or even more impressive, than his abs.

She looked back up at his face and froze. His eyes were open.

Damn, caught in the act. She muttered a very unladylike word.

"Am I dreaming?" he asked, his voice gravelly, eyes glossy from sleep, or lack thereof.

This had to be a dream. Real life never felt this good.

"You're dreaming," she told him, sliding her hand upward, through the sprinkling of silky hair on his chest.

He groaned and closed his eyes again. "If this is a dream I don't ever want to wake up."

"It is," she said, gently dragging her nails down his pecs, over his small dark nipples. The scent of his skin was inebriating, and so delicious she wanted to eat him up. "This isn't really happening."

A sleepy smile curled his lips. "So I can do this?"

He covered her hand with his own and lifted it to his lips, brushing a kiss against her wrist.

She whimpered and cupped his face in her hand, his beard rough against her palm. She brushed her thumb over his full bottom lip and his tongue darted out for a taste. It just about did her in.

"Come here," he said. He hooked his hands behind her neck and pulled her against the hard wall of his chest for a kiss. He tasted like coffee and sleep and something wild and exciting. Her heart pounded its way up into her throat and her skin felt electric. She was no longer thinking of the consequences. Screw the consequences. She wanted him, and she was going to take what she wanted.

His hand slid down her throat and slipped inside the opening of her robe, and when he cupped her breast, she stopped thinking altogether.

Seven

Her lips still pressed to Parker's, Clare climbed on the couch with him, straddling his thighs, her eyes dark with desire. He'd been fantasizing about this for so long, it was almost hard to believe it was really happening. When he first woke up to find her touching him, he thought it really *was* a dream. But if she wanted to pretend this wasn't happening who was he to shatter her illusion? If that was what it took to ease her conscience, to keep her in his arms, that was fine by him.

Then she was out of his arms, but only so she would be free to attack the zipper on his pants. She did it with the enthusiasm of someone on a time clock. Or someone trying not to change her mind. If she backed out now, the pain of what he would be missing out on would be excruciating. But it was a risk he was willing to take.

"No one can know about this," she said breathlessly

as she stripped him from the waist down. "And I mean no one."

Even if he wanted to disagree, there was no way in hell he would risk blowing this. Not now. He'd slept with a fair amount of women over the years. Sometimes the sex was fantastic, sometimes not, but they had all been missing something. The emotional connection he felt with Clare, maybe. He had never been one to chase women. The truth was he'd never had to. They always seemed to come to him. Maybe having to work for it made him appreciate the end result that much more. Because, damn, did he appreciate her right now.

"I promise I won't say a word to anyone." He tugged at the tie on her robe until it fell open. Clare whimpered softly. Either she believed him or she didn't care anymore.

"You're not worried about your aunt coming home?" he asked her.

"She's away for the week. She's always out of town."

"Good to know." Sliding his hands inside her robe, he pushed it off her slender shoulders, running his hands down her toned arms, over her soft stomach. She was all pale skin and soft curves, and everything in his being sighed with pleasure. She was perfect. Her dark blond hair hung like spun silk over her shoulders, giving him a peekaboo view of her perfectly shaped, supple breasts.

"You're amazing," he said. "I've never seen you with your hair down."

"Was it everything you hoped it would be?" She smiled at him with heavy-lidded eyes. "Because flattery will get you *everywhere*."

That was what he liked to hear.

"Will it get me here?" he asked her, cupping her firm

breasts, testing their weight against his palms, rolling the small pink tips between his fingers.

"Oh, yeah," she said, covering his hands with her own, showing him what she liked.

"How about here?" He ran his hands up her thighs, using his thumbs to tease the crevice where her legs met. She gasped as he touched her most sensitive spot. She was hot and wet and ready for him, but he wasn't about to rush this.

Clare had different ideas. She came up on her knees, and with one quick downward thrust he was inside of her. It was so erotic, and so unexpected, he nearly lost it right then. He moaned and his body arched upward to meet her, driving himself as deep as he could go.

Clare hissed with pleasure and threw her head back, her long hair brushing across his knees like the tickle of a feather. He gripped her hips, tried to slow her down as she rode him, but she was so deep in the zone, she didn't even seem to realize he was there.

Mild-mannered Nurse Clare had a naughty side after all.

She used his body, putting a friction shine on the leather sofa cushion, and he let her. When he was sure he couldn't take any more he wrapped his hands around her waist and tried to think about baseball, but she took him by the wrists and held them on either side of his head, using her weight to pin them there.

He could have easily gotten free, but why the hell would he want to? She seemed to get off on being in control, and he preferred a shameless and aggressive woman who knew what she liked. She could dominate him whenever and wherever she wanted.

Clare started to moan and ride him faster, and the

last shred of his control took a vacation. He never let himself be the first to orgasm, but he beat her to the punch by about thirty seconds. Clare didn't even seem to notice. She rode out her own release, then collapsed on his chest, breathing hard, her heart pounding in time with his own, and said, "I *really* needed that."

"Me, too," he said, folding his arms around her. Damn, she felt good. Holding her close this way was almost as good as the actual sex.

Almost.

He'd been anticipating this since the moment he'd first seen her, and she didn't disappoint.

She tucked her face into the crook of his neck, her silky hair catching on his chin stubble. "If I had known it would be this amazing I would have jumped you months ago."

"If I had any energy left, I would pin you down on the floor and do it again." He was so relaxed and so completely satisfied that he could barely keep his eyes open. Besides that catnap, which he was guessing by his intense fatigue couldn't have been more than a few minutes, he hadn't slept in more than twenty-four hours. As a resident he could function on one or two hours of sleep a night for a week or more, but he was getting too damned old now.

"Sure you won't change your mind?" she said, nibbling his earlobe.

Oh, man, did he want to. Maybe if he were ten years younger… "I wouldn't be much good to you like this."

She frowned, looking disappointed.

"I don't mean to sound ungrateful, because believe me, I'm not, but I have to know, why now?"

She shrugged. "I thought I would give the water jets in my tub a break."

Oh, damn. "Seriously?"

She grinned. "I shudder to imagine my next water bill."

The mental picture had his neurons firing and his blood boiling, but exhaustion won out. So he shelved the image for future reference. Not that he believed her. Or maybe he did.

"So," she said, disentangling herself from his arms to sit up, "I want to make sure we're on the same page."

Oh, boy, here we go. The Talk. "What? No afterglow?"

"I don't do afterglow. This isn't a relationship. This was just sex."

He'd used that same line on dozens of women and the irony of the situation wasn't lost on him. Because this time, he didn't want "just sex." He wanted her, in every way there was to want someone. It felt almost as if the force of the universe was propelling them toward one another. He knew that she felt it, too. She just wasn't ready to let herself accept it. But she would in her own time, and thankfully he was a very patient man.

"Whatever you want," he told her, and she looked as if maybe she didn't believe him.

"No one can know about us. And I mean *no one.*"

"Be careful, you're going to bruise my tender ego."

She laughed and climbed off his lap, grabbing her robe from the floor. "Somehow I doubt that."

"Where are you going?"

"I have to get dressed and get out of here. I'd like to spend some time with Janey before they take her."

"Maddie," he reminded her.

"Right. It's going to be weird calling her by a different name. I also promised I would work a few hours at the free clinic this afternoon."

"Can I see you later?"

She hesitated, then said, "That's probably not a good idea."

"Why?"

She shot him a look as she tugged the robe back on. "You know why."

"I knew it," he said, throwing his arm dramatically over his eyes. "You're ashamed of me."

She grabbed his shirt off the floor and tossed it to him. "I need you dressed and ready to go by the time I come back down."

"Sure thing," he said, but the second she was gone he tossed his shirt on the floor and dropped his head back against the arm of the sofa. He must have drifted off, only to be roused by a loud thud.

He peered out through the slits of his eyes, trying to get his bearings, then saw his clothes in a pile on the floor beside the couch and grinned. Clare must have decided to let him stay, or maybe she had tried to wake him and he hadn't responded. The house was quiet and the angle of the sunshine filtering through the closed blinds meant it had to be late afternoon. Clare had covered him with one of her quilts before she left, and it smelled like her. He knew he should get dressed and get home for a few hours of shut-eye, but he was so comfortable…

He looked back over at his clothes and a few feet away sat an unfamiliar pair of shoes. Women's shoes. He didn't recall them being there that morning. Clare hadn't been wearing them. Then one of the shoes started tapping, and he realized that there was an actual person inside of them.

And he had the sinking feeling that it wasn't Clare.

Parker bolted up on the couch, catching the blanket just before it fell to the floor.

The shoes were on an older, attractive woman, and the noise that roused him must have been the front door closing after she'd come in.

He was assuming she was Clare's aunt. So much for her being out of town.

Having heard her referred to as an old maid, Parker had formed a specific impression in his head of how Kay probably looked, but reality bore no resemblance to his imagination. Her clothes were casual but neat, fashionable and very expensive. She had long dark blond hair like Clare's, but hers was peppered with shades of silver and gray, and while Clare's hair had a sort of wild and free quality to it, this woman's was smooth and sleek.

Thankfully, she wasn't holding a gun on him. Because people in Texas loved their guns. And he was guessing she had one or two herself.

"It's not every day a woman comes home to find a naked man on her couch," she said with a heavy Texas twang. "This must be my lucky day." Then she looked him up and down, smiled and added, "Or maybe it's yours."

Boy did he hope she was joking. "You must be Aunt Kay."

"I must be."

He could only imagine what she was probably thinking, and damn would he like to put some clothes on. The blanket was feeling awfully thin and a little small.

"And who might you be?" she asked.

"Parker," he said. "Parker Reese. I work with Clare."

One brow rose slightly. "Among other things?"

No, this wasn't awkward at all. "Uh…yeah."

"You're better looking than I imagined. But that might just be the absence of clothes."

So she knew who he was? That was interesting. "Has Clare mentioned me?"

She gave him one of those *bless your heart* looks. "I'm afraid that I'm not at liberty to say."

Ooookay.

"She was right about one thing," Kay said. "They would have a field day with you."

Huh? "They who? And why would they have a field day?"

She flashed him another placating smile. "I'm not at liberty to say."

Of course she wasn't. This was too weird. He was the naked stranger in her house, yet he was the one asking all of the questions. Though she seemed to have a pretty good idea of who he was. "Maybe I should call Clare," he said.

"Maybe you should put your clothes on first."

Yeah, that would probably be a good idea. He just hoped she wasn't expecting to watch him.

"Go on up to Clare's room, and for the love of all that is holy, take the blanket with you. My heart isn't what it used to be."

Somehow he doubted that. Despite her age, she looked strong as an ox. Sturdy, yet refined. And as much as he appreciated the offer of privacy—and oh, did he appreciate it—he wasn't so sure Clare would appreciate him using her bedroom. He'd gone up there the other night to tease her, but this was different. It felt like an invasion of privacy to be in there when she wasn't around. If he was going to make this relationship work, he had to respect Clare's boundaries. "Would it be all right if I just use a bathroom down here? I don't want to invade Clare's space."

His request seemed to surprise Kay, and he was betting it earned him a few brownie points, too.

"That's awfully thoughtful of you. There's a half bath just off the kitchen."

"Thanks." He grabbed his clothes and his phone and with the blanket tucked firmly around his midsection, he hightailed it to the bathroom. Once he was in there, there was no hurry, but he threw his clothes on as quickly as possible. So fast he was pretty sure he put his boxers and socks on inside out.

When he was dressed he checked his phone, surprised to find that it was almost four o'clock. He'd slept for nearly *eight* hours. Far more than his typical five or six. And it was a deep restful kind of sleep that usually evaded him.

Must have been the sex.

He dialed Clare, and she answered her phone saying, "You had better not be snooping."

He smiled and shook his head. "Houston, we have a problem."

"What's wrong?"

"You know how you thought your aunt was still out of town?"

"Uh-oh."

Uh-oh was right. "Yeah, well, she's not. She's here."

He could feel her cringe over the phone line. "Tell me you weren't still on the couch."

"I wish I could."

"Naked?"

"As the day I was born."

She made a noise and it took a second for him to realize what he was hearing. "Oh, my God, are you *laughing*?"

"No, of course not," she said, clearing her throat. "She's not holding you at gunpoint, is she?"

He knew she had guns! "Not yet, and frankly, she's scary enough without one."

"Yeah, she can be," Clare said, and he could hear the mirth in her voice. Was she enjoying this?

"This isn't funny. Stop laughing."

"I'm sorry, but the mental picture…"

Okay, maybe it was a little funny. "I take it my name has come up before."

There was a slight pause, as if she were choosing her words carefully. "A time or two, yes."

"You don't seem too upset that our *secret* is out."

"Aunt Kay won't tell anyone. I trust her absolutely."

"She said that you were right, they would have a field day. What's that supposed to mean?"

"Long story," she said. "And I'm sorry she walked in on you like that. I really had no idea she would be home early."

"Are you coming back?"

"Not for another hour or so. I'm volunteering at the free clinic."

"So basically I'm on my own?"

"Yeah, sorry."

"You promise she's not going to hurt me?"

"If it makes you feel better, she's never actually shot anyone."

Oh, yeah, that made him feel so much better.

"However…" she said.

"What?"

"She might give you a hard time."

"*Might?* She already did!"

"Well, it's probably not over yet. Aunt Kay is very protective of me."

Swell.

"Did you see Ja—I mean Maddie?" he asked her. "I didn't get a page so I'm assuming things are good."

"I did see her, and she's doing really well. Logan and Hadley were there with Maggie. She's so much bigger and healthier, it's hard to imagine that they're the same age."

"Maddie will catch up."

"I'm going to miss her, but I know this is for the best. And I'm so glad to know that she has family."

"Did Logan say if he was able to contact his brother?"

"They left messages for him but so far they haven't heard back. Won't he be surprised to find out that not only is he a father, but to twins no less."

"And one with special needs. He'll have his hands full."

"Hold on a sec," Clare said, and he heard her talking to someone, then she was back. "Parker, I have to go. Can I call you later?"

He was hoping she would. "Of course."

"Okay, I'll talk to you then. And, Parker?"

"Yeah?"

"Good luck."

She seemed to be enjoying this a little too much.

He hung up and stuck his phone in his pocket, then folded the blanket he'd been wearing and opened the door. Clare's aunt was standing in the kitchen, sipping on a bottle of beer. She gestured to an open bottle in front of a bar stool at the kitchen island and said, "Have a seat, Parker."

"I should really get going," he said.

One brow rose slightly, and she gave him a look that said compliance was not optional.

Wow. She was tough. And a little scary.

No, she was *a lot* scary.

He handed her the blanket and did as he was told, feeling like a teenager meeting his girlfriend's parents for the first time. "I guess I can spare a few minutes."

"What are your intentions with my niece?"

Talk about getting right to the point. But who knew, maybe he would glean some insight on what made Clare tick. "I find her utterly fascinating," he said. "From the minute we were introduced I was drawn to her, and though she won't admit it, I think the feeling is mutual."

Kay neither confirmed nor denied it. "Clare is not as tough as she likes people to think."

"I know."

"She's a little broken."

"Who isn't?"

His answer seemed to satisfy her. "You're a smart man, but I'll be keeping my eye on you."

No surprise there, and he couldn't help but respect her for it. "Aunt Kay," he said, "I would expect no less."

Eight

It was just starting to get dark when Clare pulled in the driveway. Parker's car was gone, and she realized that deep down she had been hoping he was still there. Which was completely ridiculous. He had better things to do than hang around all day waiting for her.

But it would have been a little cool if he had. And a little terrifying.

She parked her aunt's car in the garage and stepped inside the house. "I'm home!"

"In here!" her aunt called from the living room.

Aunt Kay sat in her recliner, a book in her lap. She loved murder mysteries and psychological thrillers. The darker and gorier the better.

"So," Clare said, setting her purse down on the coffee table. "Is he buried in the backyard in a shallow grave?"

"Oh, please," her aunt scoffed. "There are much more effective ways to get rid of a body. And a car."

Clare gave her a look.

"I'm kidding. I like him."

Huh? Aunt Kay never "liked" anyone without getting to know them first, and that process could take weeks, and sometimes even months. "Just like that? You like him."

She shrugged. "Sometimes you just know. I would think you of all people would realize that."

"What's that supposed to mean?"

"You know *exactly* what I mean, Clare. You've got it bad for the man."

Yeah, she did. "He doesn't know that."

"He sure thinks he does."

Of course he did. He was a man. He thought he knew everything. It just so happened that in this case he was right.

Lucky guess.

"He is a little stubborn. I almost ran him to death on the jogging path the other day. Then I served him a half-frozen breakfast sandwich, which he actually ate. I should have known he would be too damned polite to complain."

"Sounds as if you've been having fun with him," Kay said.

"At his expense."

"Nothing wrong with that. Is he good in bed?"

Clare collapsed onto the sofa. "We never made it to the bed, but he's good on a couch."

"I'm just happy to hear that you're letting your hair down and having fun for a change. You need a man in your life."

"Don't get ahead of yourself." It had *bad idea* written all over it. She couldn't think straight when she was around him. All she could feel was an edgy sort of excitement, and she had been displaying a dangerously blasé attitude. She'd left him alone in her house, for God's sake. She *never* did that.

Although to be fair, removing him would have required dragging him sound asleep out the front door and leaving him on the porch. She'd tried to wake him when she was ready to go, but the man slept like the dead. "I haven't even decided if I'm going to sleep with him again," she told her aunt.

"Well, that just breaks my heart," Aunt Kay said. "A body that perfect should be put to good use."

Though she and Kay looked a little bit alike, and they both shared a deep aversion to farm life, Clare and her aunt couldn't have been more different. Kay grabbed life by the horns and didn't let go, while Clare wouldn't even venture on the other side of the fence.

"Here's something you might find interesting," Kay said. "I told him he could go up to your room to change."

Clare's jaw fell. "Why? You know I hate that."

"He apparently knows, too, because he asked to change in the bathroom down here instead. Said he didn't want to invade your space."

She blinked. "Oh."

"Sounds like he knows you pretty well already."

Yeah, it sort of did.

"And he respects your space."

Finally.

"And he's so hot."

Yes, he was.

"Maybe you should cut the guy a break and give him a chance. Not all men are liars and cheats. Something tells me that he's one of the good guys. Go out on a date or two. Have some fun, see where it goes."

"Why would I date someone that I can't even take home to my family? You said it yourself. They would have a field day with him."

"Maybe you should stop worrying about what they think."

She wished it were that easy. "How badly did you scare him?"

She shrugged. "If he scared easily you would have been rid of him months ago."

That still didn't make a relationship a good idea. It just meant that he was stubborn.

"I wish you could have seen the look on his face when he woke up and saw me standing there," Kay said with a smile. "If only I'd had my camera."

Clare would have paid big money to see that. "I hope you don't mind but I had to use your car. Mine committed suicide last night. It will cost almost as much as a new one to fix it."

"Of course I don't mind. Do we need to go car shopping?"

"I'm thinking it's time." Her aunt was a ruthless haggler. Be it a car or a refrigerator, when the salesman gave his rock-bottom price, she always managed to talk him down just a little lower. When they were rebuilding the house after the tornado she'd haggled the builder into paying out of pocket for the upgrades the insurance refused to cover. People just had a hard time telling her no.

"What brought you home so early?" Clare asked her.

"Claud and I had a fight. He asked me to marry him again."

"I take it you said no?"

She sighed, shaking her head. "Some men never learn."

She could have been talking about Parker, but Clare didn't bother to point that out.

"Are you hungry?" Kay asked. "Let's order dinner."

"I could go for sushi."

"Hmm, sounds good," she said, pulling out her phone. Neither of them cooked, so her aunt had the number of every restaurant in Royal that delivered on speed dial. "You want the usual?"

"Yes, please. While I'm waiting I'm going to go upstairs and get out of these scrubs." She was exhausted, thanks to a certain someone waking her at the crack of dawn that morning. But in all fairness it had been worth it.

"I'll let you know when it gets here," her aunt told her.

With sore, tired feet Clare climbed the stairs. A soak in the tub sounded good, but with the food on the way she took a hot shower instead. And though they were barely stubbly, she shaved her legs and cleaned up the bikini line, as well.

Just in case.

After her shower, as she was drying off, she took note of her new svelte figure. She looked damn good. Not that she'd been overweight, per se, but she hadn't exactly been healthy before.

She was still standing at the mirror naked, brushing the knots from her wet hair when her aunt knocked on the bedroom door. "Come on in! Just leave it on the bed."

She heard the door open, then close again, and a second later saw movement in the bathroom doorway. She turned and her breath caught in her lungs.

It was Parker standing there.

He grinned, his eyes raking over her from the top of her head all the way down to her pink-tipped toes, and every inch of her skin came alive all at once. He looked sexy as hell in faded jeans and a black T-shirt with the hospital logo. She had never seen him dressed so casually. She took in the way those biceps stretched the armholes of his shirt, and the way the jeans hugged his lean hips. But as good as he looked in his clothes, she knew he looked even better out of them.

He held up the sushi bag and said with a frustratingly sexy smile, "Special delivery."

Clare would have grabbed her robe to cover herself, but by the look in his eyes, and the fact that he had put the bag down and begun to peel off his clothes, she had the feeling the damage was already done.

"Your aunt sent me up," he said, taking off his shirt and dropping it on the floor. "Remind me to thank her profusely."

Aunt Kay would hear about it later, all right. Because she was meddling. Unfortunately she was really good at it.

The jeans went next, and Clare just stood there like a dummy watching, when she should have been kicking him to the curb for being so presumptuous. But then the boxers dropped and that was all she wrote. She couldn't tell him no now if her life depended on it.

"Come here," he said, taking her hand and leading her to the bed, walking backward so he didn't have to take his eyes off her. "You are so sexy."

Before she could censor herself, she said, "Look who's talking."

With a grin, he pulled her in and kissed her. And

kissed her. Oh, did she love kissing him. He smelled freshly showered and his chin was smooth. And as he hauled her up against the length of that ripped physique she was no more sturdy than her trembling hands. Lucky for her he wasted no time getting her off her feet and into bed.

He laid her on her back. Typically she didn't like being on her back, but as he climbed in beside her, she decided to let it slide. Then he started to kiss her again and she ignored that irrational need to be in control. She liked the feel of his weight pressing her into the mattress, his hands skimming her body, igniting a trail of fire across her skin. Then he began to kiss his way downward. It felt so good, and she wanted to relax and enjoy it, but as he reached the lowest part of her stomach, she automatically tensed.

Parker froze and lifted his head to look at her. "What's wrong?"

"Nothing."

He frowned and pushed himself up on his elbows. "Don't lie to me."

Damn it. Why did he have to be so intuitive? So concerned about her needs and her weird hang-ups. He needed to stop being so wonderfully thoughtful. "It's nothing."

"The hell it is. Talk to me, Clare."

The tone in his voice when he said her name sent shivers across her skin. After months of listening to the annoying nicknames he came up with for her, he had to choose *now* to start using her real name? When she was feeling most vulnerable? And did he have to say it with so much...*feeling*?

"What you're doing, what you're getting ready to do, it makes me feel very…"

"Vulnerable?"

"*Yes*. Very vulnerable."

"Do you want me to stop?"

"Yes. And no. I don't know, it's weird. I'm weird."

To his credit he didn't ask why she felt that way, because that was one big ole can of worms she would rather not spill just yet. Or maybe ever. He was just so darned open and honest, it was difficult not to give him some sort of explanation.

"You're not weird." He kissed her stomach once more, then made his way back upward. "And I don't want to do anything that makes you uncomfortable. This is supposed to be fun."

"I don't want you to think that I don't trust you."

"Clare, you barely know me. Trust is earned." He kissed her so sweetly she could have cried, or punched him, then he rolled onto his back and pulled her on top of him, grinning that devilish smile. "Better?"

"You don't mind?"

"I get to lie here while a gorgeous woman rides me like I'm a rodeo bull. What do you think?"

She leaned down to kiss him, for fear that if she didn't do something, she really would cry. Why did he have to be so wonderful? So understanding?

So damn *hot*.

He clearly had no reservations about being dominated, because she did ride him like a rodeo bull. He let her take the lead and set the pace, and even though he was on his back he didn't just lie there. He kept his hands and his mouth and his hips plenty busy making her crazy, and when he cradled her face in his hands and gasped her name as he shattered, that sent her sailing. Her own release came on like a tsunami that set her soaring headlong into ecstasy.

And he wasn't even through with her. He rolled her over and started from the top again. Her senses blurred and her body quaked and she forgot all about being in control, being nervous, and let him do his thing. And boy, did he do his thing. When she couldn't take it any longer, he was still champing at the bit to pleasure her again.

She'd rediscovered muscles tonight that she hadn't used in a long time, and it was way past time to take them out, dust them off and put them to good use. But she was going to pay for it tomorrow.

"I need to rest," she told him, flopping down on her back.

"I've heard that more than once tonight," he said with a grin, his hand teasing its way downward.

She intercepted it just above her navel. "I really mean it this time. I'm exhausted."

Looking disappointed, he rolled onto his back beside her. She didn't usually do the afterglow part, but as he took her hand, weaving their fingers together, she was too tired to move. Besides, it felt good to be near to him, their bodies close, their fingers intertwined. She liked it way too much.

"So what did my aunt say to you when you got here?" she asked him.

"She handed me the bag and said, 'Clare is in her bedroom, go on up.'"

She and Aunt Kay were going to have to have a talk about boundaries. About how it was not okay to send sexy men up to her bedroom. Although in this particular case Clare was willing to overlook the transgression.

"Your aunt is tough," he said. "But I think she likes me."

She wouldn't have sent him up here otherwise. "She has to be tough. She's been on her own most of her life. At a time when women didn't stay single and have careers instead of families."

He pushed himself up on his elbow. "She's never been married?"

"She was once, a really long time ago. But only for a few months."

"What happened? If you don't mind my asking."

"As a kid Kay hated farm life. Probably more than I do. She always dreamed of being a 'sophisticated city slicker,' as she put it. When she was seventeen she met a wealthy businessman from Tulsa. He was fifteen years older and worldly and she fell hard for him. Everyone loved him. He was charming and personable, and he showered her and her family with gifts. He took her to fancy restaurants and bought her nice clothes.

"I guess times were pretty hard and her parents were so happy to have a rich son-in-law, they didn't bat an eyelash when she turned up pregnant. So they had a shotgun wedding, then he took her to his house in Tulsa. Everyone thought he was perfect, and that Kay was such a lucky girl."

"No one is perfect."

"Yeah. They were married about a week when he started beating her."

Parker winced. "He was a predator."

"A predator with a volatile temper. She said he was like Jekyll and Hyde. The first time he hit her it was over the grocery money. He got angry because she bought a magazine. She called him stingy, and he backhanded her."

Parker cringed. "She didn't leave?"

"She had nowhere to go. Her parents were too poor to take her and her baby in, and back then a pregnant woman couldn't just go out and get a job, or even get a credit card without her husband's signature. Plus, he'd been subsidizing her family's farm. She knew that if she tried to leave, he would cut them off. Without that money, they would have fallen into poverty and lost everything. There would be no place for her parents and her five siblings to go. She was, as she puts it, in one hell of a pickle."

"Did her parents know what was going on?"

"No, of course not. If they had they would have driven to Tulsa and taken her back home, even if it meant losing everything. But she said the guilt would have hurt far worse than his fists ever could."

"That's one hell of a sacrifice. But she obviously got away."

"Yes, when he almost killed her. He came home from work angry and she said the wrong thing, so he used her as a punching bag. It was dumb luck that a neighbor had her window open and just happened to hear him screaming at her. When he stormed off the neighbor came by to see if she was okay. She found her bleeding and battered on the kitchen floor and called for help. Kay had internal injuries and would have bled to death if not for her. They got her to the hospital in time to save her life, but she lost the baby. And her uterus."

He closed his eyes and shook his head. Jesus.

"But she made sure it would never happen again. To her or anyone else."

"How?"

"Long story short, the day she got out of the hospital he said he was going to teach her a lesson, so she ran him over with his car."

His eyes went wide and his jaw fell. "Did she kill him?"

"Almost. He never walked right again. Or beat anyone else, I'm sure."

"Did she get in trouble?"

"She claimed it was self-defense, and after the way he beat her before that, people believed her. And Kay being Kay, she pulled herself up by her bootstraps and started over. When she was healed she wound up getting a job as a stewardess. She worked the international flights, so she's traveled pretty much everywhere, and has friends all over the world. When she was labeled 'too old' to do the job, she started a travel agency in Dallas. When the industry was at an all-time high she retired and sold the business for a small fortune. Now she spends most of her time traveling and volunteering for domestic-abuse organizations. She counsels young people trapped in abusive relationships."

"Wow, that's one hell of a life."

"I keep telling her that she needs to write a memoir. Her story could help a lot of people."

Parker's stomach rumbled loudly and Clare laughed. "Hungry?"

"I guess I skipped dinner," he said, rubbing a hand across his belly.

"I've got sushi and I'd be willing to share. And I could probably find a couple of beers in the fridge."

For several seconds he just looked at her, a funny little half smile on his face.

"What?"

"You surprise me, Clare."

"Why is that?"

"I thought for sure you would kick me out of your bed the second we were finished."

So did she. And normally she would have. "If I wasn't so tired I probably would," she lied, when the truth was she didn't want him to go anywhere.

She was playing a dangerous game, letting him get so close. If she wasn't careful she might do something stupid like fall head over heels in love with him.

Nine

Though she'd had only one day off work, when Clare pulled into the hospital lot the next morning it felt as if weeks had passed. So much had happened in such a short span of time.

She and Parker had had a picnic on her bed last night—sushi and beer—then had sex again. She couldn't imagine where he found the energy. He had impressive stamina, and loads of patience. She must have fallen asleep immediately afterward, and when she woke at midnight he was gone. He could have easily taken advantage of her unconscious state and hung around, but he really seemed to respect her space now. As hard as he'd pushed the past three months, suddenly he seemed to know just when to back off. It was a little disconcerting—no, make that terrifying—the way he was so attuned to her needs. Most men didn't have a clue.

Parker was in meetings all morning so she didn't see him right away, and as a result spent the first half of her day fighting the nervous excitement building in her belly. It wasn't as if she didn't see him almost every day at work. What a difference a few days could make. It felt as if her entire life had been flipped on its head. And somewhere in the back of her mind there was a nagging little voice asking her, what if it was all a game to him? What if he said something to make people believe they were an item. What if he hauled her up out of her chair behind the nurses' station and kissed her senseless?

As quickly as she had the thought, she dismissed it. Now that she knew him a little better, she didn't think he would be capable of anything so underhanded. Her aunt was right: he was one of the good guys. And Clare needed to get her priorities straight.

In her experience, the hotter the sex, the faster the relationship burned, until there was nothing left but ash. At the rate they were going, they wouldn't make it a week.

But he had been so sweet and so understanding about her reservations. Because of her hang-ups, a first intimate encounter with a man could be a bit awkward, and usually was. Men always thought they would be the one to "cure" her. As if she was broken or something. Which she was a little, she supposed. But they inevitably pushed her too far, or sometimes not far enough. It just always seemed to end in disaster for everyone. Eventually, she'd just stopped trying.

But this thing with Parker had her reevaluating that decision.

She was at the nurses' station looking up a chart on the computer when she heard his familiar footsteps, and as he neared, her heart sailed right up into her already tight throat and lodged there, pounding relentlessly.

Oh, man, this was *bad*.

She heard him talking to Rebecca. Clare knew for a fact that he'd dated the young nurse a time or two, and Clare felt her hackles rise. Though from the look on Rebecca's face when Clare glanced up, there was no love lost there. Her eyes settled on Parker for no more than a second, but the damage was done. Her heart did a nose-dive with a triple twist to the pit of her belly, knocking her insides all out of whack.

She heard him send Rebecca to check on a patient, then his footsteps as he came closer. Her heart sailed back up into her throat again and the crown of her scalp felt tingly and warm.

"Hey there, sweet cheeks," he said, which was exactly the way he would have greeted her before they slept together. And it would have annoyed the hell out of her. Now the sound of his voice strummed across her nerve endings, the friction warming her from the inside out.

"Dr. Reese," she said, not looking up from the screen. She was afraid that if she looked at him again, her true feelings would wind up on display for everyone to see. Including him. She was so beside herself her hands were trembling.

What was *wrong* with her?

He leaned down and looked over her shoulder at the computer screen, as if they were discussing a patient, and said quietly, "Have I mentioned that you're amazing?"

It was difficult not to swoon, or throw her arms

around his neck and kiss him. Hoping her voice wasn't as shaky as the rest of her, she said, "Once or twice."

"Sleep well?"

She nodded. Oh, had she ever. He had completely worn her out. "I was a little surprised that you left."

"You sound disappointed."

Yeah, she sort of did, didn't she?

"I would have stayed." He pointed at nothing in particular on the screen. "But I left because I knew that would be what you wanted."

And he was right. Or was he? If she had woken up beside him this morning, they could have had a little fun before work.

Which just goes to show how much this is clouding your judgment, you big dummy.

He really needed to get a handle on this habit he had of being so wonderful. Couldn't he say something sexist or rude? Or even better, condescending.

"Busy tonight?" he asked.

"What were you thinking?"

His breath was warm against her ear when he said, "You know exactly what I'm thinking, cupcake."

Back to the nicknames, were they? She was sort of getting used to hearing him use her name. But this time the teasing didn't bother her so much. "I promised my friend Violet that I would go to a stained-glass class with her tonight at Priceless, the antiques store just outside of town."

"Sounds like fun. Violet is Mac McCallum's sister, right? He owns the Double M Ranch."

"That's the one."

"Okay," he said. "How about afterward?"

She wanted to, she really did. It was all just moving

so fast. "I think I need some time to think. You know, about us."

"At least you're willing to admit there is an *us*."

At least.

As he straightened, his hand brushed her bare arm and her senses went into extreme overload. "Call me if you change your mind, princess."

Clare really, *really* wanted to see him tonight, and wrestled all day with what she should do. Should she be smart and reasonable, and take the time she needed to sort her feelings out, or be wildly irresponsible, say what the hell and jump him again? When Violet called later that afternoon to confirm their plans, Clare felt torn.

After small talk about the ranch she and her brother Mac owned, Violet asked, "Are we still on for tonight?"

An excuse was on the tip of her tongue, and Clare would have canceled, but the idea of seeing Parker socially four days in a row scared her a little.

"I can't wait," she told Violet with more enthusiasm than she was feeling. But she also knew she was doing the right thing. She was sure when she got to Priceless she would have a good time. She'd always had an interest in making stained glass and she'd heard that Raina Patterson's studio was impressive. In addition to teaching crafts, Raina sold antiques out of the space. Clare had shopped in Priceless, but never taken a class there.

She remembered her car situation and asked Violet, "I know it's a little out of your way, but could you give me a lift? I'm carless right now."

"Is that how you wound up at the Royal Diner with

Dr. Reese the other night?" Violet asked, a teasing lilt in her tone.

Ugh. Clare hated small towns sometimes. Violet was well aware of Parker's shenanigans and how much they irritated Clare. She and everyone else Clare knew.

She made a sound of disgust and said, "He basically kidnapped me. He offered to drive me home then took me to the diner instead. Short of walking, or calling a cab, I was stuck. But I was hungry and he paid the check, so it could have been worse, I guess."

"Why don't you just go out with him?"

"Because he's a womanizing, insufferable, mega-lomaniac."

"Yeah, but he's *so* hot."

"Then why don't you go out with him?"

There was a slight pause, then she said, "It's not me he wants."

Touché.

She heard footsteps behind her and turned to see Grace Haines, Janey's caseworker, approaching. *Madeline*, she reminded herself. For a second she thought the worst, that something was wrong, but Grace was smiling.

"I have to let you go, Violet. I'll see you tonight."

They hung up and Clare greeted Grace with a smile and a hug. "What brings you here?"

"I came to pick up some paperwork for Madeline's transfer and I thought I would stop and say hello."

"How is she doing?"

"She's great. She may get to go home in a couple of weeks. She'll have monitors, of course, but Hadley and Logan are taking a class at the center so they'll know what to do in an emergency."

"No word on the father?" Clare asked.

Grace shook her head somberly. "Either he can't be reached, or doesn't want to be. Logan doesn't speak too highly of his brother. Thankfully if Seth doesn't claim the twins, Logan and Hadley have already committed to adopting them. Honestly, I'm thinking that it would be for the best. I'm all for keeping children with their biological parents, but Seth is anything but reliable."

"After such a rotten start in life, those girls deserve a happy, stable family."

"They sure do," Grace said. "I dated Seth in high school. Even then there was nothing *stable* about him."

"Grace!"

Clare and Grace both turned to see Parker coming toward them, all smiles. "How's my favorite caseworker?"

Grace smiled. "Great, and how is my favorite pediatrician?"

"Couldn't be better," he said, not even acknowledging that Clare was standing there. Then they hugged and though it was totally platonic Clare felt the slightest twinge of jealousy. Grace was tall and curvy with chestnut hair that tumbled down in soft natural curls. She was also beautiful, and so very nice, and Clare had never met a caseworker more dedicated to the kids in her care. Standing together she and Parker made an extremely attractive couple.

"How's our girl doing?" Parker asked her.

"Still improving. I was just telling Clare that she might be able to go home in a couple of weeks."

"That makes my day," he said.

Grace looked at her watch. "I'd love to stay and chat but I have a home visit to get to. But I'm sure I'll see you guys again soon."

"It was great to see you," Parker said, then he turned to Clare and his smile disappeared. "When you get a minute I need to see you in my office."

Her heart plummeted and landed with a messy splat. He looked genuinely upset with her and she had no clue what she had done wrong.

"Um, yeah, sure," she said. "Now is good."

He nodded sternly, turned and all but marched down the hall. The two women watched him walk away in stunned silence.

"What was that about?" Grace asked, looking as taken aback by his demeanor as Clare was.

"I have no idea. I guess I'm about to find out."

"Well, good luck."

They headed in opposite directions down the hall. When Clare got to Parker's office the door was partially closed so she knocked gingerly.

"Enter."

She stepped inside expecting to see him at his desk. Then the door shut behind her and she spun around. Parker stood there grinning. "Hey there, sweet cheeks."

"Hey," Clare said, looking hopelessly confused.

Parker took her hand and pulled her against him, then proceeded to kiss her socks off. When he finally let her go she gave him a playful shove. "You creep! I really thought you were mad at me."

"Pretty good, huh?" Parker said with a grin. He probably could have made his point without sounding angry, but the crushed look on Clare's face had been worth it. If he'd snapped at her a week ago, she would have stood there stony faced and emotionless, as if she only had to listen because he was the boss. Not that he snapped at his staff all that often, but it did happen occasionally. But her reaction said something that up until now he could only hypothesize.

She cared. A lot.

She slid her arms up around his neck, pressed her body to his and pulled him down for an enthusiastic kiss. He got an instant hard-on. She was sexy as hell, and so completely unaware of it.

"Did you really need to talk to me or did you just want to make out?" she asked him. "Because the longer I'm in here the more suspicious it will look."

"I saw the way you looked at us when I hugged Grace. I thought we should talk about it."

"How did I look?" she asked, even though she knew that he knew exactly what was going on.

"A little green, actually."

She backed out of his arms, nose in the air. "That's ridiculous."

"Is it?"

She folded her arms stubbornly. "Yes, it is."

"Admit it, you were jealous."

"Why would I be jealous? We're not in an exclusive relationship."

"Well then, maybe we should be."

Her eyes went wide and up went the wall. "That's crazy. I haven't even decided if I'm going to sleep with you again."

Yeah, right. "Then what was that kiss you just laid on me all about? Are you a tease, Clare?"

She didn't seem to have a comeback for that, but her inner struggle was written all over her face.

"You do what you need to do," he told her. "But as

long as we're *involved*, I'm not going to date, or have any sort of physical relationship with anyone else."

She looked as if she might cry, or barf. As if she didn't know *how* to feel. And all she managed was a shaky, "O-okay."

He tugged her back into his arms with no resistance and tipped her chin up so he could look into her eyes. "That's a promise, sweetheart."

Something dark flashed in her eyes. "In my experience men have a very limited grasp on the concept of a promise."

"Sounds like you've been hanging around the wrong kind of men."

Clearly he'd hit a sore spot. She untangled herself from his arms and said, "This is not the time or the place to get into this. I have to get back to work. If anyone asks, we're discussing Janey—I mean, Madeline's case. Finishing up paperwork or something."

He nodded. "As you wish."

After she left, he took a seat at his desk. Boy, had he hit a nerve.

Luc popped his head in a second later. "Hey, have you got a minute?"

"Sure, what's up?"

He flopped down in the chair opposite Parker and propped his feet up on the desk. "I haven't seen you in a few days so I wasn't able to congratulate you on solving the mystery."

Mystery? Had he somehow figured out that Parker and Clare were intimate?

He decided to play dumb. "I'm not sure what you mean."

Luc looked at him as if he was an idiot. "Madeline. I hear that she's getting better."

Oh, *that mystery*. "Twin-to-twin transfusion," he said with a shrug. "Who knew?"

"Was that Clare I just saw leaving your office?"

"We were discussing a patient," he said.

"I also heard you were at the diner with her the other night. Sounds as if you're wearing her down."

It took a second for Parker to realize that Luc was referring to their bet. Parker had completely forgotten about it. What seemed like an innocent joke then could have real repercussions for his relationship with Clare if she ever caught wind of it.

"Actually I haven't made any progress at all. And I'm thinking I'm just wasting my time."

"You might want to rethink that," Luc said. "I mentioned our bet to Bruce Marsh in Radiology and he wanted in. He must have told someone, and they must have told someone else. Last night I heard a member mention it at the club."

Suddenly Parker was the one who felt like barfing. And he couldn't even get angry because it wasn't unusual for their little bets to make the rounds of their fellow doctors. To have this one running rampant through the hospital was bad enough. Now that it was out in public, God only knew who would get wind of it.

What the hell had he done?

"I'm clearly not getting anywhere with her, so let's just call you the winner and be done with it," he told Luc.

Luc frowned. "It's not like you to give up so easily. Is there something you're not telling me?"

He wrestled with his options. If he told Luc the truth

he would be breaking a promise to Clare, but if he didn't he could find himself in the hot seat.

Breaking a promise to Clare to save himself? Really? That sounded like something his father would do. There had to be a better way.

"The truth is, I've started seeing someone," he told Luc, sticking as close to the truth as possible. "She works here at the hospital and wants to keep the relationship quiet while we see where this goes."

His curiosity piqued, Luc asked, "Is it someone I know?"

"Maybe. Maybe not. But I have strong feelings for this woman, and if she hears about the bet she might take it the wrong way."

"I see what you mean," Luc said. "I'm sorry, Parker. I'll see what I can do to make this discreetly go away, but it seems to have taken on a life of its own."

Parker felt sick to his stomach. How the hell had he gotten himself in this mess? What had he been thinking? Innocent bet or not it had been sexist and chauvinistic. That was exactly the person he'd been struggling *not* to be. There was a time when he saw women as playthings…as an interesting and pleasurable way to pass the time. And while he'd never been openly or deliberately disrespectful to any member of the opposite sex, his actions spoke for themselves.

If Luc couldn't get a handle on this, Parker would have no choice but to fess up to Clare and take his lumps. Even if that meant losing her.

Ten

As promised Violet picked Clare up on the way to Priceless.

It was currently housed in a giant renovated red barn in the Courtyard, the growing artist's community on the outskirts of town. Clare used to be a regular shopper in the antiques store when it was located downtown, but it had been devastated by the tornado. Since Raina had changed locations, Clare never seemed to get out that way often enough. Seeing all of the amazing stock up front in the shop as Raina led them back to the workshop was motivating Clare to come back very soon.

Violet had been quiet for most of the drive there, which was very unusual for her. She was one of the spunkiest women Clare knew. And weirdly enough, Clare, who was usually the quiet type, couldn't seem to stop talking. She felt all bubbly and excited inside, while at the same time questioning her own sanity.

Exclusive, my ass. How could the hospital playboy make such an outrageous claim? She was betting that he'd never even been in a committed relationship. Now he wanted one with *her*? They didn't even…*match.* He should be with someone like Grace. Someone as beautiful as he was.

Once they were inside the building under the bright studio lights, Clare realized that Violet didn't look so good. Her skin looked especially pale against her thick auburn hair, and Clare could swear she was a little thinner than the last time she saw her.

When the class was under way, she leaned close to Violet. "Are you feeling okay? You look a little green."

The minute the words were out she realized that Parker had said nearly the exact same thing to her earlier today. Oh, great, he was beginning to rub off on her.

"I don't know what's wrong," Violet said, sipping gingerly on the water bottle she'd brought to class. "I'll be fine for a while, then get this weird overwhelming nausea. It must be some sort of virus."

It didn't sound like a virus to Clare. "When do you seem to feel sick the most?"

"I wake up feeling pretty lousy every day, and though I'm starving all the time, if I eat I can barely hold it down. I've been really tired, too."

Clare made her voice even lower and asked, "Is there any possibility that you're pregnant?"

Violet sucked in a breath and a myriad of emotions flashed across her face. Shock, fear, confusion. Then she shook her head and said, "No, that can't be it. I'm not even seeing anyone."

"Are you sure, because early prenatal care—"

"That's not it," she insisted. "It's just a virus or a parasite or something. I'll be fine."

Clare let it go, but a few minutes later, as she snapped a piece of glass in the wrong place, Violet nudged her with her elbow and whispered, "Oh, my God! Is that a hickey?"

Clare glanced at the people sitting around them. "Where?"

"On your neck, genius."

Clare gasped and slapped a hand across the side of her neck, felt herself starting to flush. "No, of course not."

Violet wasn't buying it. "You haven't stopped smiling since I picked you up and you practically talked my head off on the way here. No wonder you've been in such a good mood."

She was going to deny it. Say that it was… Well, that was the problem. She didn't know what to say. Besides, the inferno burning in her cheeks was a dead giveaway.

Violet leaned in close and whispered, "Did you do what I think you did? And if so, with whom?"

Clare opened her mouth but nothing came out.

"Was it Dr. Reese?"

Still speechless, Clare just looked at her, and Violet's eyes went wide. "Oh, my God, it *was* him!"

"Shhhh," Clare scolded, as people turned to look at them. "Keep your voice down."

"I knew it," Violet whispered. "I knew you had a thing for him. And who can blame you?"

"You can't tell anyone," Clare said, tugging the band from her hair so it would tumble down and cover the evidence. "And I mean *no one*."

"Why? You guys make an adorable couple."

No, he made her look good. He and Grace? *They* made an adorable couple.

"I'm not even sure if I'm going to see him again," she told Violet. "If people knew it would just be awkward. You have to promise me you won't say anything to anyone."

"Of course I promise," Violet said, laying a reassuring hand on her arm. "But you can't keep it a secret forever."

If she tried hard enough she could. The alternative was unacceptable. If her staff were to learn how flighty and irresponsible she'd been behaving, they would lose all respect for her.

Parker still on her mind, Clare could hardly concentrate on the class. And no matter how hard she tried she couldn't get the damned glass pieces cut without mangling them horribly.

First stained-glass class. Major fail.

She looked up and saw Raina's little boy Justin, dressed in a cowboy get-up, clomping around the perimeter of the room as if he was riding a horse.

Their eyes met and Clare waved. Justin changed direction and trotted over to her table.

"Hey there, partner," Clare teased, then realized almost immediately that she sounded just like Parker and his silly nicknames. He really was starting rub off on her.

But Justin giggled and stopped at her table, all smiles. "Hi, Clare."

"I like the threads," she told him, tugging on his fringed faux-suede vest.

"Santa brought it," he said, very matter-of-factly. "*And* he brought me a *daddy*."

Clare gasped. *"No way!"* Everyone knew that Raina and Nolan Dane were engaged, but Clare played along, telling Justin, "You must have been super good all year."

"Super, *super* good," he said proudly.

"Hey, mister," Raina said to her son, stopping at the table to check Clare and Violet's progress. "Do we bother the customers during classes?"

His little bottom lip rolled into a pout and he shook his head.

"Skedaddle."

He sighed and said, *"Okay."*

Raina chucked him on the chin and he trotted off on his invisible steed. Then she looked down at the mess on Clare's table and tried to smile.

"I guess stained glass just isn't my thing," Clare told her.

"It takes practice," Raina said.

Not to mention concentration and a steady hand. Neither of which Clare possessed at the moment. She still couldn't believe Parker had given her a hickey, when he knew how important it was to keep their relationship secret. If people in town got wind that she was seeing someone—*anyone*—she would be under the microscope. Because that's the way it was in Royal. Everyone was all up in each other's private business.

The longer she thought about what he'd done, the angrier she became, and by the time Violet dropped her at home she was so hot under the collar it was a wonder steam wasn't shooting out her ears. She knew she had to settle this or she would be up all night fuming.

Thankfully her aunt was home. She sat in her recliner reading one of her murder mysteries.

"Would it be okay if I use your car?" Clare asked her.

"Sure, hon, help yourself." Her head tipped a little to the left. "Are you okay? You look upset."

Upset didn't begin to say it. "You have no idea."

"Uh-oh. Parker?"

"I'll explain when I get back." She dialed Parker's number on her way to the garage.

"Hello," he answered.

"I need your address."

There was a slight pause. "You do?"

She started the car and initialized the navigation. "Yes, I do."

He recited the address and she punched it in. He was only fifteen minutes away. "Thanks."

"You don't sound happy."

"I'm not."

"So why did you want my address?"

"So I can come over there and kill you."

Parker wasn't sure what was going on, or why Clare would be unhappy, but it didn't take long to find out. She got there in ten minutes flat and started pounding on his front door. He opened it and there she stood on his porch looking *incredibly* unhappy. After they'd hung up he'd wondered if this was some sort of revenge for pretending to be mad at her earlier that day.

Apparently not.

"Whatever you're unhappy about, I'm certain it's not the door's fault."

She glared at him. "You gave me a *hickey*?"

Was that what had gotten her panties in such a twist? He stepped back and gestured her inside. "Come on in. Let's talk."

She charged past him. "Violet saw it, and she made me admit I'm seeing someone. And she knows it's *you*."

"Clare, I didn't give you a hickey."

She made a rude noise. "Well, I didn't give it to *myself*."

"Let me see," he said.

She took her coat off and dropped it over the back of the couch, baring her neck to him. "See? How do you explain that?"

He examined her neck. "Explain what?"

"What do you mean, what? Don't tell me you don't know what a hickey looks like."

"Clare, there's nothing here."

Her lips pressed into a tight line. "That's not funny."

"I'm not trying to be funny. Is it maybe on the other side?" Frowning, she turned so he could look. "Sorry, nothing there either."

"How can that be? Violet said—" She blinked, then blinked again. "Oh, my gosh, that little sneak."

"I don't get it," he said.

She collapsed onto the couch, dropping her head in her hands. "She suspected that I was seeing someone so she lied about the hickey to make me spill my guts. And I fell for it, hook, line and sinker."

Was that all?

"I'm sorry," she said.

"It's okay." He sat down beside her, took her hand, which she promptly retracted.

"No, it's not. I'm an intelligent person. You'd think that I would have the good sense to at least confirm it in a mirror before I started flinging accusations."

"I could think of a few ways you could make it up to

me," he said, but he didn't get the smile he'd been hoping for. He wasn't sure if she'd even heard him.

"This is ridiculous," she said, and was up on her feet again, pacing the rug. "I'm acting like a crazy person."

He took her hand to hold her still. "Don't you think you might be overreacting a little? I'm assuming you told Violet the truth because you trust her." Or because deep down, she actually wanted the truth to come out. It was too soon to say.

She looked up at him. "Did you mean what you said today? About being exclusive? It wasn't just a line to get me back into bed?"

They were back to that? He should have known that this wouldn't be easy, that she would question his every move. What had made her so afraid to follow her heart?

"Come here," he said, pulling her down into his lap, surprised when she didn't resist. He looked her dead in the eyes, so she would know he was telling the truth, and said, "It was not a line. I meant every word I said."

She looked as though she really wanted to believe him but wasn't quite there yet. Which was a little frustrating, but not a deal breaker. She would get there.

"Have you ever even been in a committed relationship?" she asked him.

He shook his head. "Nope."

"Then how can you promise to be exclusive to me? Do you even know how?" She paused then said, "Don't answer that."

Oooookay.

She looked around his living room, as if actually seeing it for the first time since she got there. "Nice condo. Although I would have imagined you in something a lot bigger. I like the decor, though."

"It's an executive rental—it came this way."

"Oh."

"I'll buy something eventually. I just thought I should settle into the job first, before I tied myself here."

"So you're not sure you're staying?"

Definitely not what he'd said. "I wasn't sure *then*." He picked up her hand and kissed the inside of her wrist. "But I am now."

"If you tell me you're staying because of me, I'll probably have a panic attack. Just sayin'."

He grinned. "No panic attacks tonight."

"I'm sorry."

"Would you *stop* apologizing?" He rearranged her on his lap so she was straddling his thighs. "I have a great idea. Why don't you kiss me."

"You're just trying to shut me up."

He grinned. "Pretty much."

She tried to look offended, but laughed instead. "There is such a thing as *too* honest, you know. But this time, I guess I'll let it slide."

"I think it's time for a tour of the house," he told her. "Specifically my bedroom, though I do have a fairly sturdy desk in my office. Just sayin'. Or there's the trundle bed in the spare room—"

She folded a hand over his mouth, a saucy grin on her glossy lips. "We can do it wherever you want. Now, shut up and kiss me."

Despite all the options Parker had mentioned, they went to the bedroom first, then never left. Every time she told herself that the sex couldn't possibly get better, he pulled out the stops, making her even crazier than he had the time before. It was as if someone had written a handbook on her emotional and sexual needs, and he'd read it from cover to cover. Twice.

Afterward he pulled on a pair of flannel pajama bottoms and headed to the kitchen for a snack. Which wound up being leftover reheated spinach and bacon quiche—coincidentally, her favorite kind—and a huge bowl of grapes. And it was delicious. They sat side by side on his bed, eating the quiche and feeding each other grapes.

"This is so good," she said, and always on the lookout for palatable frozen fare, asked, "What brand is it?"

"It's not," he said.

"Oh. Did you get it from a restaurant?"

He looked at her a little funny. "No."

"Does someone cook for you?"

He shook his head. "Guess again."

"Elves?"

He laughed. "Is it really so hard to believe that a man can cook?"

In her family it was. "The men in my family don't cook."

"How about you?"

"I was banned from the kitchen a long time ago. Forget to turn off the burner under the frying pan and almost burn down the kitchen *one time*, and you're branded for life." Which was fine because she had always hated cooking. And still did. "You really made this?" she asked.

"I really did." He popped a green grape in her mouth. She bit down and the sweet juice exploded onto her tongue. Lately food seemed to taste so much better than before. In fact, everything about her life felt pretty darn good.

If only she could let go and just trust it. Trust him.

"Can you cook anything else?" she asked him.

"Anything you want, as long as I have the ingredients. And a recipe."

"Did you take classes?"

"I dated a chef. We saw each other on and off for about six months, I guess. She would cook for me and I would watch. Then I started experimenting on my own. I realized I was pretty good at it, and I found it incredibly relaxing. And I'm not gonna lie, the chicks dig it."

"Hit me again," she said, nodding to the grapes.

"For someone so trim you sure can put the food away." He fed her another grape, the pad of his thumb grazing her lower lip.

"I've lost almost twenty pounds since December."

He looked genuinely surprised. "Seriously?"

"Seriously."

"That's a lot."

"Did you not notice that I was a bit on the chubby side?"

He shrugged. "You looked good to me. Besides, chubby is okay."

Was this guy for real? "Aside from your weird fascination with me, I was under the impression that you were more attracted to the Barbie-doll type."

"So was I."

What the hell was that supposed to mean? Was he deliberately trying to confuse her?

"So what changed?" she asked him.

"I saw you."

If it was a lie, it was the sweetest lie anyone had ever told her. And the idea that it might be true scared her half to death. "Haul out the boots and shovels," she said. "The BS is getting deep."

He laughed. "Why is it so unbelievable?"

"Because everyone knows the kind of man you are. You're a womanizer and a serial dater. That sort of guy doesn't settle down. He conquers. And when he gets bored he moves on. And even if he does eventually settle, it never lasts."

"Yep, that pretty much sounds like me."

She blinked, taken aback by his honesty. He sure wasn't helping his case. "So I'm right?"

"I didn't say that."

"What *are* you saying?"

"People change. Priorities change. I'm not the man I used to be."

In her experience, people could change, but not that much. "So you're telling me that you're ready to settle down?"

"I don't know. Maybe. There was a time when I never would have considered a wife and kids. Now it doesn't seem so far-fetched."

He would make an excellent husband and father, and she envied the woman who snagged him. And she wished that it could be her. Even though she knew it was impossible.

"As much as you love kids, I'm surprised you don't have any," he told her. "Just haven't found the right man?"

She hadn't even been looking. "My patients are my children," she said. "Besides, I'm only thirty-three. I still have a few good childbearing years ahead of me. Or maybe I'll follow in my aunt Kay's footsteps and never have any. God knows there are enough of us already. Another baby in the family would be like white noise. Especially a child of mine."

Eleven

"Why is that?" Parker asked Clare.

"Forget it," she said with a shake of her head, as if she were clearing away an unpleasant memory. "It's a long story."

Something told him not to push the issue of her family, but eventually they were going to talk about it, and he was going to get to the root of the problem. Even if he had to take drastic measures. The key to her heart was in there somewhere under all the baggage, and he was going to find it.

But for now he would let it slide.

"By the way, I noticed last night that the toilet in your bathroom was running like crazy," he said.

"I know. I have to call a plumber."

"You want me to take a look at it?"

"You know how to fix a toilet?"

"Yup."

"What kind of millionaire are you?"

He laughed. "Not a very good one, I guess."

"You sure don't act like a rich guy."

"Are you forgetting? I drive a luxury import."

"That you put a Santa hat and antlers on for Christmas."

He grinned. "I like Christmas."

"And you are the least pretentious person I know. There's a rumor going around that you give a lot of your money to charity."

"My *dad's* money," he said. "And my reasons are not as philanthropic as you might think. I give his money away to charity because I know that's the last thing he would want me to do with it."

"Not the charitable type?"

"For him it was all about making more money. It was never enough. He died a very wealthy man, but his money never did anyone much good. Not even him."

"And now it does."

"Exactly. I may have to live with the millionaire label, but that doesn't mean I have to like it."

"So, when did you learn to fix a toilet?"

"My father believed I should know everything about running his business, from the ground up. Including building maintenance. So instead of letting me volunteer for Greenpeace during summer break—which is what I really wanted to do—I was forced to follow George the maintenance guy around for three months. I thought it was all a total waste of time. As a doctor I wouldn't need to know how to fix a toilet or unclog a drain."

"Unless your home toilet breaks and the plumber can't make it over for a week."

"Exactly. Looking back, I'm thankful for everything I learned. I really have used a lot of that knowledge in my adult life. Not everything he taught me was a total waste of time. His tyrannical way of running his business taught me the best way not to talk to my staff. He thought that he was better than anyone who had less money than him. I was supposed to take over his business. Instead, I sold it all off before the body was cold."

Her brows rose.

"I know that sounds crass, and probably a little selfish, but the offer was made and I took it. I never wanted his business. From the time I was small I was into nature and conservation. There was a time when I seriously considered becoming a veterinarian."

"No way."

"I loved animals, and it got me into trouble sometimes."

"How so?"

"When I was a kid, maybe thirteen or fourteen, I got wind of a project my dad and his company would be working on. They were trying to buy land and develop on a nature preserve. I went on a campaign to stop them."

"You must have been a really confident kid to take on not only a huge company but also your own father."

"I'm not sure if it was confidence, stupidity or just a glaring lack of common sense, but when he figured out what I was up to he grounded me for a month."

"And you said that your mother wasn't around?"

"It was a pretty strange situation actually. My father

hired my mother as a surrogate. He wanted an heir, a mini me, if you will. Long story short, they fell in love."

"Wow, it sounds like the plot of a romance novel or movie. What could be more romantic?"

"Shortly after my birth she left us both for the limo driver."

Clare cringed. "Okay, so not that romantic," she said. "How sad that must have been for your father, especially with a newborn baby."

"I think he was more angry than sad. For pretty much my entire childhood he drilled into me that women were all liars and cheaters and were not to be trusted. He considered them playthings."

"And you believed him?"

"You hear something enough times, you can't help but believe it. He more or less had me brainwashed."

One bad experience and Parker's father felt the need to judge all women? "What a horrible thing to do to you," she said.

"I had money to burn, a career I loved and women champing at the bit, willing to do pretty much anything to land me. And I let them, knowing damn well I would never settle down. In my eyes, life should have been perfect. In reality I felt empty, and disgusted with myself. At that point I knew things had to change. I can't really blame my mother for leaving," Parker said. "If you knew my father you would understand why. To put it in simple terms, he was a bully. It was his way or the highway."

"So you've never even met her?"

He shook his head. "I haven't even seen a picture. I thought I might find some when he died, but he probably burned them."

"If she thought your father was that terrible, why did she leave you there with him?"

"I've asked myself that same thing a million times."

"I just… I don't understand. I'll *never* understand how a woman could leave her own child."

"I'll probably never know why she did it, but I'd like to think she left out of her love for me. That I was somehow better off without her. I guess I'll never know for sure."

"You've never tried to find her? It probably wouldn't be that difficult."

"I'm not difficult to find either."

There was so much buried pain and bitterness in those words it hurt her heart.

"Why don't we talk about something else?" he said, stretching out across the bed and pulling her down with him. "Or better yet, let's not talk at all."

Tempting, but there was something she had to say to him, something he deserved to hear, hard as it would be. She untangled herself from his arms and sat up. "No, we do need to talk."

He sat up, too. "What?"

"I need to explain to you why I'm the way I am. You know, my need to be in control of myself at all times. Especially in bed."

"Clare, you don't have to explain."

"No, I do. I want you to understand." She took his hand between her two and squeezed it. "I trust you."

The smile he flashed her made her feel all warm inside. She was starting to believe that he genuinely cared about her. Which was awful, of course, and wonderful. And she didn't have a clue what to do about it.

One step at a time, Clare.

"This happened a long time ago, at my first job out of nursing school. Before I started working at the hospital I worked very briefly at an OB-GYN practice. It was my first real job besides working on my parents' farm and I was incredibly naive. One of the doctors sort of took me under his wing. Then into his bed."

Parker looked pained, but stayed quiet.

"He was older, and way more sophisticated. I felt so honored that he picked me. For a month he was my entire world. We had to keep it a secret, of course. For my sake, he said. So it wouldn't look like favoritism. I thought we were falling in love, then his pregnant wife showed up at the office."

Parker mumbled a curse. "I take it you didn't know he was married?"

She shook her head. "He never talked about her, or even had a picture in his office. I didn't have a clue. Needless to say I ended it the second she was gone. I never would have gone near him if I knew. He came on strong and was so persistent."

"And I did the same damn thing, didn't I?" His laugh was a wry one. "All the time I thought I was being charming, you thought I was a total creep."

She cracked a smile. "Well, not a *total* creep."

"I'm really sorry, Clare."

"There's no way you could have known. Besides, I'm not the person now that I was back then. I'd been so sheltered up to that point. My family is really big and very traditional. My parents wouldn't even talk about letting me date until I was seventeen, and by then I was cramming to get on the honor list so I could get a scholarship and get the hell out of there. Nursing school was brutal, so I spent most of my time studying. I didn't have much experience with boys, and I had virtually no experience with men. It never even occurred to me that a married man would initiate an intimate relationship. Where I was from men didn't do that sort of thing. Or if they did, no one talked about it."

"So what happened? Did the pregnant wife find out?"

"She found an old text that he'd saved. A very personal and explicit text."

"You were sexting."

She nodded. "She was not happy about it. It was a huge blowout. He said that *I* seduced *him*. Needless to say I lost my job. And my dignity. No one believed me when I said I didn't know he was married."

"It wasn't your fault."

"Most people didn't see it that way, my family included. I was devastated and I needed someone to talk to. My aunt was away on business and I couldn't get ahold of her. I called my sister Sue instead. Growing up, she was the one I was closest to. I made her swear that she would take it to the grave. Two minutes after we hung up my mother called in hysterics. She said that I should have known better and I should come right back to the ranch where I belonged. I was a simple country girl and people would always try to take advantage of me. And it was high time I realized that I would never make it on my own, and I needed my family. She wouldn't even let me try to explain. She ended the conversation by saying how disappointed she was in me."

"That's a tough one," he said.

"It gets worse. My dad called me later that day to say that the family had had a meeting and everyone agreed that I had to come home."

His eyes went wide. "Your mom told the whole family?"

Clare nodded. "Of course I told my dad no, I wouldn't be coming home. I was too ashamed and mortified to show my face. No one even bothered to ask if I was okay. Then my siblings started calling me, trying to shame me into coming back home, saying how much everyone missed me. It's horrible when everyone you love and care about turns their back on you. I was devastated."

"You had every right to be. They betrayed your trust."

"They would tell you that I betrayed theirs."

"They're dead wrong. And shame on your brothers and sisters for not being there for you."

"Aunt Kay was the only one who believed me. Who cared. She invited me to come stay with her until I was back on my feet. I spent most of the first month in bed. But Kay was friends with the hospital administrator at Royal Memorial and she got me an interview. I didn't want to go, but she insisted. It was probably the best thing she could have done for me. With work to focus on I was able to put what happened behind me. Originally I had planned to get my own place, but we realized that it didn't make sense. Kay only uses the house as a home base when she isn't traveling, which isn't very often. She likes having someone here to keep an eye on things. It ended up being a perfect situation for both of us."

He shook his head, looking baffled. "I don't even know what to say."

"You don't have to say anything. Besides, I'm not finished."

"It gets worse?"

"I've only ever told Aunt Kay, because I knew she of all people would understand. It's very difficult to talk about the things that he did to me. But I have to tell you."

He looked pained. "You don't have to tell me."

She took a deep breath and blew it out, trembling from head to toe. "No, I want to. I *need* to."

He put his hand on her shoulder. "Only if you're ready."

"He was my first. And I know that sounds crazy considering my age, but I wanted to save myself for someone special. It's how I was raised. I honestly thought he was the one. That's why I let him do what he wanted to do."

"Which was?"

She swallowed hard. *You can do this.* "He liked it… rough."

Parker winced. "But not your first time. Right?"

Though she wanted to bow her head in shame, she held it high instead. "He didn't force me, and I could have said no, but I was so head over heels for him, I would have done anything he asked. Even though it terrified me. He got off on my fear."

Looking confused, Parker asked, "So, am I to understand that every time you had sex with him, you were scared? Or am I way off base?"

She took a deep breath and blew it out. "*Every* time. Some more than others. It depended on his mood. Near the end of the relationship he had begun to get very aggressive. And again, I could have walked away. I chose to stay."

"This doctor have a name?" Parker asked, jaw

clenched. "In honor of your dignity and self-respect, I'd like to kick his teeth in."

"He wouldn't be worth the effort. He was a sleazebag. He'll probably always be one. It was just poor judgment on my part."

"Listen to me," Parker said, gently cradling her face in his hands. "It's not your fault."

She folded her hands over his. "I know that now, but it still stings after all this time. I'm still humiliated. Without fail, every time I'm visiting the farm someone makes a snide remark about the relationship. They'll never let me live it down."

"You're giving them way too much power," he said.

"Probably. And I hope that someday I can let it go. I'm just not ready yet."

"What can I do?" he said.

"Just be patient with me. "

"I can do that," he said with a smile. After everything she'd just revealed, all the pain she had spilled out, she could smile, too. It felt good to talk about it. To let off some of the pressure.

"After it was over, it took years before I wanted to have sex again," she told him, "and a long time after that before I could let myself enjoy it. I've come a long way since then, but I'm still not one hundred percent there. Maybe I'll never be."

"No, you will be."

Twelve

Parker sounded so sure, Clare wanted to believe him. If anyone could pull her back from the dark recesses of her mind, it would probably be him. For whatever reason, he seemed to "get" her. And she was nowhere close to ready to admit that to him.

"I'm thirsty. You want something to drink?" she asked him. She needed a minute to regroup, and could see the understanding in his eyes.

"I could go for a beer," he said.

"I'll be right back." She hopped up from the bed and headed downstairs to the kitchen. It was a very nice condo, but as she got a better look around, it seemed a little barren and impersonal. Definitely temporary. She wondered what sort of place he would be looking for…

Nope, she didn't even want to know, because what if it was exactly the same thing she wanted? That would just be awkward.

The refrigerator was well stocked with a variety of foods. Lots of fruits and vegetables and cheeses. She grabbed two beers off the door and headed back up. After this beer she had to go home. She'd never done well sleeping in strange places. She was a creature of habit. If she stayed here, in an unfamiliar bed, she would probably toss and turn all night long.

Yeah, Clare, just keep telling yourself that.

The truth was that she was scared, plain and simple.

And wasn't she being a little presumptuous? He hadn't even asked if she wanted to stay. It was possible that he didn't even want her to.

As if. He would probably love it. It would make him very happy.

A cold chill raised the hair on her arms. Wasn't that exactly what had gotten her into trouble before?

Don't you want me to be happy? her ex would ask when something he did made her uncomfortable. *You know I would never do anything to hurt you.*

It was a lie. He wasn't happy *unless* he was hurting her.

But this was different. Parker went out of his way to make *her* happy. She thought that telling him the truth about her past would make her feel vulnerable and weak, but in reality she felt empowered. And it was a *good* feeling. She felt good when she was with him. So why was she still fighting this? Everything about their relationship felt right. He seemed like someone she could really learn to trust. She was already partway there. Didn't she owe it to herself to at least *try*?

When Clare stepped back into the bedroom Parker was sound asleep and snoring softly. And here she thought he'd worn her out, when it looked as if it was the other way around. She considered waking him, but he looked so adorable when he slept.

She set the beers down on the night table and slid into bed beside him. He was facing her, so she could lie there and watch his beautiful face all night if she wanted to.

She thought about his mother abandoning him and her heart broke. It was so sad she wanted to cry. No wonder he didn't let himself get close to women. The most important woman in his life had walked away without looking back. And his horrible father had only exacerbated the problem by filling his head with lies.

It made her wish things could be different for him, that she could be the one to make him see that mother or no mother, he was an amazing human being. Truly one of the good ones.

She must have dozed off, because when she opened her eyes again the lights were out and she was in the exact same position on the bed. Parker was gone.

She rubbed her eyes and rolled over to grab her phone, which was almost dead. Six o'clock.

She'd done it. She'd spent the night and the world hadn't come to an end. And she hadn't slept lousy either.

She leaned over and switched on the lamp, temporarily blinding herself. As her pupils adjusted, Parker walked into the room wearing his flannel pajama bottoms, holding two steaming cups of coffee.

"Good morning, sleepyhead," he said, his usual chipper, cheerful self. He may have been the most positive, upbeat person she had ever known.

She pushed herself up into a sitting position. "Good morning."

He handed her one of the cups, sat on the edge of the mattress beside her and kissed her forehead. There was something so sweet about it, so deeply affectionate. "Sleep well?"

Amazingly well. "I must have been in a coma," she said. "I didn't move once. I don't even think I dreamed."

"I did," he said, wiggling his brows, "but we'll save that for later."

Hmm, something to look forward to.

"Did you mean to stay, or did you fall asleep before you could leave?"

"A little of both."

"Are you sorry that you stayed?"

She smiled and shook her head. "But I can't stay long. I have to go home and get ready for work. And return my aunt's car."

"How are you planning to get to the hospital?"

"Kay can drive me."

"Or you can shower here. I'll follow you home, wait while you change, then take you to work."

And risk being seen together? That would most certainly get the rumor mill spinning.

She was getting sick of living afraid, always worried about what people would think of her. Maybe it was time she got her priorities straight. Maybe it should be about what she wanted for a change.

"Okay."

He looked a little taken aback, but he smiled. "Really?"

"Really. It's on your way. Why not."

"If you want I can drop you around the block, so no one sees us together."

She did and she didn't. And what did that say about her? She was acting as though he was some dark, dirty secret when really, their relationship was far from controversial. They were two consenting adults and what they did outside the hospital was no one else's business. As long as they didn't let the physical relationship bleed into their work relationship. She already lost one job that way.

"I have to stop worrying what other people think. Like you said, I give people too much power."

"True story," he said with a smile. "So, you want me to shower first? Or we could even shower together."

"One step at a time," she said. Though most people wouldn't consider something as innocuous as sharing a shower a "step," they probably hadn't been brutally shoved face-first into a shower stall and pinned against the cold, hard tile.

Parker accepted her decline with a smile, because that's who Parker was. "I'll go first."

Her eyes glued to his tight behind as he walked to the closet to pick out clothes, she felt around the bedside table for her phone so she could check the weather. The low battery warning flashed, then the screen went black.

Damn.

"Do you know what the temperature is supposed to be today?" she asked as Parker laid his clothes out on the bed. "My phone just died."

"Look it up on my phone," he said. He leaned over to grab it off the bedside table and held it out to her.

She hesitated.

"I promise it won't bite."

She took it. "You really don't mind me looking at your phone?"

"Why would I? The code is 0613, my birthday."

"You were born on the thirteenth of June?"

"And yes, it was a Friday. I looked it up."

Well, that explained a lot.

"To me a phone is a very personal thing," she said. "I would never give out my code. Practically my whole life is on this phone."

"Me, too. If you did feel the need to snoop, you would probably find something interesting. You might even see something you wished you hadn't. Or you could just not snoop. Your choice."

She looked at the phone, then back at him. "You have my word, I definitely won't snoop."

He laughed. "I'll be out in ten minutes."

The following week Clare got a surprise call from her sister Jen. "I'm going to be in the area this afternoon picking up a mare, and I want to come see you," she told Clare.

Clare cringed, thankful Jen couldn't see her through the phone. Every visit with a family member seemed to end in disaster, and things had been going so well lately, she hated to push her luck. The past week and a half had been weird but wonderful. Clare *felt* wonderful. All her family ever did was bring her down. "I'm working today," Clare told her sister.

"I know, but you can take a quick break, right?"

"I have patients to care for. I can't just leave them." It was a lie. She could have asked someone to cover for her.

"But we haven't seen you in months. I miss you."

Don't have anyone else to embarrass and shame? she wanted to ask. "I'm sorry. Maybe if you would have given me a little advance notice."

"I only found out this morning that I had to go."

"Oh."

"You can't spare five minutes to see your own sister?"

Clare could feel herself caving. It was the guilt that always got her. "Tell you what. Call me when you get to Kay's house and I'll let you know if I can get away."

"I'll call you in about an hour."

And Clare wouldn't answer the phone. Problem solved.

She stuck her phone in her pocket. Maybe she was being selfish, but she wanted to be happy just a little while longer before she opened that wound again. She was learning that it was okay to be selfish every once in a while.

She got a text and looked at her phone again. It was from Parker, asking to see her in his office. They were extremely careful to keep their relationship platonic and professional at the hospital, but every so often they would meet in his office to steal a kiss or two. Sometimes more. Once when they were both working late he summoned her to his office and she found him sitting behind his desk wearing nothing but his lab coat and stethoscope.

His door was closed when she got there, so she knocked.

"Come in."

He was fully dressed—darn it—and sitting at his desk, his laptop in front of him. "Come in and close the door."

"What's up?"

"I need your opinion on something." He turned the laptop around so she could see the screen. "I've been on this site. It's called Family Finder. They help people connect with their biological family."

"Are you thinking of contacting your mom?"

He took a breath and blew it out, brow furrowed. "Since we talked about her it's been on my mind. I was thinking about Maddie and Maggie. They'll never get the opportunity to meet their real mom. But I can meet mine, and I can't deny that I'm curious."

"I think it would be a great idea."

"All I need to do is fill out a form with the information I have, which thankfully is extensive. If she's already posted on the site looking for me, I'll be notified."

"So, if she's already on the site, you'll know it right away."

He nodded. "I'm not sure how I feel about that. On the one hand I feel as if it's time to deal with this, and on the other I can't help but worry that I'll be disappointed. The forms are all filled out and ready to go. I'm just having a little trouble hitting Submit."

She loved that he wasn't too macho to let her see his vulnerabilities. He was very honest about his feelings. Sometimes too honest, so much so that it made her squirm a little. He knew the *L* word was currently off the table, but that didn't stop him from creatively hinting around. But he did it with so much charm it was difficult to be annoyed.

"I don't know what to say."

He snapped his laptop shut. "I have to think about this."

"There's no rush."

He pushed himself up from his chair. "Sorry to drag you in here for nothing."

She rose up on her toes and kissed him. "No problem."

They both walked out to the nurses' station. She sat

down, ready to get back to work, and Parker asked, "Are you expecting company?"

How could he possibly know that? "Did you bug my phone or something?"

"No, but there's a woman who just stepped off the elevator and she looks like she could be your twin."

Oh, crap! Clare shot up in her chair, and sure as anything there stood her sister by the elevator. How had she gotten there so fast?

Jen saw Clare and waved.

Parker was looking at her, waiting for an explanation.

"It's my sister Jen," she said. "I asked her not to come, but that's my family. Constantly ignoring what I say."

"Hey, sweetie," Jen said, and Clare walked around the station to hug her.

"An hour away?"

"Okay, I lied. I was already in Royal when I called you. And I didn't come for a horse. I came to see you."

Thirteen

"Dr. Reese," Clare said, hoping he would play along. "This is my sister Jen."

"Pleasure," Parker said, shaking her hand.

"Dr. Reese is my boss," she told her sister, hoping she would be less likely to say something embarrassing or inappropriate. Of all her siblings, Jen, six years her senior, was the most vocal, and the most blunt.

"You must be proud of your sister," he said, "being chief nurse of one of the highest-rated children's wards in the state."

"We all are," Jen said, shooting Clare a look.

Somehow Clare found that very hard to believe. They had never supported her in her career.

"We would be lost without her." Parker laid a hand on Clare's shoulder, giving it a reassuring squeeze. Then he flashed one of those charming smiles. "If you'll excuse me, ladies, I have a patient to check on."

"That man is like a cool glass of lemonade on a hot day," Jen said.

My *cool glass of lemonade, thank-you-very-much.* "Last I checked you were a married woman."

Jen grinned. "It doesn't hurt to look, honey. As long as I bring my appetite home."

Clare grimaced. "Ew."

Her sister laughed. "Can we go somewhere private and talk?"

Alarm made her heart skip a beat. Was Jen here because something bad had happened? "Sure, we can use the break room."

"Sounds good."

She showed her sister down the hall to the break room, which thankfully was empty, and said, "Have a seat."

Jen made herself comfortable in a chair. "So, are you and the doctor…?"

Oh, boy, here we go. "What makes you think that?"

"He was a little defensive, and you didn't seem to like me lookin' at him. And he squeezed your shoulder. That was a little personal."

"You noticed all that?"

"Honey, I have four boys. I don't miss a thing."

Clare raised her chin a notch, ready to take her lumps. "As a matter of fact, we're dating."

Jen nodded approvingly. "He's cute."

Clare waited for more. For a rich-doctor crack. Or some other disparaging remark.

"Is it serious?" Jen asked.

"We've only been dating for two weeks."

"Beau proposed to me on our second date. Fifteen

years later and we're still going strong. I think if you know, you just know. You know?"

Clare laughed, remembering why, of all her siblings, Jen was by far the most honest and outgoing. "You're weird."

She smiled. "That's what my boys tell me."

Times like now, Clare missed being a part of her family, wished she wasn't such an outsider. "So, you said you needed to talk to me. About what?"

"The seven of us had a family meeting."

"Seven?"

"Just the siblings."

"About what?"

"You mostly, and the fact that you never come around. And when you do you're so defensive."

Confused, she asked, "What about Mom and Dad? Were they at this meeting?"

"They weren't included."

As far as Clare knew, the family never made a group decision without first getting their parents' blessing. "You had a family meeting without Mom and Dad?"

"It's been known to happen. It wouldn't surprise you if you came around, or called."

"I'm busy."

"You want to talk about busy, try being the mom of four rambunctious boys, and I still make it to dinner at Mom and Dad's once a month. If we at least knew why you're so distant..."

"*Why?* Are you kidding me?"

"I know that something happened between you and Mom and Dad. I know what a pain they can be, but you have a very large family who misses you."

A kernel of anger popped in Clare's belly, causing

a chain reaction, until she felt like exploding. She'd always hated confrontation, but right now she was too furious to think straight. To be afraid. The new Clare stood up for herself, and didn't take any crap from anyone, damn it. "You miss me? Well, where the hell were you all when I needed you? When my entire world fell apart. You didn't miss me so much then."

"Clare—"

"I'm not stupid, you know. I know what you all think of me. What Mom and Dad think of me. You've made it obvious that I'm a huge disappointment."

"Clare—"

"People make mistakes, you know, but they shouldn't have to pay for it forever! It wasn't even my fault!" she shrieked, and for the first time actually believed it. "I was young and stupid and he took advantage of me. He lied to me. End of story."

"Clare, shut up!" Jen shouted.

Startled, Clare closed her mouth.

"What the *hell* are you talking about?"

She was going to play dumb? Seriously? "I know Mom and Dad told everyone. They said there was a family meeting. She said that everyone agreed I should come home. I was a simple country girl who could never make it on her own."

"We all knew something was wrong," Jen said. "But there was no family meeting. If Mom and Dad said there was, they were lying. They told everyone that you were in trouble, but they refused to say how or why. They just wanted us all to call and try to get you to come home. We were all worried sick about you. We still are. We want you back in the family."

"If Sue had kept her mouth shut, no one would have

known anything. She promised me she would take it to her grave, then she turned around and told Mom."

Jen frowned. "No, she didn't."

"*Yes*, she did."

"No, Clare, she did not. She heard Mom on the phone with you and assumed you had called her."

"If she didn't tell her, how did Mom find out?"

"If I had to guess, I would say she was listening on the extension. She used to do it all the time."

Taken aback, Clare blinked and said, "Since when?"

"Since my entire childhood. That's how she kept tabs on all of us."

Clare had no idea. But she hadn't spent much time on the phone as a kid either. And if she did it was to discuss homework, or equally innocuous things. She hadn't had much of a social life.

"She did it to everyone?"

"Yup. She was always listening to our calls and going through our stuff. There was no privacy in that house."

And Clare had thought it was just she who had no privacy. Had it not occurred to her that her brothers and sisters felt the same way?

"Sue seriously didn't tell them?"

"No, Clare. She wouldn't tell *anyone*, and we badgered her, believe me. We wanted to know what was wrong. Anytime we tried to bring it up, you went on the defensive. Then you stopped coming around. We were all very hurt."

Clare could barely wrap her head around it. All these years she had stayed away, thinking everyone was judging her, and they didn't even know what had happened? "She really didn't tell anyone?"

"No, hon," Jen said patiently. "She didn't."

Tears stung Clare's eyes. Was it possible that what she had conceived as wisecracks and ribbing from her family had in reality only been their way of trying to figure out what was wrong? Were they just trying to *talk* to her?

How could her mom go all this time letting her believe Sue had ratted her out? Was it possible she didn't even know that Clare blamed Sue?

Clare shook her head, still having trouble grasping this. How could she have been so wrong about her family? She could only imagine all the things that she had missed out on over the years. How much fuller and richer her life would be.

She felt sick inside. She'd lost out on so much, just because she had been afraid to speak her mind.

"I thought everyone abandoned me," she told Jen. "That no one cared."

"Oh, honey." Jen rose from the chair, wrapped her arms around Clare and hugged her hard, and Clare hugged her back just as firmly. "Everyone cared. We always have. You know what this is?"

Clare sniffled and shook her head.

"This is one big cluster eff," she said, patting Clare's back. She was such a *mom*.

Clare smiled in spite of herself. "Cluster eff?"

Jen held her at arm's length and said, "I'm the mother of four boys. I have to set a good example."

"I miss the boys," Clare said. "I've missed out on so much…"

"So things will be different now."

"It might take some time to forgive Mom and Dad for lying to me." It had begun a chain reaction that left

Clare feeling isolated and alone. Like an outcast. How did you forgive someone for that?

"For what it's worth, I truly believe that they thought they were doing the right thing. They didn't want to hurt anyone. They just didn't think about the consequences of their actions."

"That doesn't make it okay."

"No, but you should talk to them about it and tell them how you feel. They won't be around forever."

Jen was right of course. Clare did need to talk to them. And her siblings needed to know what really happened. She didn't even know why she wanted to tell them. She just felt as if she needed to get it off her chest. Or maybe, after all this time, she just needed their acceptance.

"I want to tell you what happened," Clare said.

"Are you sure?"

"Very sure."

"I swear I won't tell a soul."

"No, this time I actually want you to."

Parker stood at the nurses station pretending to work on a chart, keeping his eye on the door of the break room. Clare and her sister had been in there for a while now and he was beginning to worry. Clare hadn't looked happy to see her. Things had been going so well, he hated to see something like this set them back.

"I'm sure she's fine," Rebecca said from behind the desk.

Parker turned to her. "Who?"

"Clare. You've been on edge since she went in there."

He didn't realize that he was being that obvious, or that careless. "It's complicated."

"You seem to be spending a lot more time together lately."

That was none of her business and he didn't justify it with a response.

"I'm sorry I got snippy with you," she said. "I was jealous, I guess. It's been pretty obvious that you have a thing for Clare."

"Since when?"

"Pretty much since you started at the hospital."

Had it really been that noticeable?

"I knew you and I didn't have a chance. And the truth is, you're a little old for me."

"And feeling older every day," he said, but that was okay. He felt more settled, and more content than he ever had in his life. There was no way that was a bad thing.

Convincing Clare would be another matter altogether. She was so terrified to trust this. To trust *herself*. Who knew how long it would be before she felt okay with taking their relationship to the next level. Maybe never. She was so worried about what other people would think, how they would judge her. When would she learn that it didn't matter what anyone else thought? He was in love with her. There was no other explanation for this inexorable need to protect her. He wanted to spend the rest of his life with her. He knew somewhere deep down in his soul she was the one for him. His perfect match. And he couldn't even tell her. He was paying the price for all the other people who had hurt and betrayed her.

It was frustrating as hell. And it wasn't fair. Not to her and not to him.

When Clare introduced him to her sister, his first

reaction had been to go on the defensive, and he was afraid he'd been a little rude. He was hoping to apologize to the both of them.

The break room door finally opened and Clare and her sister walked out. He could tell from where he stood that they had both been crying. But he couldn't tell if that was a good or bad thing.

Clare and her sister embraced, holding each other tight. After a moment they parted and started to walk toward him and he met them halfway. He must have looked confused, or concerned, because Clare told him immediately, "Everything is okay."

"So you'll definitely be there for dinner?" Jen asked her.

Clare smiled and nodded. "I promise."

"And you'll bring this guy along?" she asked, gesturing to Parker.

"It's a distinct possibility. If he wants to go."

"Of course he wants to go," Jen said, giving his arm a playful nudge with her elbow. "Don't you."

"Go where?" he asked.

"To meet Clare's family. There are so many of us, it can be a bit intimidating."

She wanted him to meet her family? Since when? Was it something she'd said just to placate her sister? Knowing the way they treated Clare, he wasn't sure if he wanted to meet them. It would be difficult to keep his feelings hidden.

She and her sister said goodbye, then she turned to him and smiled. "You are not going to believe what just happened to me."

Fourteen

The Texas Cattleman's Club meeting wasn't due to start for another hour, but Clare was working late and Parker was bored so he showed up early. He sat at the bar at the clubhouse, sipping his usual drink, the Family Finder app open on his phone, his profile taunting him. As it had for nearly two weeks now. It would take one tap on the screen to submit his request, but he still couldn't seem to make himself do it. Which wasn't at all like him. When he wanted something, he went after it. This time something was stopping him. The question was what.

The idea of family, and possibly one of his own, weighed heavily on his mind since the impromptu family gathering he and Clare had attended at her parents' farm this past weekend. At first she'd hemmed and hawed about bringing him, which he had tried not to take personally. He'd learned that in that sort of situation it was best to step back and let her work it out alone. If she asked for input he gave it, but trying to convince her to do something usually had her digging her heels in to do the exact opposite. But her siblings, whom she'd had a very open and honest dialogue with lately, nagged and cajoled her for a week until she finally agreed to bring him.

On the morning of the party she'd called him with the idea to bring overnight bags in case they were too tired, or more likely too hammered, to drive the hour back to Royal.

His second surprise, when they'd arrived at her parents' farm, was the sheer size of her family. He'd met countless nieces and nephews, aunts and uncles, and more cousins than should be allowed in one family. He'd tried to keep up with all the new names and faces, but somewhere around his fourth beer he'd given up. From that point on he'd addressed everyone as *sir* or *ma'am*. Even the children, who'd seemed to get a big kick out of that.

The food had been incredible, and there'd been so much of it. Roasted pig and smoked ribs and of course authentic Texas chili. Clare had told him that it was customary to bring either a side dish or dessert to share, which explained the rows and rows of platters and casserole dishes on the serving tables. There was literally enough food for a small army.

Parker had eaten himself into a food coma, and drank way more than he should have. From around dusk on, his memory had been a little spotty. He remembered a huge bonfire out in the field, and Clare's brothers joking around that they were going to throw Parker into it.

He remembered live music, and square dancing badly. Really, *really* badly. But what he remembered most was the constant smile on Clare's face, and her laugh, and how happy she'd seemed. And how sexy she'd looked when she jumped him later that night in the tent she'd borrowed from her parents. And she hadn't been exaggerating when she said her family was traditional. The fact that she and Parker were sharing a tent out of wedlock had raised a few eyebrows from the older set.

Despite his vow to never ride any breed of four-legged animal again, Clare had talked him into going horseback riding the next morning and given him a proper tour of the land. They'd stayed for a lunch of leftovers, and her mom had sent bags and bags of food home with them.

Though much of the party was a blur, he distinctly recalled thinking about his biological mother. And though meeting Clare's entire gargantuan family all at once had had him feeling a little intimidated at first, it made him realize what he had missed out on all these years. Was it possible that he had siblings somewhere, too? Would they be interested in meeting him? Did they have gatherings like Clare's family?

To find out, he would have to hit Submit. Just one tap of the mouse.

Cursing under his breath, he shut the app again.

Maybe he just wasn't ready. With everything else in his life going so well, would he only be tempting fate?

It still astounded him a little that after a lifetime of having no desire to settle down, much less have a family, he could be so sure in less than a month's time that Clare was the *one*. She was smart and sexy and fun. She challenged him emotionally and intellectually. And in the bedroom, as well. She had a sharp wit and snarky sense of humor.

She was still hesitant about their relationship going public, but they had been spending almost all of their free time together, and he knew that people were beginning to notice.

Parker heard his name called and turned to see Luc gesturing him over to a table in the back of the bar. Parker had been so lost in thought he hadn't even seen him come in. He stuck his phone in his pocket and walked over. Though Parker was far from knowing all the members of the club, he recognized the men sitting at the table with Luc. Case Baxter, who was the recently elected president of the club, and beside him Nathan Battle, the sheriff of Royal.

The men shook hands and Parker sat down, asking Luc, "How was Mexico?"

He and his wife, Julie, had just returned from a long-overdue vacation. Which had Parker thinking that maybe he and Clare should take a few days away, just the two of them.

"Hot," Luc said. "But relaxing. We got back this afternoon."

"Do anything fun?"

"We slept a lot. And caught up on our reading. Our last day there we chartered a boat."

"Sounds like the perfect vacation."

"I'd go back tomorrow if I could."

"Parker," Case said, "we were discussing the Samson Oil land grab. We still have no idea why any oil company would buy up land with no oil. Any thoughts?"

Parker shook his head. "I'm afraid I don't know

enough about the town to be much help. But I agree that it's suspicious."

"Listen and learn," Nathan said, spreading a map out across the table that marked the property the company had purchased so far, and all the land it was still trying to obtain. Parker tried to pay attention so he would appear at least slightly informed during the meeting, but his mind kept wandering.

When Case and Nathan left the bar to get ready for the meeting, Luc asked him, "Everything okay? You seem awfully distracted tonight."

"I have a lot on my mind," he said, and told Luc about his desire to meet his biological mother.

"Why now?" Luc asked.

"Let's just say that lately I've been reevaluating my priorities."

"This wouldn't have anything to do with Clare, would it?"

There was really no point in denying it. "Almost exclusively. Who told you?"

"I can tell you who didn't tell me. It's a much shorter list. If you haven't noticed by now, secrets are tough to keep in a town this small and tight-knit."

"I know." And he was okay with that. The question was how Clare would feel about it.

"I had a feeling, when you mentioned the new woman you were seeing, that it was probably Clare," Luc said. "Once you set your mind to something you don't just give up."

"I'm in love with her."

"Wow. That's the first time I've ever heard you say that."

"That's because I've never said it before. Until I met

Clare I didn't think I would ever settle down. Now I want it all. A wife and a child, or even two. I want to be everything to my kids that my father never was for me."

"Have you told her how you feel?"

"Not yet."

"What are you waiting for?"

"The right time. I'll know it when I see it."

"On the subject of marriage and family, Julie and I have a little news of our own to share. We've been throwing around the idea of starting a family for a while now, so she quit taking her birth control. We were assuming it would take at least a couple of months for her system to regulate."

"How long did it actually take?"

He grinned. "Closer to two weeks. We found out just before we left for Mexico."

Parker laughed. "Congratulations. That's great news."

He was happy for Luc, and at the same time he was a little jealous. Maybe it was time he stopped tiptoeing around the issue and told Clare how he felt. It had taken him a long time to get to this place, and he didn't want to waste a minute of it.

When Clare made it to Parker's house after work he wasn't home yet. She parked her new car in the driveway and, using the key he'd given her last week, let herself into his condo. It still felt a little strange being there alone, but he would hopefully be home soon. It had been a hellish day at work. The kind that had her questioning humanity. An unresponsive eight-month-old infant with severe brain swelling had been brought in to emergency. Though they'd done everything they could, the child had died shortly after. The worst part was that it was a textbook case of shaken-baby syndrome. The parents had been arrested, and their two other children taken by protective services. Clare had called Grace only to learn that both kids, ages two and four, had signs of abuse, as well. It was so heartbreaking that she gave herself permission to sit in the stairwell and sob, but even that didn't help much.

Clare shed her coat and dropped her purse on the cluttered coffee table, feeling depressed, her heart breaking for that poor little baby. At least she was at peace. Even if she'd survived she would have been severely mentally disabled. She probably would have spent her life in a group home, since her own parents clearly had no business raising children.

At least little Maddie's story had a happy ending. She was getting stronger every day, and would hopefully get to join her twin sister at home.

What Clare really needed was one of Parker's hugs. Feeling his arms around her somehow always managed to make the bad stuff go away for a while. Besides, she had an awful lot to be happy about these days.

She grabbed herself a beer from the fridge and flopped down on the sofa to wait for Parker.

Her relationship with her family was the best it had ever been, though things with her parents were still a little strained. It would just take her time to forgive them for lying to her. She believed that they had been truly afraid for her, and had had her best interests in mind, even though their actions had seemed to say the opposite. They had hurt her deeply, even if they hadn't meant to, and it would take a while to sort those feelings out. On the bright side, Parker had been extremely well received by her entire family, and though she'd been a bit hesitant to bring him at first, she was glad she had. For all her fears about "rich doctor" cracks, no one had said a disparaging word. And though Parker had looked thoroughly overwhelmed by the number of relatives there when they first arrived, he'd fit right in.

Only after seeing everyone all together like that had she realized how much she missed being part of a family. Before they'd left the next day her siblings had made her promise to regularly attend the monthly family dinners. She'd promised, and this time she meant it. So much had changed.

She had changed.

She'd been insistent that she and Parker continue to keep their relationship a secret, but people were beginning to put two and two together. Though no one had the guts to come right out and ask her about it, it was only a matter of time. Besides, all of her reasons for keeping it quiet seemed a little silly now. She had tried to convince herself that it would put her job in jeopardy, sleeping with the boss. But that was just a lame excuse to not let him close.

She tried putting herself in Parker's place, tried to imagine how she would feel if the tables were turned, if he wanted to keep it a secret. The truth was, it kinda sucked.

Maybe deep down she felt as if she didn't deserve someone like him, that people would see them as mismatched, and her as pathetic. She realized today, with complete certainty, that she didn't give a damn what anyone thought. She was so happy these past few weeks that sometimes she wanted to shout it from the rooftops. So tonight she planned to tell him that she wanted to take things public. She was tired of hiding, tired of watching what she said, and whom she said it in front of.

There was something else she wanted to say to him, something that she had never said to anyone but her family. The *L* word. Up to now, in her mind, love had always meant obligation, and sacrifice, and often heartbreak. It meant giving without getting anything in return.

With Parker it was different. He gave as much as he took. More even. And he must have been a saint to put up with all of her weird hang-ups and personality quirks. But without fail he accepted her for exactly who she was, no question.

Until now the only place she'd ever felt truly in her element was at work. For the first time in forever, with her family and with Parker, she felt as if she truly belonged. As if she fit in.

She heard the garage door open and her heart leaped up into her throat. Despite being with one another nearly every day, the excitement of seeing him walk through the door was a thrill that never went away. She met him at the door, greeting him with a kiss, and as his arms went around her she felt the stress of the day slipping away. She held him as tight as she could.

"If you let go for a second and let me take my coat off I could hug you properly," he teased, and she held him even tighter. "Hey, is everything okay?"

She looked up at him, into his beautiful eyes, and though she meant to tell him about her crummy day, and say how happy she was that he was home, something altogether different came out.

"I love you, Parker."

He blinked. Then blinked again. Then he grinned and said, "I love you, too, Clare."

That wasn't all that hard. And she liked that he didn't make a big deal out of it.

"How was your meeting?" she asked, loosening his tie.

"Good. Luc and Julie are expecting."

"No kidding."

"Yeah, he seems pretty excited. They want me to be the baby's doctor."

"Of course they do. You're the best."

He grinned and kissed her. "Thanks. You're not so bad yourself. How was work?"

"Not so good."

"Let me grab a beer and you can tell me about it."

They snuggled on the sofa, her head resting on his shoulder as she told him about her rotten afternoon. "It was a very stressful day."

"Do I need to pull out the coloring books?" he teased. She did in fact have a few there, as well as a set of colored pencils. But right now she just wanted to be with him.

"Are you staying over tonight?" he asked.

She should probably head home, but she didn't feel like going back out into the cold. "If you don't mind."

He gave her a *yeah right* look. "Do I ever mind when you spend the night?"

"I'm warning you, I'm too tired to do anything but sleep."

He laughed. "Okay."

"I'm serious. I'm exhausted."

"Yet somehow you always manage to find the energy."

After they finished their beers they went up to his bedroom and he switched on the news while they undressed. Then she remembered her purse was still downstairs with her phone in it.

"I left my phone downstairs," she told him. "I'm going to grab it."

He patted the pockets of his pants. "I think I left mine in the kitchen. I'm pretty sure I set it down when I was taking my coat off."

"I'll get yours, too." Her feet ached as she trudged down the stairs. She hooked her purse over her shoulder, then grabbed his phone, which was sitting on the kitchen counter. She was almost to the stairs when his phone buzzed. She glanced at the screen and saw that it was an incoming text message from Luc Wakefield.

The two-word preview on his locked screen said, About Clare...

She stopped at the bottom of the stairs. *About Clare* what? Had Parker told Luc about his relationship with Clare? Even though he *swore* he wouldn't? Or had Luc just heard about them through the hospital grapevine.

She itched to read the rest of the text, then thought about their conversation regarding his phone, and the dangers of snooping. But it probably wasn't a big deal. He wouldn't have given her his code if he had something to hide.

She tapped in the code and the text flashed on the screen.

She read it once, then read it again, then read it a third time.

Well, he'd been right about one thing. She definitely wished she'd never seen it.

Fifteen

Parker was sitting on the edge of the mattress watching CNN when something hit him hard in the back. "Ow! What the…"

He turned to see his phone lying on the blanket behind him, then he looked up to see Clare standing in the bedroom doorway. That had really hurt, not to mention that if she'd missed she might have broken his phone. "Thanks, I think."

At first he thought she was teasing him, and had just underestimated her own strength. Then he saw her face. She was wearing a look like he'd never seen before. As if someone had died. Or worse.

His heart skipped a beat. "What's wrong?"

"You got a text from Dr. Wakefield."

Uh-oh. What the hell had Luc said?

She didn't move from the doorway. "Aren't you going to read it?"

"Um, sure." He punched in his code and the text flashed on the screen.

About Clare... I know we ended the bet, but since you slept with her before that, you technically win. I'll stop by the bank on my way to work. You want that in small bills?

He cursed under his breath. Then cursed again.

"It was a bet?" she asked, her voice trembling. "You bet Luc that you would sleep with me?"

He wanted to deny it, but he couldn't.

The outrage and devastation were written all over her face, making him feel like the giant ass that he was. He tried to think of something to say, anything to make her stop looking at him like that.

"I know it sounds awful," he said. "But if you let me explain—"

"Did you or did you not bet Luc that you would sleep with me?"

Shit.

"I did. But it's not... It isn't..." He didn't even know what to say. He had no excuse, no logical explanation. He wanted to kill Luc, but this was his own fault. He'd done a bad, stupid thing and now he had to own up to it and take his lumps.

"I was going to tell you, it just never seemed like the right time."

"No, you're just a coward."

"Clare, I'm sorry."

"So am I, Parker." She turned around and he jumped up to follow her.

"Clare, wait!"

He caught up with her at the bottom of the stairs. He grabbed her arm and she violently jerked it away. "*Do not* touch me. You don't get to touch me *ever again*."

She was so furious, her face was bright red and her hands were trembling as she shoved her arms into her coat sleeves. "I am so stupid. I can't believe I let myself trust you."

"No, I'm the stupid one, Clare. And I cannot begin to tell you how sorry I am. I wasn't thinking. I didn't know—"

She raised a hand to stop him midsentence. "Save your breath, I'm not buying it. Not anymore."

She walked out the door and he let her go. She was too angry to listen to reason, even if he did have some sort of reasonable excuse. Which he didn't. He'd worked so hard to earn her trust, and in a matter of seconds he'd lost it.

Maybe she just needed time to think it through. Maybe after a day or two she would give him a chance to explain. Maybe, if he was totally honest from now on, she could learn to trust him again.

Or maybe it was just over.

Yeah, it was over.

In this day and age, with all the communications technology available, it was still possible to go radio silent and drop completely off the map. He knew because that's what Clare had done. She'd taken a week's vacation then disappeared.

Every time he let himself remember the way her face had looked when she'd walked out the door—the bitterness and hurt—his gut tied itself into knots. Which was probably why he hadn't been able to eat in two days. Nothing would go down.

Having never had a broken heart, he'd had no idea just how dreadful it could feel. He wished he could go back and apologize profusely to all of the women he'd seduced then discarded over the years. If any of them felt even a fraction of what he was feeling now...

In a word, it *sucked*.

His days of using and manipulating women to get what he wanted were officially over.

He'd left a few things at Clare's house, things he would really like to have back, like his tennis shoes, but knowing Kay had guns, he wouldn't dare. He knew how it worked in that family. He hurt Clare, so Kay would hurt him. She had brothers, too. Big ones, who could snap him like a twig, or throw him off a cliff. With all that land they had, no one would ever find the body...

But killing him would mean putting him out of his misery, and he deserved every bit of misery he was feeling. And he was sure they knew that.

He took Wednesday off and lay around the house in his pajamas flipping through the TV channels. He didn't even have anyone to talk to. Luc was the one he called with a problem. But if Parker told him it was his text that had blown everything wide-open, Luc would never forgive himself.

There was nothing on TV so he grabbed his laptop. Out of habit he clicked on the Family Finder link in his browser and the page popped up. It was times like this when having a family would come in handy.

He read through the letter section of his profile. He'd written a few short passages about himself, describing his career and his various degrees. It sounded...wrong.

Awkward or forced or something. He highlighted all the text and hit Delete. He sat for a second, looking at the blank page, wondering what it was he really wanted to impart to the woman who'd abandoned him.

He typed five words, but they pretty much said it all.

I want to meet you.

And before he could change his mind he hit Submit.

It was finally done. He'd sent it. Now all he could do was sit back and wait. He wasn't sure if he felt excited or nervous.

He wondered how long it would take—

The computer beeped as a message window popped up on his screen. I want to meet you, too.

Apparently not that long.

After exchanging phone numbers and one very short and awkward conversation, Rachel Simpson, his biological mother, had immediately purchased a plane ticket for her trip to Texas from her home in Nebraska.

Heavy traffic made him a little late picking her up, and when he walked into the baggage-claim area where they planned to meet, she was already there. Though he had never even seen a picture of her, he knew her the moment he saw her. They looked alike. And the second her eyes landed on him, it was obvious that she could see it, too.

She looked younger than he expected. But she had been only eighteen when he was born, putting her at fifty-six now.

She was very attractive—tall and slender, with long dark hair streaked with gray.

Suddenly his feet felt glued to the floor, but she came to him. And for some strange reason her uncertainty was a comfort. At least he wasn't the only one flying blind.

Then she was standing in front of him, saying, "Parker."

She held a hand out and he automatically took it, but instead of shaking it, she held it tight. "I've been looking forward to this for a very long time," she said. "It's so good to see you."

He wished he could say the same, but right now he wasn't sure how he felt. He was feeling so many things he couldn't sort them all out. All he could manage was, "How was your flight?"

"It was good. My return flight leaves in three hours. I'd have stayed longer but I couldn't get the time off work. Is there somewhere that we can go and talk?"

They chose a coffee shop close to the airport, and she asked him question after question about himself. He waited to feel some sort of connection, or affection.

"You must have questions about me," she said finally.

He did, but all he could think to say was, "You answered my request so fast."

"I've been registered on the site since it was created. I figured that if you wanted to see me, this would be one of the first places you looked."

"You could have just contacted me."

"I didn't think it would be fair to disrupt your life. I knew that you had the resources to find me if you wanted to."

"Why didn't you want me?"

His blunt question seemed to surprise her, and he surprised himself. But he had never been one to dance around an issue. He'd met with her to get answers, and he was going to get them.

"I did want you, I swear, but I was only eighteen when you were born and I had signed a contract. He told you that I was a surrogate?"

Parker nodded.

"I only agreed to do it to make money for college, but your father was so charming and sweet to me. I was very young and naive, and it was the late seventies so that sort of thing wasn't common, and not looked upon too favorably. My family would have been horrified to learn what I did. Your grandparents were very old-fashioned."

His grandparents? The ones that he hadn't even known existed? "Were?"

"They were over forty when they had my brother and me. They passed years ago."

He hoped she wasn't expecting any sympathy from him.

"So you just disappeared for nine months? Didn't your parents wonder where you were?"

"I told them that I got a job as a nanny to save money for school."

He picked up his coffee cup to take a sip, but put it back down untouched. The truth was, he felt a little sick to his stomach. "Did you love him?"

"I thought I did. I wanted to, and not just because he was rich. Though that was what everyone believed. It was wonderful at first. You know how charming he could be. He could also be cold and cruel. But by that time I wanted you so much, I was willing to stay with him."

"Yet you left."

"Parker, he didn't give me a choice. He *made* me leave."

"Was it true what he told me about the limo driver?"

"Darren was the only friend I had."

"I heard it was more than that. He said you ran off with him."

"Your father and I had a terrible fight. He was never around, and when he was, though he claimed to love me, he treated me like a subordinate."

Parker could certainly relate to that.

"Darren was just consoling me, but your father got the wrong idea. He accused me of cheating on him. He kicked me out, said I broke the terms of our agreement, and sent me away without a penny to my name. I hadn't earned the money. You were only two weeks old. I was devastated."

"What did you do?"

"The only thing I could do. I went home to Nebraska and tried to convince everyone that my heart wasn't breaking. I tried to forget."

"It would seem you did a pretty good job."

There was regret and pain in her voice when she said, "No, Parker, I haven't. In thirty-eight years a day hasn't passed that I didn't think of you, and wonder what you were doing."

"But you didn't try to see me."

"I signed a contract saying I wouldn't. And at the time I thought I was doing the right thing. I thought that he could give you a better life than I ever could. But once I got to know him, when I realized how wrong I was about him, it was too late."

"I'm no attorney, but I'm fairly certain that any contract would become null and void the day I turned eighteen. Yet here we are *twenty* years later."

She winced, as if his words actually stung, and he felt a stab of guilt. "As I said, I didn't want to disrupt your life. I felt as if I had no right."

"Because thinking that you abandoned me for the limo driver was so much better."

"You have every reason to be angry. And I will never forgive myself for robbing you of the opportunity to be a part of our family."

"Family?"

"You have two brother and two sisters. You also have seven nieces and nephews. Your brother David is thirty-five. He's a country vet. He has three boys. Jeanie is thirty-two. She's a schoolteacher, and she has four children. Two of each. Now, the twins, Aaron and Ashley, came along later. They graduate high school next year."

It was hard to imagine that he could have a brother and sister still in high school. The whole situation was making him feel weirdly left out. And resentful. "Do they know about me?"

"They do. And they would have all flown here with me if I let them. They can't wait to meet you. If that's something you want."

He didn't know what he wanted. He just felt angry and annoyed. "Did your husband know about me?"

She nodded. "It took me years to work up the courage to tell him. But he was one hundred percent supportive. He was a good man, Parker. A good father. I wish you could have known him."

"He's not...?"

"He passed away last year. Lung cancer."

It was so much to take in all at once. There were years' and years' worth of things he'd missed.

"There's something else that you need to know," she said, her tone ominous. "Something you probably don't know about your father. He was sterile. He couldn't have children of his own."

"So how am I here?"

"I was already pregnant when I met him."

Sixteen

The coffee shop spun around him. Of all scenarios he had imagined over the years regarding his mother, this had never even crossed his mind. But it sure did explain a lot. Why he and the man he thought was his father were so completely different. Somewhere deep down Parker had always felt an odd detachment from his father. Now he knew why.

"So who is my real father?"

She wrapped her hands around her coffee cup looking so sad. "I didn't know him very well. I had just graduated high school and we were on vacation. Every summer my parents would rent a cabin at the lake and we would spend a month there. Your father's name was Michael Johnson. He was eighteen, and on vacation with his grandparents. He had joined the army and was leaving for boot camp as soon as their vacation was over. It was love at first sight for both of us. We were inseparable for two weeks. We spent every second we could together. I was back in Nebraska when I discovered I was pregnant."

"Did you try to contact him?"

"He was in basic training by then. I didn't have a clue *how* to get in touch with him, and by the time I found him, it was too late. He was dead."

So his biological father was dead.

He wanted to feel remorse, or regret, or pride, but he just felt numb. "How did he die?"

"I don't know much, only that he was on a rescue mission and the helicopter he was in was shot down. Everyone on board was killed. He died a hero."

That meant more to him than she could possibly understand. Since his father—the man who raised him—had never done a decent thing in his life.

"I've used the internet to follow your career over the years," she told him. "I know this probably doesn't mean much, but I'm so proud of the man you've become."

His laugh was a bitter one. "Don't believe everything you read. The truth is, I'm a screw-up."

The sympathy in her eyes nearly did him in. She really cared. "Do you want to talk about it?"

Though he hadn't planned to bring up his relationship with Clare, or anything else about his life, he heard himself spilling his guts. And once he got started, he couldn't seem to stop. He told her the entire sordid story.

"She sounds very special," his mother said when he was all talked out. "What are you planning to do to get her back?"

"There's nothing I can do," he said. "I betrayed her trust. It's over."

"But you love her, don't you? And she loves you?"

He nodded. "Or she used to."

"Then you have to at least try." She laid a hand over his and squeezed gently, and in that instant he felt a connection. A sense of familiarity. It was…nice. So he left his hand there. "Trust me when I say people don't fall out of love overnight. She probably just needs time to sort things out."

"You have no idea how stubborn she is."

"It sounds to me as if you're a little stubborn, too. Or you're just afraid of being rejected again."

Maybe she was right. He'd never been rejected before, so he had no idea how to handle it, or what to do to get her back. He was stumbling around in the dark, and his instincts were failing him.

"Okay," he said, "tell me what I should do. How I can fix this."

"Parker, only you know the answer to that question."

But that was the problem. He didn't. "I don't even know where she is."

"Don't you?"

Of course he did. She was at her parents' ranch. But talking to her meant going there and facing her entire family.

Jesus. Clare was right. He really was a coward.

He and Rachel talked up until the minute it was time to take her back to the airport, and all the way to the terminal, where he dropped her outside the doors. They parted with a promise that they would keep in touch, and he gave her permission to give his contact information to his brothers and sisters.

He drove home, weighing his options, and he realized Rachel was right. Clare was worth fighting for.

And if he failed, he would live the rest of his life regretting it. But at least he could say that he'd tried. He would stop home and pick up a few things, then drive to her parents' farm. If she refused to talk to him, he would camp out with the horses until she changed her mind. He would even take on her brothers if he had to. He was willing to go to any lengths to get her back.

But when he pulled down his street, her car was in his driveway and he felt a rush of hope that made his scalp tingle.

He hit the brake and stopped in the road. He had planned to use the hour's drive to the farm to figure out what he was going to say to her. It looked as if he would have to wing it.

He pulled in beside her car. She wasn't in it. Then he remembered that she still had his key. He shuddered to think what she might be doing in there. Setting his house on fire maybe?

He parked in the garage, then let himself inside, nerves roiling in his belly. He hadn't been this nervous, or this determined, in his life. She may have been stubborn, but so was he, and he refused to let her leave until he'd had the chance to explain.

She was sitting on the sofa, and the deep love and respect that he felt for her propelled him forward when what he really wanted to do was turn around and run. Never in his adult life had he been intimidated by a woman, but Clare scared the hell out of him right now.

As he walked into the room she stood. She didn't say a word; she just looked at him, her expression blank. And he couldn't think of a damned thing to say. He stood there, trying to make his brain work.

She walked over, until she was standing in front of

him. She had her hair up in one of those messy buns, and he itched to pull the band out so it would tumble out over her shoulders.

For several excruciating seconds she just looked at him. Searching his face. He waited for her to punch him, or scratch his eyes out. Instead, she threw her arms around him.

He was so stunned that for a second he just stood there, speechless.

"I'm so sorry," she said, laying her cheek against his chest, holding him so tight.

Wait a minute. Had she really just apologized to *him*?

"Clare, you have nothing to be sorry for. I betrayed your trust. I'm the bad guy here."

She looked up at him. "And I betrayed yours."

He blinked. What the hell was she talking about? "I don't understand."

"I said I loved you, and at the first sign of trouble I exploded. I didn't even give you a chance to explain. I was so wrapped up in my own feelings I didn't even stop to think about yours."

"Clare, this was my fault."

"Not completely. I should have been more understanding. I was just scared, and feeling vulnerable."

"You had every right to be. I screwed up."

"And I forgive you."

He blinked. "Just like that?"

"You made a mistake."

"It was a stupid move. I don't even know what I was thinking. I guess I wasn't."

"After all the soul-searching you've done, and the changes you've made, you were bound to have a setback and do something the old Parker would have done.

But I'm not in love with that guy. I'm in love with you, right now, just the way you are."

"I never meant to hurt you. And I was a coward for not telling you about the bet. It was stupid and childish."

"And I'm sorry that I overreacted so badly. And I don't want to fight. I want to fix this. Fix me."

"There's nothing to fix," he said, pulling her close and holding her tight, hardly able to conceive that she was giving him a second chance. "You're perfect."

"Far from it." She rose up on her toes and kissed him gently. "All I know is that I love you, and the past few days I've been miserable without you. The idea that I might never kiss you again, or feel your arms around me…" Her voice wavered and tears swam in her eyes. "We can figure this out."

"Yes," he said, "I want that, too."

She cupped his face in her hands, smiled up at him. "I really love you, Parker. So much."

"I love you, too. And I have so much to tell you. I met my mother today."

Clare gasped and her eyes lit. "You did?"

"You're not the only one with a big family. Turns out I have two half brothers and two half sisters. But we can talk about that later. Right now I just want to hold you."

After another long and wonderful embrace, she looked up at him and said, "I was thinking that since you won the bet because of me, it would only be fair to give me half of the prize."

"You can have it all," he said, letting go of her so he could take out his wallet. He pulled out a ten-dollar bill and handed it to her.

She looked at the bill, then back to him. "Ten bucks?"

"Yup."

"That's it?"

"'Fraid so. They're not serious bets. We always goof around."

She laughed, and shook her head, and it was the most beautiful thing he'd ever heard. They were okay. And he was never letting her go again.

"You know, this is all Maddie's fault," he said.

Clare looked at him funny. "Why do you say that?"

"Sharing in her care brought us together in a way no other patient has before. It's because of her that we connected."

"That's true," she said. "Remind me to thank her someday."

"I know things moved pretty fast with us, and to ask you to marry me right this minute would be pushing it."

"A little," she agreed.

"I just want you to know that I have every intention of spending the rest of my life with you. Whether you like it or not."

She grinned. "I think I like it."

"I don't care if we wait ten years to get married, as long as I know I have your heart." He cradled her face in his hands, kissed her gently. "Because, cupcake, you definitely have mine."

* * * * *

Erika wasn't at all what he expected when he'd spotted a foreign princess on the guest list.

He'd envisioned either a stiff-necked dignitary or a football groupie bent on a photo op and a chance to meet his players. He didn't come across many people who dared tell him they didn't like football.

How contrary that her disinterest in his world made her all the more appealing. Yes, she aroused him in a way he couldn't recall having felt about any woman before.

And quite possibly some of that allure had to do with the fact that for once in his life he wasn't under the scrutiny of the American media.

Perhaps if he was careful he could do something impulsive without worrying about the consequences rippling through his family's world.

* * *

His Pregnant Princess Bride
is part of the Bayou Billionaires series—
Secrets and scandal are a Cajun family
legacy for the Reynaud brothers!

HIS PREGNANT PRINCESS BRIDE

BY
CATHERINE MANN

First Published in Great Britain 2016
By Mills & Boon, an imprint of HarperCollins*Publishers*
1 London Bridge Street, London, SE1 9GF

© 2016 Catherine Mann

ISBN: 978-0-263-91848-9

51-0216

Our policy is to use papers that are natural, renewable and recyclable products and made from wood grown in sustainable forests.The logging and manufacturing processes conform to the legal environmental regulations of the country of origin.

Printed and bound in Spain
by CPI, Barcelona

USA TODAY bestselling author **Catherine Mann** lives on a sunny Florida beach with her flyboy husband and their four children. With more than forty books in print in over twenty countries, she has also celebrated wins for both a RITA® Award and a Booksellers' Best Award. Catherine enjoys chatting with readers online—thanks to the wonders of the internet, which allows her to network with her laptop by the water! Contact Catherine through her website, www.catherinemann.com, find her on Facebook and Twitter (@CatherineMann1) or reach her by snail mail at PO Box 6065, Navarre, FL 32566, USA.

To my dear friend and former neighbour
from Louisiana—Karen.
Thank you for all the Mardi Gras cakes
and celebrations!

Prologue

"I have to confess, I don't care for the football at all."

Princess Erika's declaration caught Gervais Reynaud off guard, considering they'd spent the past four hours in the private viewing box overlooking Wembley Stadium, where his team would be playing a preseason exhibition game two months from now.

As the owner of the New Orleans Hurricanes NFL team, Gervais had more important things to do than indulge this high-maintenance Nordic princess he'd been seated beside during today's event, a high-stakes soccer match that was called "football" on this side of the globe. A game she didn't even respect regardless of which country played. Had it been sexist of him to think she might actually enjoy the game, since she was a royal, serving in her country's army? He'd expected a military member to be athletic. Not unreasonable, right? She was definitely toned under that gray, regimented uniform decorated with gold braid and commendations.

But she was also undoubtedly bored by the game.

And while Gervais didn't enjoy soccer as much as American football, he respected the hell out of it. The athletes were some of the best in the world. His main task for today had been to scout the stadium, to see what it would be like for the New Orleans Hurricanes when they played here in August. He'd staked his business reputation on the team he owned, a move his financial advisers had all adamantly opposed. There were risks, of course. But Gervais had never backed away from a challenge. It went against his nature. And now his career was tied to the success of the Hurricanes. The media spotlight had always been intense for him because of his family name. But after he'd purchased the franchise, the media became relentless.

Previewing the Wembley Stadium facilities at least offered him a welcome weekend of breathing room from scrutiny, since the UK fan base for American football was nominal. Here, he could simply enjoy a game without a camera panning to his face or reporters circling him afterward.

He only wished he could be watching the Hurricanes play today. He'd put one of his brothers in charge of the team as head coach. Another brother ran the team on the field in the quarterback position. Sportswriters back in the United States implied he'd made a colossal mistake.

Playing favorites? Clearly, they didn't know the Reynauds.

He wouldn't have chosen from his family unless they were the best for the job. Not when purchasing this team provided his chance to forge his own path as more than just part of the Reynaud extended-family empire of shipping moguls and football stars.

But to do that successfully, he had to play the political game with every bit as much strategy as the game on the field. As a team owner, he was the face of the Hurricanes. Which meant putting up with a temperamental princess who hadn't grasped that the "football team" he owned wasn't the one on the field. Not that she seemed to care much one way or the other.

Sprawled on the white leather sofa, Gervais tossed a pigskin from hand to hand, the ball a token gift from the public relations coordinator who'd welcomed him today and shown him to the private viewing box. The box was emptying now that the clock ran out after the London club beat another English team in the FA Cup Final. "You don't like the ball?"

She waved an elegant hand, smoothing over her pale blond hair sleeked back in a flawless twist. "No, not that. Perhaps my English is not as good as I would wish," she said with only the slightest hint of an accent. She'd been educated well, speaking with an intonation that was unquestionably sexy, even as she failed to notice the kind of football he held was different than the one they'd used on the field. "I do not care for the game. The football game."

"Interesting choice, then, for your country to send you as the royal representative to a finals match." Damn, she was too beautiful for her own good, wearing that neat-fitting uniform and filling it out in all the right places. Just looking at her brought to mind her heritage—her warrior princess ancestors out in battle side by side with badass Vikings—although this Nordic princess had clearly been suffering in regal silence for the past four hours. The way she'd dismissed her travel assistant had Gervais thinking he wouldn't even bother playing the diplomat with this ice princess.

"So, Princess Erika, were you sent here as punishment for some bad-girl imperial infraction?"

And if so, why wasn't she leaving now that the game had ended? What held her here, sipping champagne and talking to him after the box cleared? More important, what kept *him* here when he had a flight planned for tonight?

"First of all, I am not a reigning royal." Her icy blue eyes were as cool as her icy homeland as she set down her crystal champagne flute. "Our monarchy has been defunct for over forty-five years. And even if it was not, I am the youngest of five girls. And as for my second point, comments like yours only confirm my issue with attending a function like this where you assume I must be some kind of troublemaker if I don't enjoy this game. I must be flawed. No offense meant, but you and I simply have different interests."

"Then why are you here?" He wanted to know more than he should.

The PR coordinator for the stadium had introduced them only briefly and he found himself hungry to know more about this intriguing but reticent woman.

"My mother was not happy with my choice to join

the military, even though if I were a male that would not be in question. She is concerned I am not socializing enough and that I will end up unmarried, since clearly my worth is contingent upon having babies." Rolling her eyes, she crossed her long, slim legs at the ankles, her arms elegantly draped on the white leather chair. "Ridiculous, is it not, considering I am able to support myself? Besides, most of my older sisters are married and breeding like raccoons."

"Like rabbits."

She arched a thin blond eyebrow. "Excuse me?"

"The phrase is *breeding like rabbits*." Gervais couldn't quite smother a grin as the conversation took an interesting turn.

"Oh, well, that is strange." She frowned, tapping her upper lip with a short, neat fingernail. "Rabbits are cute and fuzzy. Raccoons are less appealing. I believe raccoons fit better," she said as if merely stating it could change a colloquialism on her say-so.

"You don't like kids?" he found himself asking, even though he could have stood and offered to walk her out and be done with any expectation of social nicety.

When was the last time he exchanged more than a few words with a woman outside of business? He could spend another minute talking to her.

"I do not believe I must have a dozen heirs to make a defunct monarchy stable."

Hmm, valid point and an unexpected answer. "So I take that to mean you're no threat to hitting on the players?"

Down on the field, the winning team was being mobbed.

"You assume correctly," she blurted so quickly and emphatically, she startled a laugh from him.

It was refreshing to find a woman who wasn't a sports groupie for a change.

He found himself staying behind to talk to her even though he had a flight to catch. "What do you do in the military?"

"I am a nurse by degree but the military uses my skills as a linguist. In essence, I'm a diplomatic translator."

"Say again?"

"Is that so shocking? Do I not appear intelligent?"

She appeared hot as hell, like a blue flame, the most searing of all.

"You're lovely and articulate. You speak English fluently as a second language. You're clearly intelligent."

"And you are a flatterer," she said dismissively. "I work as a translator, but now that I'm nearing the end of my time in military service, I'll be taking the RN degree a step further, becoming a nurse-practitioner, with a specialty in homeopathic treatments, using natural herbs and even scents, studying how they relate to moods and physiological effects. Stress relievers. Energy infusers. Or immune boosters. Or allergy relievers. Any number of combinations to combine an alluring perfume with a healthier lifestyle."

"Where do you study that?"

"I've been accepted into a program in London. I had hoped to pursue nursing in the military to increase my experience, but my government had other plans for me to be a translator."

A nurse, soon to become a nurse-practitioner? Now, *that* surprised him. "Very impressive."

"Thank you." She nodded regally, a lock of hair sliding free from her twist and caressing her cheek. She tucked it behind her ear. "Now, explain to me what I need to know to speak intelligently about what I saw down on the field with all those musclemen when I return home."

Standing, he extended an arm to her. "By all means, Princess, I know a little something about European football even though the team I own is an American football team."

She rose with the elegance of a woman who'd been trained in every manner to grace high-end ballrooms not ball games. And yet she chose to further her education and serve her country in uniform.

Princess-Captain Erika Mitras wasn't at all what he expected when he'd spotted a foreign dignitary on the guest list. He'd envisioned either a stiff-necked VIP or a football groupie bent on a photo op and a chance to meet the players. He didn't come across many people who dared tell him they didn't like football—European or American. In fact, he didn't have many people in his life who disliked sports. The shipping business might be the source of Reynaud wealth, but football had long been their passion.

How contrary that her disinterest in sports made her all the more appealing. Yes, she aroused him in a way he couldn't recall having felt about any woman before.

And quite possibly some of that allure had to do with the fact that for once in his life he wasn't under the scrutiny of the American media. Perhaps if he was careful, he could do something impulsive without worrying about the consequences rippling through his family's world.

He stepped closer, folding her hand into the crook of his arm, and caught a whiff of a cinnamon scent. "And while I do that, what do you say we enjoy London? Dinner, theater, your choice. Just the two of us."

Flights could be rescheduled.

She paused to peer up at him, her cool blue eyes roaming his face for a moment before the barest hint of a smile played over her lips. "Only if, after a brief outline of the differences in these football sports, we can agree to no football talk at all?"

"None," he vowed without hesitation.

"Then it sounds lovely."

Who knew cinnamon would be such a total turn-on?

One

2 ½ Months Later
New Orleans, Louisiana

Princess Erika Birgitta Inger Freya Mitras of Holsgrof knew how to make a royally memorable appearance.

Her mother had taught her well. And Erika needed all the confidence she could garner striding onto the practice field full of larger-than-life men in training. Most important, she needed all her confidence to face one particular man. The leader of this testosterone domain, the owner of the state-of-the-art training facility where he now presided. Players dotted the field in black-and-gold uniforms, their padded shoulders crashing against each other. Shouts, grunts and curses volleyed. Men who appeared to be trainers or coaches jogged alongside them, barking instructions or blowing whistles.

She'd finished her military stint a month ago, her hopes of serving her country in combat having been sidelined by her parents' interference. They'd shuffled her into some safe figurehead job that made her realize the family's Viking-warrior heritage would not be carried on through her. She'd been so disillusioned, adrift and on edge the day she attended the soccer game, she had been reckless.

Too reckless. And that weekend of indulgence brought her here. Now. To New Orleans. To Gervais.

Her Jimmy Choo heels sank into the most plush grass ever as she stepped onto the practice field of the New Orleans Hurricanes. She'd assumed this particularly American game was played on Astroturf. And assumptions were what she had to avoid when it came to her current adventure in the United States.

She had not intended to see Gervais Reynaud again after he left the United Kingdom. Their weekend of dates—and amazing, mind-blowing sex—had been an escape from rules and protocol and everything else that had kept her life rigidly in check for so long. She'd had relationships in the past, carefully chosen and approved. This was her first encounter of her own choosing.

And it had turned out to be far more memorable than she could have ever imagined.

She felt the weight of his eyes from across the open stretch of greenery. Or perhaps he had noticed her only because of the sudden silence. Players now stood still, their shouts dimming to a dull echo.

The rest of the place faded for her while she focused on Gervais Reynaud standing at the foot of the bleachers, as tall as any of the players. He was muscular, more so than the average man but more understated than the men in uniform nearby. She knew he had played in his youth and through college but had chosen a business route in the family's shipping enterprise until he had bought the New Orleans Hurricanes football team. The *American* football team. She understood the difference now. She also knew Gervais's purchase of the team had attracted a great deal of press coverage in business and sports media alike.

He had not told her much about his life, but before she made her trip here she had made a point of learning more about him and his family.

It certainly was amazing what a few internet searches could reveal.

Tracing their ancestry deep into Acadian history, the Reynaud family first built their fortune in shipping, a business that his grandfather patriarch Leon Reynaud had expanded into a thriving cruise ship company. Leon also turned a love of sports into another successful venture when he'd purchased shares in a Texas football team, learning the business from the inside out. His elder son, Christophe, inherited the shares but promptly sold them to buy a baseball team, creating a deep family rift.

Leon passed his intense love of football to his younger son, Theo, whose promising career as a quarterback in Atlanta was cut short due to injury and excess after his marriage to a celebrated supermodel fell apart. Theo had three sons from his marriage, Gervais, Henri and Jean-Pierre, and one from an earlier affair, Dempsey. All of the sons inherited a passion for the game, playing in college and groomed for the NFL.

While the elder two sons broke ties with their father to bring corporate savvy to the front office of the relatively new team, the younger two sons both continued their careers on the field. The Reynaud brothers were especially well-known in Louisiana, where their football exploits were discussed—as much a topic of conversation as the women in their lives. She'd overheard references to each in the lobby of the five-star hotel where she'd spent the night in New Orleans.

Would she be the topic of such conversation once her "encounter" with Gervais became public knowledge? There would be no way to hide it from his football world much longer.

Football. A game she still cared very little about, a fact he had teased her about during their weekend together, a weekend where they had spent more time undressed than clothed. Her gaze was drawn back to that well-honed body of his that had made such passionate love to her.

His dark eyes heated her with memories as he strode toward her. His long legs ate the ground in giant slices, his khakis and sports jacket declaring him in the middle of a workday. He stopped in front of her, his broad shoulders blocking the sun and casting his handsome face in shadows. But she didn't have to see to know his jaw would be peppered with the stubble that seemed to grow in seconds after he shaved. Her fingers—her body—remembered the texture of that rasp well.

Her breath caught somewhere in her chest.

He folded his arms over his chest, just under the Hurricanes logo stitched on the front of his jacket. "Welcome to the States, Erika. No one mentioned your intention to visit. I thought you didn't like sports."

"And yet, here I am." And in need of privacy out of the bright Louisiana sun and the even brighter curious eyes of his team and staff. She needed space and courage to tell him why she'd made this unexpected journey across the Atlantic to this muggy bayou state. "This is not an official royal visit."

"And you're not in uniform." His eyes glided over her wraparound dress.

"I'm out of the service now to begin furthering my studies." About to return to school to be a nurse-practitioner, the career field she'd hoped to pursue in the military, but they would not allow her such an in-the-field position, instead preferring to dress her up and trot her around as a figurehead translator. "I am here for a conference on homeopathic herbs and scents." A part of her passion in the nursing field, and a totally made-up excuse for being here today.

"The homeopathic scents for healing, right? Are you here to share specially scented deodorant with my players? Because they could certainly use it." His mouth tipped with a smile.

"Are you interested in such a line?" Still jet-lagged from the transatlantic flight, she was ill prepared to exchange pleasantries, much less ones filled with taunts at her career choice.

"Is that why you are here? For business before you start your new degree?"

She could not just banter with him. She simply could not. "Please, can we go somewhere private to talk?"

He searched her eyes for a long moment before gesturing over his shoulder. "I'm in the middle of a meeting with sponsors. How about supper?"

"I am not here for seduction," she stated bluntly.

"Okay." His eyebrows shot upward. "I thought I asked you to join me for gumbo not sex. But now that we're talking about sex—"

"We are not." She cut him short. "Finish your meeting if you must, but I need to speak with you as soon as possible. Privately. Unless you want your personal business and mine overheard by all of your team straining to listen."

She definitely was not ready for them to hear she was pregnant with the heir to the Reynaud family dynasty.

She was back. Princess Erika, the sexy seductress who'd filled his dreams since they'd parted ways nearly three months ago. And even though he should be paying attention to the deal with his sponsors, he could not tear his eyes away from her. From the swish of her curves and hips. And the long platinum-blond hair that made her look completely otherworldly.

He needed to focus, but damn. She was mesmerizing.

And apparently, every team member on the field was

also aware of that fact. From their top wide receiver Wildcard to running back Freight Train.

Gervais turned his attention back to finishing up his conversation with the director of player personnel—Beau Durant—responsible for draft picks, trades, acquiring the right players and negotiating contracts. An old college friend, Beau shared his friend's interest in running a football team. He took a businesslike, numbers approach to the job and wed that with his personal interest in football. Like Gervais, he had a position in his family's multinational corporation, but football was his obsession.

"Gervais, I'd love to stay and chat, but we have another meeting to get to. We'll be in touch," his former college roommate promised.

"Perfect, Beau. Thank you," he said, offering him a sincere handshake. Beau's eyes were on the princess even if he didn't ask the obvious question. Beau was an all-business kind of guy who never pried. He'd always said he didn't want others sticking their noses in his private life, either.

The eyes of the whole damn team remained on the princess, in fact. Which made Gervais steam with protectiveness.

He barked over to his half brother, the head coach, "Dempsey, don't your boys have something better to do than stand around drooling over a woman like pimply teenage boys?"

Dempsey smirked. "All right, men. Back to practice. You can stare at pretty girls on someone else's time. Now, move!" Henri Reynaud, the Hurricanes' quarterback and Gervais's brother, shot him a look of half amusement. But he slung his helmet back on and began to make his way into formation. The Bayou Bomber, a nickname Henri had earned during his college days at LSU, would not be so easily dissuaded from his obvious curiosity.

Dempsey scratched some numbers out on his paper. Absently, he asked, "What's with the royal visit?"

"We have some…unresolved issues from our time in England."

"Your time together?" Dempsey's wicked grin spread, and he clucked his tongue.

He might as well come clean in an understated way. The truth would be apparent soon enough. "We had a quiet…relationship."

"Very damn quiet if I didn't hear about it." Crossing his arms, he did his best to look hurt.

"You were busy with the team. As it should be."

"So you have some transcontinental dating relationship with Europe's most eligible princess?"

"Reading the tabloids again, Dempsey?"

"Gotta keep up with my players' antics somehow." He shrugged it off.

"Well, don't let her hear you discussing her eligibility. She's military. She might well be able to kick your ass."

"Military, huh? That's surprising."

"She said male royals serve. Why not females? She just finished up her time." Which had seemed to bother her. He understood well about trying to find where you fit in a high-profile family.

"Carole Montemarte, the Hurricanes' press relations coordinator, will have a blast spinning that for the media. Royalty for a girlfriend? Nice, dude. And she chased you clear across the ocean. You are quite the man."

Except that didn't make sense. She'd ignored his calls after he left the country. Granted, what they'd shared blew his mind, and he didn't have the time or energy for a transcontinental relationship. So his calls had been more…obligatory. Had she known that? Was that the reason she'd ignored him?

So why show up here now?

He sure as hell intended to find out.

Two

Limos were something of the norm for Erika. Part of the privilege of growing up royal. This should feel normal, watching the sunset while being chauffeured in the limo Gervais had sent to retrieve her from her hotel. Half of her childhood had been spent in the backseat of a limo as she and her family went from one event to another.

But today was anything but normal. As she pulled at the satin fabric of her dress, her mind began to race. She had never pictured herself with a brood of children like her sisters. Not that she didn't want them, but this was all happening so fast. And with a man she wasn't entirely sure of. Just the thought of Gervais sent her mind reeling. The thought of telling him about their shared interest made her stomach knot. She began to wonder about what she would tell him. How she would tell him. News she could barely wrap her brain around. But there were secrets impossible to keep in her world, so if she wanted to inform Gervais on her terms, she would have to do so soon.

Tonight.

And just like that, Erika realized the vehicle had stopped. Reality was starting to set in, and no amount of finery and luxury was going to change that. She had chosen the arctic-blue dress because it reminded her of her heritage. Of her family's Viking past. Of the strength of her small country. She needed these reminders if she was going to face him.

Try as she might, Erika couldn't get the way he looked at her out of her mind. His eyes drinking her in. The memory sent a pleasurable shiver along her skin.

The chauffeur opened the door with a click, and she stepped out of the limo. Tall and proud. A light breeze danced against her skin, threatening her sideswept updo. Fingers instinctively flew to the white-crusted sapphire pin that, at the nape of her neck, not only held her hair together but also had been in her family for centuries.

Smoothing her blond hair that cascaded over one of her shoulders, she took in the Reynaud family compound in the meeting of sunset with the moon, the stars just beginning to sparkle in the Louisiana sky. Though she had to admit, the flood of lights leading up to the door diminished the starlight.

She lifted her gaze to the massive structure ahead of her. Greek Revival with white arches and columns— no other word than *massive*, and a girl who grew up in a palace wasn't impressed easily.

As she walked up the stairs to the home, the sureness from touching her family heirloom began to wane. But before she could lose her nerve and turn back, the limo pulled away and the grand door opened in front of her. This was officially happening.

Though the lights outside had been clinical and bright, the foyer was illuminated by bulbs of yellow. The warmth of these lights reflected on what appeared to be hand-painted murals depicting a fox hunt. American royalty.

A servant gestured for her to walk through the room on the left. Gathering the skirt of her dress, Erika crossed the threshold, leaving behind the foyer and its elaborate staircase and murals.

This room was made for entertainment. She had been in plenty of grand dining halls, and this one felt familiar and impersonal, with wisps of silk that told their secrets to the glass and windows.

Erika had always hated dinners in rooms like this.

Quickly scanning the room, she noted the elaborately carved wooden chair and the huge arrangements of flowers and the tall marble vases. But Gervais wasn't here, either.

She pressed on through the next threshold and found herself in a simpler room. It was clear that this was a family room. The opulent colors of the grand dining room softened, giving way to a creamy palette. The kind of colors that made Erika want to curl up on the plush leather sofa with a good book and some strong tea with milk.

The family room sported an entertainment bar with

Palladian windows overlooking the pool and grounds. But if she turned ever so slightly she could also see an alcove that appeared to lead to a more private section.

The master bedroom and bath? She could envision that space having doors out to the pool, a hot tub, perhaps. She bit her lip and spun away.

It was not as if she was here to gawk at furniture. She had to tell a man she barely knew that they were having a baby. And that the press would have a field day if she and Gervais didn't get a handle on this now.

And there. She saw him. Chiseled. Dark hair, ruffled ever so slightly. His lips parted into a smile as he met her gaze.

Nerves and something else jolted her to life. Pushed her forward. Toward him and that wolfish smile.

She looked around and saw housekeeping staff, but no one else. Erika waved an elegant hand to the expansive room they stood in and the ones she'd already passed through. "Where's the rest of your family?"

"Dempsey owns the other home on the compound grounds, next door. My younger brothers Jean-Pierre and Henri share the rights to the house to the northwest on the lake. Gramps has quarters here with me, since this house has been in our family the longest. It's familiar. He has servants on call round the clock. He's getting older and more forgetful. But we're hoping to hold back time as long as we can for him."

"I am so sorry."

"They make great meds these days. He's still got lots of life and light left in him." A practiced smile pressed against his lips. It was apparent he was hopeful. And used to defending his grandfather's position.

"And where does the rest of your family live?"

"Are you worried they'll walk in on us?" He angled a brow upward, and she felt the heat of his eyes graze across her body. A flush crept along her face, heating her from the inside out. Threatening to set her nerves bounding out of control. She needed to stay calm.

"Perhaps."

"My father's in Texas and doesn't return often. Jean-Pierre is in New York with his team for the season and Henri lives in the Garden District most of the time, so their house here is vacant for a while."

Stepping out onto the patio, he nodded for her to follow. She hastened behind him. Intrigued. He had that way about him. A quality of danger that masked itself as safe. That quality that made him undeniably sexy.

And that, she reminded herself, was how she'd ended up in this situation.

Gervais surveyed the patio. She followed his gaze, noting the presence of a hot tub and an elaborate fountain that pumped water into the pool. The fountain, like the house, was descended from a Greek aesthetic. Apollo and Daphne were intertwined, water flowing from the statues into the pool.

Over the poolside sound system, the din of steel drums competed with the gentle echo of rolling waves on the lakeshore.

"You arranged dinner outside." Erika breathed in the air on this rare night of low humidity. She looked around at the elaborate patio table that was dressed for dinner with lights, fresh flowers, silver and china. Ceiling fans circled a delicious breeze from the slight overhang of the porch.

"I promised you gumbo—" he gestured broadly, before holding the seat out for her "—and I delivered."

She settled into the chair, intensely aware of his hands close to her shoulders. The heat of his chest close to her back. Blinking away the awareness, she focused on the table settings, surprised to realize he planned to serve her himself from the silver chafing dishes. "Your home is lovely."

"The old plantation homes have a lot of character." He slid into the seat across from hers. "I know our history here doesn't compete with the hundreds of years, castles and Viking lore of your country, but the place has stories in the walls all the same."

"The architecture and details are stunning. I can see why you were drawn to live here." When Americans talked about their colonial towns, they always spoke of the old-world charm they'd possessed. But that was selling it short. Cities like New Orleans were the distillation of cultures haphazardly pressed against each other. And that distillation yielded beauty that was so different from the actual Old World.

"If you would prefer a restaurant…" He paused, tongs grasping freshly baked bread.

"This is better. More private." She held up a hand. "Don't take that the wrong way."

"Understood. You made your point earlier."

Seafood gumbo, red beans and rice, thick black

coffee and powdery doughnuts—beignets. It was a spread that sent her taste buds jumping.

"Did you have a nice ride from the Four Winds Resort?"

"I did. The trees heavy with Spanish moss are beautiful. And the water laps at the roads as if the sea could wash over the land at any moment." The languid landscape was so different than her country's rugged and fierce Viking past. She'd liked learning about New Orleans so far.

"You could stay here, you know."

"I did not come here for that." She laced her words with ice even as her body burned with awareness of the man seated across from her.

"Then why are you here after walking out on me without a word or backward glance?"

So that hadn't escaped his notice. She began to prepare the speeches that had replayed in her mind since she had boarded the plane to make the transatlantic journey.

"I'm sorry about that. I thought I was making things easier for both of us. It was a fling with no future, given we live across an ocean from each other. I saved us both a messy goodbye."

At that time she had been thinking about the life she needed to get on track. But all her carefully laid plans were shifting beneath her feet, now that she was pregnant.

"And when I called you? Left messages asking to speak to you?"

"I thought you were being polite. Gentlemanly. And

do not get me wrong, I believe it honorable of you. But that is not enough to build a relationship."

"How much would it have hurt to return one call? If we're talking about polite, I expected as much from you." He cocked an eyebrow.

"You are angry. I apologize if I made the wrong decision."

"Well, you're here now. For your conference, right?"

"Actually, that wasn't the truth." She fidgeted with her leather band bracelet, inspirational inscriptions scrolled on metal insets providing support. Advice. And if ever she was in need of help, the moment was now. "I only said that in case others overheard. I'm here to see you. I want to apologize for walking out on you and have a conversation we should have had then."

"What conversation would that be?"

Oh, what a loaded question, she thought. "How we would handle it if there were unexpected consequences from our weekend together."

He stared at her, hard. "Unexpected consequences? How about you spell it out rather than have me play Fifty Questions."

She dabbed the corners of her mouth as if she could buy herself a few more seconds before her life changed forever. Folding the napkin carefully and placing it beside her plate, she met his dark brown eyes, her own gaze steady. Her hands shaky. "I am pregnant. The baby is yours."

Of all the things that Erika could have said, being pregnant was not what Gervais had been preparing himself for. He ought to say something. Something fast, witty and comforting. But instead, he just looked at her.

Really looked at her as he swallowed. Hard.

She was every bit as breathtaking as that first night they'd met. But there was something different in the way she carried her body that should have tipped him off.

Her face was difficult to read. She'd iced him out of gaining any insights in her eyes. Gervais examined the hair that trailed down her shoulder, exposing her collarbone and slender neck. This was the hairstyle of a royal, so different than the girl who had let her hair run wild over their weekend together.

And what a weekend it'd been. Months had passed since then and he still thought about her. About the way she'd tasted on his tongue.

He had to say something worthy of that. Of her. He collected his thoughts, determined to say the perfect thing.

Despite all of that, only one word fell out of his mouth.

"Pregnant." So much for a grand speech.

Her face flashed with a hint of disappointment. Of course, she had every right to expect more from him. But more silence escaped his lips, and the air was filled not with sounds of him speaking, but with the buzz of waves and boats.

The trace of frustration and disappointment had left her face. She looked every bit a Viking queen. Impassive. Strong. Icy. And still so damn sexy in her soft feminine clothes and that bold leather bracelet.

"Yes, and I am absolutely certain the child is yours."

"I didn't question you."

"I wanted to be clear. Although in these days of DNA tests, it is not a subject that one can lie about." She frowned. "Do you need time to think, for us to talk more later? You look pale."

Did he? Hell, he did feel as if he'd been broadsided by a three-hundred-pound linebacker, but back in his ballplaying days he'd been much faster at recovery. And the stakes here were far higher. He needed to tread carefully. "A child is always cause for celebration." He took her hand in his, as close as he could let himself get until he had answers, no matter how tempted he was for more. "I'm just surprised. We were careful."

"Not careful enough, apparently. You, um, did stretch the condom, and perhaps there was a leak."

He choked on a cough. "Um, uh…I don't know what to say to that."

"It was not a compliment, you Cro-Magnon." She shook her hand free from his. "Simply an observation."

"Fair enough. Okay, so you're pregnant with my baby. When do you want to head to the courthouse to get married?"

"Are you joking? I did not come to the United States expecting a proposal of marriage."

"Well, that is what I am offering. Would you prefer I do this in a more ceremonial way? Fine." He slid from his chair and dropped to one knee on the flagstone patio. "Marry me and let's bring up this child together."

Her eyes went wide with shock and she shot to her

feet. Looking around her as if to make sure no one overheard. "Get up. You look silly."

"Silly?"

For the first time since he'd met her, she appeared truly flustered. She edged farther away, sweeping back her loose hair with nervous hands. "Perhaps I chose the wrong word. You look…not like you. And this is not what I want."

"What do you want?"

"I am simply here to notify you about your child and discuss if you wish to be a part of the baby's life before I move forward with my life."

"Damn straight I want to bring up my child."

"Shared custody."

He reached to capture her restless hands and hold them firmly in his. "You are not hearing me. I want to raise my child."

"*Our* child."

"Of course." He caressed the insides of her wrists with his thumbs. "Let's declare peace so we can make our way through this conversation amicably."

Her shoulders relaxed and he guided her to a bench closer to the half wall at the end of the patio. They sat side by side, shoulder to shoulder.

She nodded. "I want peace, very much. That's why I came to you now, early on, rather than just calling or waiting longer."

"And I am glad you did." He slid his hand up her arm to her shoulder, cupping the warmth of her, aching for more. "My brother Dempsey grew up thinking our father didn't want him and it scarred him. I refuse to let that happen to my child. My baby will know he or she is wanted."

"Of course our child will be brought up knowing both parents love and want him or her."

"Yes, and you still haven't answered my question."

"What question?"

"The *silly* question that comes with a guy getting down on one knee. Will you marry me?"

Three

"Marry you? I do not even know you." Erika's voice hitched. Marriage? She had wanted him to be supportive, sure. But…marriage? The words tumbled over and over in her head in a disjointed echo.

"We knew each other well enough to have sex. Call me old-fashioned, but I'm trying to do the right thing here and offer to marry you. We can have a civil ceremony and divorce in a year. As far as our child knows, we gave it an honest try but things didn't work." His voice was level. Calm. Practical.

Her fears multiplied. This seemed too calculated. And she would not land in a family environment that was all for show again. Being raised royal had taught her she was not meant for a superficial existence. She had already chosen a meaningful career. A future where she could make a difference.

Swallowing back the anxiety swelling in her chest, she reminded herself to be reasonable.

"You figured all that out this fast? Or have you had practice with this sort of business before?" The notion cut her with surprising sharpness. She did not want to think about Gervais involved with other women after the way they'd been together.

"I am not joking." His hand inched toward hers.

She scrutinized his face, studied the way his jaw jutted. The play of muted lights on his dark hair, the way it was thickest on top of his head. Even now, he was damn attractive. But that fact wasn't enough to chase reason from her mind.

"Apparently not."

"I'll take that as a no to my proposal." Retreating his hand, he leaned forward, elbows on his knees.

"You most certainly can. It is far too soon to speak of marriage. And have you forgotten? I have plans to pursue my education in the UK."

Tilting his head, he lowered his voice. It became soft. Gentle. "You won't even consider my offer? Not even for the baby's sake? Let me take care of you while you're pregnant and recovering, postpartum and such. You can get to know my family during the football season. Afterward, we can spend more time with yours."

Even if the monarchy was defunct, she was a royal and sure of herself. She shot to her feet. "Do I get any say in this at all? You are a pushy man. I do not remember that about you."

He stood and stepped closer, very close, suggestively. His hips and thighs warm against hers. "What do you remember about our time together?"

"If you are trying to seduce me into doing whatever you want—" Erika needed to focus. Which was tougher than ever with him pressed up against her and that smolder in his eye setting her on fire.

"If? I must not be working hard enough." He slid his hands up her arms.

Her eyes fluttered shut, and for a moment she felt as if she could give in. But thoughts of her future child coursed through her mind. A ragged breath escaped her lips, and she reopened her eyes.

She clasped his wrists. "Stop. I am not playing games. I came here to inform you. Not demand anything of you. And certainly not to reenact our past together."

His hands dropped and he scowled. "Let me get this straight. If I hadn't wanted anything to do with the baby, you would have simply walked away?"

"You never would have heard from me again." The words escaped her as an icy dagger. She would have no use for such a man. And she had to admit that even if his proposal felt pushy, at least Gervais was not the sort of person to walk away from his child.

"Well, not a chance in hell is that happening this time. You may have brushed me off once before, but not again."

Had he genuinely wished to see her again after their weekend together? She had been afraid to find out at the time, afraid of answering his call only to discover that his contact was a perfunctory duty and social nicety. After what they had shared, she was not sure she could bear hearing that cool retreat in his voice. Now, of course, she would never know what his intentions had truly been toward her.

She took a deep breath. Regrouped.

"And you cannot command me to your will," she warned him, her shoulders stiff with tension. "I will not be forced into marriage because you think that is the best plan. I have plans, as well."

How many people had underestimated her resolve over the years because she had that label of "princess" attached to her? Her commanding officers. Teachers. Her own parents.

She would simply have to show Gervais her mettle.

"I understand that," he murmured, his voice melting into the sounds of waves and steel drums. "Now we need to make plans together."

Some of the tension in her eased. "Nice to know you can be reasonable and not just impulsive."

With a shrug, he began again. "In the interest of being reasonable, let's spend the next four weeks—"

"Two weeks," she corrected him. She had already disrupted her life and traveled halfway across the globe for him.

He nodded slowly. "Two weeks getting to know each other better as we make plans for our child. You could stay here in my home, where there are plenty of suites for privacy. I won't make a move that isn't mutual. We'll use this time to find common ground."

"And if we are not successful in your time frame?"

This felt like a business deal. But the time frame might be enough to bring him to reason.

"Then I guess I'll have to follow you home. Now, how about I call over to the hotel for them to send your things here? You look ready to fall asleep on your feet."

"You're honestly suggesting I give up my plans completely and stay here?" She gestured back toward the house. Two weeks. Together. Under the same roof.

That part sounded decidedly *less* like a business deal. The very idea wisped heatedly over her skin.

"Not in my bed—unless you ask, of course." He smiled devilishly. "But if we're going to make the most of these two weeks, it's best we stay here. There are fantastic graduate school programs in the area, too, if you opt for that later down the road. And I can also provide you with greater protection here."

"Protection?" What in the world did she need his protection for? And from what? And what was this later-down-the-road notion for her plans?

"We're a professional NFL family. That brings with it a level of fame and notoriety unrivaled in any other business domain. The fans are passionate. And while most of them are supportive, there is a segment that takes the game very personally. Some of the more unstable types occasionally seek revenge for what they perceive as bad decisions." His jaw flexed. "Since your child is my child, that puts our baby at risk as a Reynaud. If you won't stay here for yourself, then stay for our child. We are safe here."

He had found the one reason she couldn't debate. But she needed to be careful. To give herself time to think through the consequences of what she was agreeing to, and she couldn't do that now when she was so tired.

"I am weary. It has been a long, emotional day. I would appreciate being shown to these guest suites that you speak of and I will consider it."

"Of course." He picked up his phone and tapped the screen twice before setting it down. "You'll find all the toiletries you need at your disposal. I'll have someone show you to a room and make sure you have everything you need."

Before he finished speaking, a maid had arrived at the door, perhaps summoned by his phone.

Apparently, Gervais was serious about giving her some space if she elected to stay in the house with him. And while she appreciated that, she was also surprised at his easy efficiency. Hadn't her pregnancy announcement rattled this coolly controlled man even a little?

"Thank you." She looked at him, her breath catching at the raw masculinity of the man. She backed up a step, needing boundaries. And sleep.

"And I'll have a long Hurricanes jersey sent up for you to sleep in." His eyes remained on hers, but his voice stirred something inside her.

The last time they had slept under the same roof, there hadn't been much sleeping accomplished at all. And somehow, as she took her leave of him, she knew that he was remembering that fact as vividly as she did.

The door closed behind her, and she loosed a breath that she didn't realize she'd been holding.

This was…different from what she had grown up

with. The billowy sheer curtains thinly veiled a view of Lake Pontchartrain. Heels clacked against the opulent white marble as she made her way to an oversize plush bed. Instinctively, she ran her hand over the white comforter as she took in the room.

A grand, hand-carved mahogany-wood nightstand held a score of toiletries.

It was luxurious. She unscrewed the lid on one of the lotion bottles, and the light scent of jasmine wafted up to her. She set it down, picked up the shampoo, popped the lid and breathed in mint and a tropical, fruity flavor.

This house was old, not as old as her castle, of course, but it still had history. And such a different feel than her wintry homeland. This was grander, built more for leisure than practicality.

Plopping onto the bed, Erika was somewhat surprised to note the bed was every bit as comfortable as it looked. The bed seemed to wrap her in a hug.

And she needed a hug. Everything in her life was undergoing a drastic change. Untethered. That was where she was. Her career in the military was over. It left her feeling strange, adrift. The past few years, her path had been set. And now? A river of conflicting wants and obligations flooded her mind.

Yes, she wanted to pursue her dream. She wanted to be a nurse-practitioner and pursue her studies in the UK, wanted that so badly. But that dream wasn't as simple as it had been a couple months ago.

Even now, thousands of miles away, she felt the tendrils of familial pressure. When they learned she was going to have a child, they would be pressuring her.

Probably into marriage. And Gervais seemed to have the same ideas. How was she supposed to balance all of it?

In her soul, she knew she'd be able to take care of her child. Give her baby everything and have her dreams, too. But the weight of everyone's expectations left her feeling anxious. First things first, she needed to figure out what she wanted. How she would handle all of this. And then she could deal with the demands of her family and Gervais.

Lifting herself off the bed, she made her way to the coffee table where a stack of old sports programs casually dressed the table.

Dragging her fingers over the covers, she tried to get a feel for Gervais. For his family. The Greek Revival hinted at wealth but shed little on his personality. Though, from her brief time in the halls, she noticed how sparsely decorated the place was. On the wall, directly across from where she stood, were some photos in sleek black frames. They were matted and simple. The generic sorts of photographs that belonged more in a cold, impersonal office than a residence.

She walked over to investigate them further. The two images that hung on the wall were formal portraits, similar to the kinds she and her family had done. But whereas her family bustled with Viking grace and was filled with women, these pictures were filled with the Reynaud men.

The sons stood closer to the grandfather. Strange. A man who looked as if he could be Gervais's father was on the edge of the photograph, an impatient smile curling over his face.

Gingerly, she reached out to the frame, fingers finding cool glass. Gervais. Handsome as the devil. A smile was on her lips before she could stop it. She dropped her hand.

No, Erika. She had to remain focused. And figure out how to do what was best for her—their—child that didn't involve jumping into bed with him. Again.

Pulling at the hem of the jersey that cut her midthigh, a jersey she'd found on her bed and couldn't resist wearing, she resolved to keep her hands off him. And his out from under her jersey. Even if that did sound…delicious.

Father.

The word blasted in his mind like an air horn.

Gervais tried to bring his mind back to the present. To the meeting with Dempsey, who had stopped by after Erika retreated to a vacant suite for the night. Just because Erika was pregnant didn't mean his career was nonexistent. He needed to talk with his brother about the Hurricanes' development. About corporate sponsorships and expanding their team's prestige and net worth.

But that was a lot easier said than done with the latest developments in his personal life.

He swirled his local craft beer in his glass, watching the mini tornado foam in the center as he made himself comfortable in the den long after dinner had ended. Back when this house had still belonged to his parents, most of the rooms had been fussy and full of interior decorator additions—elaborate crystal light fixtures that hung so low he and his brothers broke a part of it every time they threw a ball in the house. Or three-dimensional art that spanned whole walls and would scrape the skin off an arm if they tackled each other into it.

The den had always been male terrain and it remained a place where Gervais felt most comfortable. The place where he most often met with his brothers. Dempsey had headed for this room as soon as he'd arrived tonight.

Now, sipping his beer, Gervais tried like hell to get his head focused back on work. The team.

Dempsey took an exaggerated sip from his glass and set it on the table in front of them. Cocking his head to the side, he settled deeper in the red leather club chair and asked, "What's the deal with the princess's arrival? She damn near caused Freight Train to trip over his feet like a first-day rookie."

"She came by to see me." Gervais tried to make it sound casual. Breezy.

"Because New Orleans happens to be right around the corner from Europe?"

"Your humor slays me." He tipped back his beer. Dempsey was a lot of things, but indirect? Never.

"Well, she obviously came to see you. And from what I'm starting to hear now from the gossip already churning, the two of you spent a great deal of time together in the UK. Are you two back together again? Dating?" A small smile, but his eyes were trained on Gervais. A Reynaud trait—dogged persistence.

"Not exactly dating."

"Then why is she here?" He leaned forward, picking up his glass. "And don't tell me it's none of my business, because she's distracting you."

He wanted to argue the point. But who the hell would he be kidding?

Instead, he dropped his voice. "This goes no further than the two of us for now."

"I'm offended you have to ask that."

"Right. Well, she's pregnant. It's mine."

"You're certain?" Dempsey set his glass on the marble side table, face darkening like a storm rolling out.

Gervais stared him down. Not in the mood for that runaround.

"All right. Your child. What next?"

"My child, my responsibility." He would be there for his child. That was nonnegotiable.

"Interesting choice of words. *Responsibility*." Something shifted in Dempsey's expression. But Gervais didn't have to wonder why. Dempsey was Gervais's illegitimate half brother. Dempsey hadn't even been in the picture until he turned thirteen years old, when Yvette, Dempsey's mom, had angled to extort money from their father, Theo, at which point Theo brought Dempsey to the family home.

To say the blending had been rough was generous. It was something that felt like the domestic equivalent of World War Three. Gervais's mother left. Then it was just a houseful of men—his brothers, Theo and Gramps. And it was really Gramps who had taken care of the boys. Theo was too busy shucking responsibilities.

"I'm sure as hell not walking away." He'd seen too

well the marks it left on Dempsey not knowing his father in the early years, the sting of growing up thinking his father didn't care. Hell, their father hadn't even known Dempsey existed.

Not that it excused their father, since he'd misled Dempsey's mother.

"I'm just saying that I understand what it feels like to be an inconvenient mistake. A responsibility." His jaw flexed, gaze fixed over Gervais's head.

"Dad loves you. We all do. You're part of our family."

"I know. But that wasn't always the case."

"We didn't know you then."

"He did. Or at least he knew that he'd been with women without considering the consequences." Dempsey's eyes darkened a shade, protectiveness for his mother obvious, even though the woman had been a negligible caregiver at best. "Anyhow, it took us all a long time to come back from that tough start. So make sure you get your head on straight before this baby's born. Better yet, get things right before you alienate the child's mother. Because if you intend to be in the kid's life, you're not going to want to spend years backtracking from screwing up with words like *responsibility* at the start."

The outburst was swift and damning. Dempsey shot up and out of his seat. He began to storm away, heading for the door.

Gervais followed.

"Dempsey—wait, I…" But the words fell silent as he nearly plowed into his brother's back.

Dempsey had halted in his tracks, his gaze on the

staircase in the corridor. Or, more accurate, his gaze on the woman now standing on the staircase.

Erika. In nothing but his jersey that barely reached midthigh. And she looked every bit as tantalizing as she had in her dress.

Gervais's eyes traced up, taking in her toned calves, the slope of her waist. The way her breasts pushed on the fabric. That wild hair of hers... She was well covered, but he couldn't help feeling the possessive need to wrap a blanket around her to shield her from his brother's gaze.

"I heard noise and realized there was someone wandering around." She drifted down a step, gesturing toward a shadowed corner of the hallway outside the den, where Gervais's grandfather stood. "I believe this is your grandfather?"

Gramps must have been wandering around again. Leon Reynaud was getting more restless with the years, and forgetful, too. But it was Erika who concerned him most right now. Her face was emotionless, yet there was a trace of unease in her voice. Had she overheard something in their conversation in the den?

Gramps Leon shook a gnarled finger at them. "Somebody's having a baby?" He shook his head. "Your father never could keep his pants zipped."

A wave of guilt crashed against him. For years he had tried to avoid any comparisons between himself and his father. Purposely setting himself on a very different path.

His father had been largely absent throughout his childhood and teen years. Theo Reynaud was a woman chaser. Neglectful of his duties to his children, his wife and the family's business.

Gervais would make damn sure he'd do better for his child. Even if Erika wasn't on board. Yet. He'd be an active presence in his future child's life. Everything his father failed to be.

Dempsey moved toward their grandfather, face slightly flushed. He stood and clapped Leon on the shoulder. "Dad's not expecting another child, *Grandpère*."

"Oh." Leon scratched his sparse hair that was standing up on end. "I get confused sometimes. I must have misunderstood."

Dempsey looked back at Gervais, expression mirroring the same relief Gervais felt. Crisis avoided.

His brother steered Gramps toward the door. "I'll walk with you to your room, Gramps." He gave Erika a nod as they passed her, though his focus remained on Leon. "I programmed some new music into your sound system. Some of those old Cajun tunes you like."

"Thank you, boy, thank you very much." They disappeared down the hall. Leaving Gervais alone with Erika.

Her arms crossed as she met his gaze. Unflinching bright blue eyes.

"You look much better in that jersey than anyone on the team ever did." God, she was crazy sexy.

"Whose jersey is this?" She traced the number with one finger, tempting him to do the same. "Whose number?"

He swallowed hard, a lump in his throat. "It's a retired number, one that had been reserved for me if I joined the team. I didn't." He shook off past regrets abruptly. He'd never played for the team, so he'd bought it, instead. "So shall I escort you back to you room?"

He couldn't keep the suggestive tone from his voice. Didn't want to.

She tipped her haughty-princess chin. "I think not. I can find my own way back."

That might be true enough. But they weren't done by a long shot. He wouldn't rest until the day came when he peeled that jersey from her beautiful body.

Four

She was really doing it. Spending two weeks with Gervais in his mansion on the shores of Lake Pontchartrain. She'd slept in his house and now that her luggage had been sent over from the hotel, she had more than a jersey to wear. She tugged at the hem, the fabric surprisingly soft to the touch, the number cool against the tips of her breasts.

This was actually happening. Last night had been more than just an overnight fluke. True to his word, Gervais hadn't been pushy about joining her here. But she felt his presence all the same.

And she was here to stay. A flutter of nerves traced down her spine as she fully opened the pocket doors to get a better look at the guest suite. She crossed the threshold from the bedroom to the sitting room, clothes in hand.

But she paused, toes sinking into the rich texture of the red Oriental rug. The way the light poured through the window in the sitting room drew her eye. Stepping toward the window, she took a moment to drink in the twinkled blue of Lake Pontchartrain.

The morning sun warmed her cheeks, sparking prisms across the room as it hit the Tiffany lamps. Glancing at her reflection in the gilded-gold mirror that was leaning on the mantel of the fireplace, she tucked a strand of hair behind her ear.

Mind wandering back, as it had a habit of doing lately, to Gervais. To the way his eyes lingered on her. And how that still ignited something in her...

But it was so much more complicated than that. She pushed the thought away, moving past the cream-colored chaise longue and opening the cherrywood armoire. As if settling her belongings in drawers gave her some semblance of normalcy. A girl could try, after all.

Her hand went to her stomach, to the barely perceptible curve of her stomach. A slight thickening to her waist. Her body was beginning to change. Her breasts were swollen and sensitive.

And her emotions were in a turmoil.

That unsettled her most of all. She was used to being seen as a focused academic, a military professional. Now she was adrift. Between jobs. Pregnant by a man she barely knew and with precious little time to settle her life before her family and the world knew of her pregnancy. She had a spot reserved for her in a graduate nursing program this fall, and she wanted to take coursework right up until her due date. But then what?

A knock on the door pulled her back to the present. She opened the paneled door and found a lovely, slender woman, wearing a pencil-thin skirt and silky blouse, tons of caramel-colored hair neatly pinned up. A large, pink-lipstick smile revealed brilliant white teeth.

She extended her hand. "Hello, I'm Adelaide Thibodeaux. Personal assistant to Dempsey Reynaud—the Hurricanes' coach. Gervais asked me to check in on you. I just wanted to make sure, do you have everything you need?"

Erika nodded. "Thank you. That is very kind of you to look in on me."

"I've been a friend of Dempsey's since childhood. I am happy to help the family." She wore sky-high pumps that would have turned Erika into a giantess—exactly the kind that she enjoyed wearing when she wasn't pregnant and less sure-footed.

"Did you have my things sent over?"

Adelaide's brow furrowed, concern touching the corners of her mouth. "Yes, did we miss anything?"

"Everything is perfect, thank you," she said, gesturing to the room behind her. "The home is lovely and comfortable, and I appreciate having my personal belongings sent over."

"We want you to enjoy your stay here in the States. It will be a wonderful publicity boon for the team to have royalty attending our games."

Erika winced. The last thing she wanted was more

attention from the media. Especially before she knew how she was going to handle the next few months.

Adelaide twisted her hands together, silver bracelets glinting in the sunlight. "Did I say something wrong?"

"Of course not. It is just that I am not a fan of football, or competitive sports of any kind." It was a half-truth. Certainly, no matter how she tried, she just didn't understand the attraction of football. But she couldn't tell Adelaide the real reason she didn't want to be a publicity ploy.

"And yet clearly you're quite fit. You must work out."

"I was in the military until recently, and I do enjoy running and yoga, but I have to confess, team sports have never held any appeal for me."

"No?" Adelaide frowned. "Then I am not sure I understand why you are here— Pardon me. I shouldn't have asked. It's not my business."

Erika searched for a simple answer. "Gervais and I enjoyed meeting each other in England." Understatement. "And since there is a conference in the area I plan to attend, I decided to visit." Okay, the conference was a lie, but one she could live with for now.

"Of course." Understanding lit her gaze, as if she was not surprised that Gervais would inspire a flight halfway across the world. "If you need anything, please don't hesitate to ask."

"Thank you. I appreciate your checking on me. But I am independent." She had always been independent, unafraid of challenges.

"I wasn't sure of the protocol for visiting royalty," Adelaide said, her voice curling into a question of sorts.

As if a princess couldn't fend for herself. "You are a princess."

"In name only, and even so, I am the fifth daughter."

"You're humble."

"I have been called many things, but not that. I am simply…practical."

Pink lips slipped back up into a smile. "Well, welcome to New Orleans. I look forward to getting to know you better."

"As do I." She had a feeling she was going to get to know everyone exceptionally well. Erika's thoughts drifted back to Gervais. She certainly wanted to get to know him better.

Adelaide started to leave, then turned back. "It might help you on game days if you think of football as a jousting field for men. You were in the military and come from a country famous for female warriors. Sure, I'm mixing time frames here with Vikings and medieval jousters, but still, if you see the game in the light of a joust or warrior competition, perhaps you may find yourself enjoying the event."

The door closed quietly behind her.

A joust? She'd never considered football and jousting. Maybe…maybe she'd give that a shot.

Her gaze floated back to the window, back to Lake Pontchartrain. It stretched before her like an exotic promise. Reminded her she was in a place that she didn't know. And it might be in her best interest to find any way into this world.

To make the most of these days here, to learn more

about the father of her child, she would need to experience his world.

And that meant grabbing a front-row seat.

Yet even as she plucked out a change of clothes, she couldn't help wondering… Had Adelaide Thibodeaux welcomed many other women into this home on Gervais's behalf?

Today was quite the production. Gervais watched the bustle of people filling the owners' suite at Zephyr Stadium for a preseason game day. Tickets for special viewing in the owners' box were sold at a premium price to raise money for a local charter school, so there were more guests than usual in the large luxury suite that normally accommodated family and friends.

His sister-in-law Fiona Harper-Reynaud was a renowned local philanthropist, and her quarterback husband was the golden boy of New Orleans, which added allure to her fund-raising invitation. Henri—beloved by fans as the Bayou Bomber—was the face of their franchise and worth every cent of his expensive contract. He was a playmaker with the drive and poise necessary to make it in the league's most closely dissected position.

The fact that female fans loved him was a bonus, even though it must be tough for Fiona sometimes. But she seemed to take it in stride, leveraging his popularity for worthy causes. Today her philanthropic guests sat casually on the dark leather chairs that lined the glass of the owners' suite. Half-eaten dishes with bottles of craft beer peppered the table in front of them as the clock ticked down the end of the second quarter that saw the Hurricanes up by three points.

Yet Gervais's eyes sought only one person. Erika.

He'd been busy greeting guests and overseeing some last-minute game-day business earlier, so he hadn't gotten to spend any time with her yet. She was tucked away, in a leather sofa by the bar, sipping a glass of sparkling water with lemon, wearing a silky, fitted turquoise dress that brushed her knees and caressed her curves with understated sex appeal. He knew full well where those enhanced curves came from.

From carrying his baby inside her.

She scrunched her toes in her heeled sandals, reaching down to press her thumb along the arch of her foot. The viewing box was cool—downright chilly. But was the New Orleans heat bothering her? The climate was a far cry from where she lived. He wanted to help her feel more comfortable, to love his home city as much as he did so they wouldn't be forced into some globe-hopping parenting situation. He wished they could have had a private breakfast to talk, but he'd been called away to the game. Thank goodness Adelaide had offered to check on her personally. Dempsey's assistant and long-time friend remained the one good thing that had come from Dempsey's early years spent living a hardscrabble life before their father had found him.

Adelaide had texted Gervais this morning, assuring him that Erika had everything she needed.

Now he watched Erika eyeing the food the servers carried. Caviar nachos and truffles pizza. Delicious delicacies, but she declined the offerings whenever the waitstaff stopped in front of her. Though she certainly looked hungry.

"Is the food not to your liking?" He stepped toward her, smoothing his tie and wondering if he should look into the foods native to her homeland. "We ordered a special menu for the event today, but we can have anything brought in."

Nearby, a group of women cheered as Henri connected with one of the rookie receivers running a slant route down on the field. No doubt, it would be one of Henri's last big plays of the game, since they needed to test the depth of the quarterback position with some of the backup talent.

Erika stood, moving closer to him, the scent of magnolia pulling his focus away from the game and slipping under his guard, making him recall their weekend together. Making him remember the view of her long legs bared just last night in a jersey that had covered her only to midthigh. He'd barely slept after that mouthwatering visual.

"Gervais, this is all incredible and definitely far more elaborate than I would have expected at a football game. Thank you."

Her response had been polite, but he could see something tugging at her. So he pressed, gently, "But…"

She took a few steps toward the glass, gesturing to the seats below, where fans were starting to crowd the aisles as halftime neared. "Honestly? My mouth is watering for one of those smothered hot dogs I see the vendors selling. With mustard and onions."

"You want a chili dog?" He couldn't hide a grin.

Right from the start she'd charmed him with the un-expected. She was a princess in the military. A sexy rebel. And despite all the imported fare weighing down the servers' trays, she wanted a chili dog.

"If it is not too much trouble, of course." She frowned. "I did not think to bring my wallet."

"It's no trouble." He wouldn't mind stepping out of the temperature-controlled suite into the excited crowd. How long had it been since he'd ventured out from behind the tinted-glass windows during a game? It had been too long.

He leaned to whisper in her ear, hand bracing her on the small of her back. "Pregnancy craving?"

She blinked quickly, her breath quickening under his touch. "I believe so. Mornings are difficult with nausea, but then I am starving for the rest of the day. Today has been difficult, with all the travel yesterday and jet lag."

"Then I will personally secure an order for you." He smiled. "I have to say I wouldn't mind having one for myself." He touched her shoulder lightly, aching to keep his hands on her. "I'll be right back."

Erika moved closer to the glass and took a seat, looking down into the field, her eyes alert.

There was no fanfare in yoga or running, so Erika looked on at the halftime show with a sense of wonder. LSU's band performed in tandem with a pop star local to the area, sending the fans into wild cheers as a laser light show sliced the air around her. The scents of fog and smoke wafted through the luxury suite's vents, teasing her oversensitive nose.

This box was quite different from the Wembley luxury suite where she'd met Gervais. The Reynaud private domain was decorated with family memorabilia, team awards and lots of video monitors for comfortable viewing in the back of the box right near the bar.

But she enjoyed her front-row seat, watching intently.

So this really did have a form of old-world pageantry mixed with a dash of medieval jousting. Her military training made her able to pick out various formations on the field below, the two teams forming and re-forming their lines to try to outwit one another. Viewing the game this way had been a revelation—and definitely not as boring as she'd once thought. And she couldn't wait to taste one of the chili dogs once Gervais returned.

Fiona Harper-Reynaud, the quarterback's wife and Gervais's sister-in-law, if Erika remembered correctly, tilted her head to the side. "Princess Erika, you look pensive."

"I have been thinking about the game, trying to understand more about what I've seen so far, since I am actually quite a neophyte about the rules. My sisters and I were not exposed much to team sports."

A few of the other women laughed softly into their cocktail napkins, eyeing Erika.

Fiona smiled, crossing her elegant legs at the ankles. "What an interesting choice, then, to spend time with Gervais when you're not a football enthusiast."

"I am learning to look at the game in a new light." She would read more about it now that she knew her child would be a part of this world.

She couldn't allow her son or daughter to be unprepared for their future, and that meant football. She could
not sit in this box overflowing with Reynauds and fail to
realize how deeply entrenched they were in this sport.

"How so?" Fiona traced a finger on her wineglass,
her diamond wedding ring glinting in the light from a
chrome pendant lamp.

Erika pointed down to the field, where the head
coach and his team were now returning to the sidelines. "Adelaide Thibodeaux suggested I think of this
as a ritual as old as time, like an ancient battle or a medieval jousting field. The imagery is working for me."

"Hmm." Fiona lifted one finely arched eyebrow.
"That's quite a sexy image. And fitting. Armor versus
shoulder pads. It works. I'll have to spin that for a future fund-raiser."

"That sounds intriguing." And it did. If it helped
Erika to appreciate the game more, it could certainly
appeal to someone else.

"Perhaps I should rethink the menu, too, as I may
have overdone things with this event." She picked up a
nacho and investigated it.

"The food is amazing. Quite a lovely, fun spread,"
Erika offered, smiling at her.

"But you want a chili dog—or so I overheard you
say."

"I hope you did not take offense, as I certainly did not
mean any." Erika fought the urge to panic. She bit down
her nerves—and a wave of nausea. This was easily ex-
plainable. "I am in America. I simply want to experience American foods served at a regular football game."

A server walked by with another fragrant tray of caviar nachos—too fragrant. She pressed her hand to her stomach as another wave of indigestion struck, cramping her stomach.

Fiona's eyebrows rose but she stayed silent for a moment. "If you need anything, anything at all, please don't hesitate to ask."

Did Fiona know somehow, even though she didn't have children? There seemed to be an understanding—and a sadness in her eyes.

For a brief, fleeting moment, she wondered if Fiona had ever found herself in Erika's situation. Not the pregnant-with-a-handsome-stranger situation, but the other one. The one where she was an outsider who shouldered too much responsibility sometimes.

The weight of that thought bore down on her, making her stomach even more queasy. She fought back the urge, praying she could get to her feet and to the ladies' room before she embarrassed herself.

Erika bit her lip, shooting to her feet, only to find the ground swaying underneath her. Not a good sign at all, but if she could just grab the back of her seat for a moment to steady herself… There. The world righted in front of her and she eyed the door, determined. "I will be right back. I need to excuse myself."

And the second she took that first step, the ground rocked all the harder under her, and she slumped into unconsciousness.

Five

Gervais pushed through the crowds, eyes set on the chili dog vendor. As he weaved in and out, he saw recognition zip through their eyes.

The media had done a nice job planting his image in the minds of the fans even though he would have preferred a quieter role, leaving the fame to the players. But the family name also sold tickets and brought fans to their television screens, so he played along because he, too, loved the game and would do whatever was needed for the Hurricanes.

Many of the fans smiled at him, nudged a companion and pointed at Gervais. He felt a little as if he was in a dog-and-pony show. And while part of him wouldn't mind pausing to speak to a few fans and act as an ambassador for the team, he really just wanted to get Erika that chili dog. Pronto.

So he flashed a smile as he continued, stopping in front of the food vendor, the smell of nacho cheese and cayenne peppers sizzling under his nose. Of all the things Erika could have asked for, he was strangely intrigued by this request. It was the most un-princess-like food in the whole sports arena. He loved that.

Gervais's phone vibrated. He juggled the two chili dogs to one hand as he fished out his cell while taking the stadium steps two at a time. He glanced at the screen and saw his sister-in-law's name. Frowning, he thumbed the on button.

"Yes, Fiona?"

"Gervais—" Fiona's normally calm voice trembled "—Erika passed out. We can't get her to wake up. I don't know—"

"I'm on my way." Panic lanced his gut.

His hand clenched around the hot dogs until a little chili oozed down his fingers as he raced up the steps faster, sprinted around a corner, then through a private entrance to the hall leading to the owners' viewing box.

A circle of people stood around a black leather sofa, blocking his view. A cold knot settled in his stomach. He set the food on the buffet table and shouldered through the crowd.

"Erika? Erika," he barked, forgetting all about formalities. He dropped to his knees beside the sofa where she lay unconscious. Too pale. Too still.

He took her hand in his, glancing back over his

shoulder. "Has anyone called a doctor? Get the team doctor. Now."

Fiona nodded. "I called him right after I called you."

He brushed his hand over Erika's forehead, her steady pulse throbbing along her neck a reassuring sign. But still, she wasn't coming around. There were so many complications that could come with pregnancy. His family had learned that tragic reality too well from his sister-in-law's multiple miscarriages.

Which made him wince all the more when he needed to lean in and privately tell Fiona, "Call the doctor back and tell him to hurry—because Erika's pregnant."

Erika pushed through layers of fog to find a group of faces staring down at her. Some closer than others.

A man with a stethoscope pressing against her neckline while he took her pulse must be a doctor.

And of course she should have known that Gervais would be near. He sat on the arm of the sofa at her feet, watching her intently, his body a barrier between her and the others in the room staring at her with undisguised interest.

Curiosity.

Whispering.

Oh, God. Somehow, they knew about the baby and she hadn't even told her parents yet.

"Gervais, do you think we could have some privacy?"

He looked around, started, as if he hadn't even realized the others were still there. "Oh, right, I'll—"

Fiona stepped up. "I've got this. You focus on Erika."

She extended her arms, gesturing toward the door. "Let's move to the other side of the box and give the princess some air…"

Her voice faded as she ushered the other guests farther away, leaving behind a bubble of privacy.

She elbowed up, then pressed a hand to her woozy head. "Doctor, what's going on?"

The physician wearing a polo shirt with the team's logo on the pocket said, "Gervais here tells me you're pregnant. Would you like him to give us some privacy while we talk?"

She didn't even hesitate with her answer. "He can stay. He has a right to know what is going on with the baby."

The doctor nodded, his eyes steady and guarded. "How far along are you?"

"Two and a half months."

"And you've been to a doctor?"

"I have, back in my homeland."

"Well, your pulse appears normal, as do your other vital signs, but you stayed unconscious for a solid fifteen minutes. I would suggest you see a local physician."

Gervais shot to his feet. "I'll take her straightaway."

Erika sat up, the world steadier now. "But you will miss the rest of the game."

"Your health is more important. We'll take the private elevator down and slip out the back." He shifted his attention to the physician. "Doc, can you send up a wheelchair?"

She swung her feet to the ground. "I can walk. I am not an invalid. I simply passed out. It happens to pregnant women."

"Pregnant women who don't eat," Gervais groused, sliding an arm around her waist for support. "You should take care of yourself."

Even as she heard the grouchiness in his voice, she saw the concern in his eyes, the fear. She wanted to soothe the furrowed lines on his forehead but knew he wouldn't welcome the gesture, especially not right now.

So she opted to lighten the mood instead. Heaven knew she could use some levity after the stress she had been under. And how strange to realize that in spite of being terrified, she felt safer now with Gervais present.

She looked up at him and forced a shaky smile. "Don't forget my chili dog."

Gervais paced the emergency room. The hum of the lights above provided a rhythm to his pacing. He tried to focus on what he could control.

Which was absolutely nothing at this point. Instead of being in the know, he was completely in the dark. He couldn't start planning, something he liked to do.

Sitting still had never been his strong suit. Gervais wanted to be in the midst of the action, not hanging on the sidelines. That was how he'd been as a football player, how he dealt with his family. Always engaged. Always on.

But now? No one would tell him anything. He wasn't a family member. Not technically, even though that was his unborn child.

God, he hated feeling helpless. Most of all he hated feeling cut off from his family. His child.

What the hell was taking the doctor so long?

Sure, the place was packed with weekend traffic. To his left was a boy with what appeared to be a broken arm and a cracked tooth. His sister, a petite blonde thing, wrinkled her nose in disgust as he shoved his arm in her face.

The man on his right elevated a very swollen ankle. He was in the ER alone, sitting in silence, hands rough with calluses.

Gervais could hear snippets of the conversation going on in the far corner of the room. A young mom cooed over her baby, holding tight to her husband's hand. They were probably first-time parents. Nervous as hell. But they were tackling the problem together. As he wanted to with Erika, but the lack of information was killing him.

The whole ride over, Erika had been woozy and nauseated. He tried to tell himself that fainting wasn't a big deal. But he wasn't having much luck calming down his worries.

The possibilities of what could be wrong played over and over again in his head. He hated this feeling. Helplessness. It did not sit well with him.

A creak from the door called his attention back to the present moment. Snapping his focus back to the ER. And to the two men heading for him. His brothers Henri and Dempsey. Henri's sweat-stained face was grave as he caught Gervais's eye. Hell, he knew time had passed. But that much? And he hadn't even watched the rest of the game on the waiting room television.

He charged over to his brothers.

Henri hauled him in hard and fast for a hug, slapping him on the back. Smelled of Gatorade. Heavily.

The leftover jug must have been poured over his head, signifying victory. "What's the news?"

"I'm still waiting to hear from the docs." He guided both of his brothers over to the privacy of a corner by a fat fake topiary tree. "We won?"

Dempsey didn't haul him in for a brotherly hug, but he thumped him on the back. They were brothers. Not as close as Henri and Gervais, but the bond was there. Solid. "Yes, by three points. Even though we sidelined most of our starters to test depth at various positions. Henri's backup did a credible job marching the offense downfield for one more TD in the closing minutes. But that's not what matters right now. We're here for you. Is everything okay?"

Gervais shrugged. "We don't know yet. Nobody's talking to me. I'm not tied to her in any legal way."

Dempsey's voice lowered till it was something barely audible. He looked squarely into his brother's eyes. "Do you plan to be there for your child?"

"Yes." Gervais didn't hesitate. "Absolutely."

Henri shifted his weight from foot to foot. The three Reynaud men stared at each other, no one daring to utter so much as a syllable for a few moments.

Dempsey nodded. "Good. You know what? I'm going to get coffee for us. Who knows how long we will be here. ER visits are never short."

"Great. Thanks," Henri said as Dempsey walked back toward the doors. "Is she considering giving the baby up for adoption?"

"I didn't bring that up." Truth be told, he hadn't even

thought of that as a real option. It was his child. He wanted to provide for his child.

"Did she?" Henri crossed his arms, voice lowered so only they could hear each other.

"No. I'm not even sure how the royalty part plays into this." God, what if his power, prestige, money, wasn't worth jack and she took his child away altogether? "She discussed shared parenting."

Henri shrugged. An attempt at nonchalance that fell flat. "I just want you to know that if things change, Fiona and I are willing to raise the baby as our own."

Gervais looked over at his brother quickly, thinking of all the miscarriages his brother and sister-in-law had been through, the strain that had put on their marriage. This baby news had to be hitting his normally happy-go-lucky brother hard. "Thank you, my brother. That means a lot to me. But this is my child. Not some mistake. Not just a responsibility. My child."

Henri nodded and hooked an arm around his brother's shoulders. "I look forward to meeting my niece or nephew. Congratulations."

"Thank you." Gervais noticed how Henri's face became blank. Distant. "Are you and Fiona okay?"

"Sure, we're fine," Henri replied a bit too quickly.

"We need your total commitment to the season. If you're having any problems, you can come to me." And he meant it. He wanted to be there for his brother. For his whole family. They meant everything to him.

Henri shook his head, looking his brother in the eyes. Offering a smile that refused to light his cheeks or touch his eyes. "No problem."

Gervais shook his head, raising an eyebrow at him. "You never were a good liar."

Wasn't that the truth? When they were kids, Henri always cracked under pressure. His eyes would widen when he fibbed.

"No problems that will distract me from the game. Now stop being the owner of the team and let's be brothers."

Gervais was about to protest, but suddenly the ER waiting room was alive with movement. Dempsey strode back over to them, cups of coffee on a tray. A damn fine balancing act going on.

And following closely on his heels was a doctor. The same old, frazzle-haired doctor that had been treating Erika. His gut knotted.

The doctor cleared his throat. "Mr. Reynaud— Gervais Reynaud," he clarified. The whole town knew the Reynauds, so no doubt the doctor recognized them. "Ms. Mitras is asking for you."

All he could do was nod. Deep in his chest, his heart thudded. Afraid. He was afraid of what was wrong with Erika and his child.

The doctor opened a thick pinewood door to a small exam room and gestured for Gervais to enter.

In the center of the room, Erika was hooked up to a smattering of machines. Lights flashed from various pieces of equipment. Her blond hair was tied back into a topknot, exposing the angles of her face. Somehow making her seem impossibly beautiful despite the presence of the machines.

Within moments he was at her side. He wanted to

show her he was here. He was committed to their child and would not abandon her. Stroking her hand, he knelt beside her. "You're okay? The baby's okay?"

Her face was pale, but she smiled, her eyes serene. "We are fine. Absolutely fine."

"This child is important to me. You are important to me." She was damn important. He had to make her see that.

"Because I am the baby's mother." The words spilled from her mouth matter-of-factly. As if there was no other reason he'd be here right now.

"We had a connection before that."

A dramatic sigh loosed from her pink lips. "We had an affair."

"I called you afterward." She'd been imprinted on his brain. A woman he could not—would not—forget.

"You are a gentleman. I appreciate that. In fact, that was part of what drew me to do something so uncharacteristic. But it was only a weekend."

"A weekend with lasting consequences." A weekend that had turned him inside out. Given time, he could make her see that, too.

"More than we realized," she said with a shaky laugh.

"What do you mean?" Head cocking to the side, he tried to discern the cause of the uneasy laughter.

She gestured to the ultrasound machine next to her. "I am pregnant with twins."

Gervais tore his gaze from Erika, focusing on the screen. Sure enough, there were two little beans on the ultrasound. He and Erika were going to have twins.

Six

Exhausted, Erika relaxed back into the passenger seat of Gervais's luxury SUV. The leather seat had the smell of a woodsy cologne, a smell she distinctively recognized as Gervais. It was oddly comforting, a steadying moment in a day that had been anything but stable.

As the car pulled away from the hospital, she glanced out the window, craning to see the collection of Reynaud brothers who stood at the entrance. Her sisters would swoon over the attractive picture they presented, those powerful, broad-shouldered men. They had all come rushing to the hospital, filled with concerns. And likely, with questions.

But they had been polite in the lobby after her release. They didn't press for information—the conversation had been brief. They'd wanted to know if she was okay. And neither Gervais nor Erika had offered any information about twins. That was something that they still had to discuss together. Something she still hadn't processed.

But how should she broach this new development in an already emotionally charged day? How in the world could she bring up everything in her whirring mind? Her eyes remained fixed out of the car, even though the scene of the hospital had faded from vision, framed by wrought-iron fences and thick greenery. Now the vibrant pinks and yellows of the old French houses populated her view.

Glancing at an elaborate wood-carved balcony, she let out an emotional sigh. What had happened today had left her shaken. She'd never passed out like that before, never felt so disoriented in her life. She'd been blessed with good health, and she had pushed her physical endurance to the limit during her military training. Yet this pregnancy was only just beginning and it had already landed her flat on her back. But, thanks to Gervais's quick action, she and her children—*children*, plural, oh, God—were safe.

It was all that mattered. That her children were okay. The twins were fine. *Twins*. She turned the word over. Was it possible to love them both so much already, even though she'd just learned about them? And yet, she did. In spite of her nerves, in spite of not having a plan figured out. Sure, she was scared about the future, about having to deal with her family…but she was overwhelmed with a deep love for her children already.

She peered over at the man in the driver's seat beside her. Perhaps he felt her eyes on him, because soon Gervais's throat moved in a long swallow. "Twins?" he mused aloud. "Twins."

The simple utterance seemed to linger on his tongue and echo through the quiet interior of the luxury vehicle. Not that she could blame him for being overwhelmed by the news. There was a lot to take in. Still, even under Gervais's audible processing of the fact that he was about to be a father not to one but two children, she could hear a glow of pride in his tone. A protectiveness that caught her attention.

Of course, the raw, masculine appeal of his muscular body taking up too much space beside her might have something to do with how thoroughly he held her notice. How easy it would be to simply lean closer. Lean on him. She could almost imagine the feel of his suit jacket beneath her cheek if she laid her head on his shoulder and curled up against his chest.

She forced herself to focus on the conversation they needed to have instead. On their children.

"Yes, there are two in there. I even heard the heartbeats." Her heart fluttered with joy as she remembered the delicate beating of her—*their*—children. The sound had made her spring to life in a way she didn't know was possible. She felt bad he'd missed that. They were his children, too, and he'd deserved to have that same feeling of awe. Looking at him sidelong, she said cautiously, "Next time you can come with me if you wish."

"I wish." There was no mistaking the sound of his commitment.

"Then you should be there." She couldn't hold back

the smile swelling inside her as she drank in his eyes alight with honest excitement. "It is too early to distinguish the sex, you know."

He shrugged, clearly unconcerned. "That doesn't matter."

"It did in my family." It came out in a whisper, something almost like a secret. And each word hurt.

He glanced over at her briefly before turning his eyes back to the road as they drove west toward his home. "Be clearer for me."

She smoothed the skirt of her dress, wrinkled beyond recognition after being crumpled into a hospital bag during her exam. If only she could smooth over her past as easily. This was knowledge she carried every day. Knowledge that ate at her and had her entire lifetime. "A line of girls was always cause for concern in my home. The monarchy is technically inactive, but even so there is no provision for a female ruler. There are no male heirs. I am afraid…"

"Oh, no. No way in hell is anyone taking my children away." His brow furrowed, anger simmering in his eyes, the joyous warmth gone.

"Our children. These are our children." She felt all the same protective instincts he did, and she felt them with a mother's fierce love.

"And we can't afford to forget for even a moment how important it is that we work together for the children. If there's a chance we can have more than a bicoastal parenting relationship, don't you think it's worth figuring that out as soon as possible?" The look he gave her was pointed. Sharp.

But Erika wasn't about to back down. She hadn't decided how to handle whatever was between them. And that meant she had to think a bit more. She wouldn't be rash and impulsive. One of them had to think through their actions.

"I will let you know when I schedule my doctor visit. I will want to visit the doctor again before returning home."

He scowled. "Can we not talk about you leaving? We're still settling details."

"You know I do not live here." New Orleans was lovely, with its vibrant history, loud colors and live music that seemed to drift up from every street corner. But it was not home. Not that she really knew where home was these days...

"One day at a time. And today we are dealing with a big change, the reality of two children. I know that happens. I just never expected..." His voice trailed, his words ebbing with emotion.

"I have twin sisters." She had always envied them their closeness, like having a built-in best friend from birth. "Twins—how do you say?—walk in my family."

"Run in your family. Okay."

She blinked at him, filing away the turn of English phrasing that brought a funny image to her mind of twins sprinting through her family tree. This was all happening so fast, she'd never stopped to consider the possibility of twins. There was so much to figure out still. "My oldest sister also has twin girls. I should have considered this possibility but I have been so overwhelmed since I realized I was expecting."

"Thank you for coming to tell me so soon." He covered her hand on the center console. "I appreciate that you didn't delay."

"You are the father. You deserve to know that." Erika lifted her chin up, tilting her head to the side to get a better look at him. He was a good man. She knew that much.

"We're going to make this work." He lifted her hand and kissed the back, then the inside of her wrist over her rapidly beating pulse.

The press of his mouth to her skin was warm and arousing, stirring memories of their weekend together. The air crackled between them now as it had then. Her emotions were already in turmoil after the scare at the game. She ached to move closer, to feel his arms around her. To have those lips on her body again. Everywhere. Arousing her to such heights her head spun at the thought. How quickly she could simply lose herself in what he could make her feel.

But doing so would take away any chance of objectivity. And now she had twice the reason to tread carefully into the future.

The silver stain of moonlight washed over the lake. The water was restless. Frothy. Uneasy. A lot like the restlessness inside Gervais. But he had to pull it together in order to make this phone call.

He thumbed through his phone, finding his father in his contact list. How long had it been since they'd spoken? Months, no doubt. The bright screen blared at him.

He knew he had to call him about Erika's pregnancy.

Theo was in Paris for the week with his latest girlfriend. Which was, in some ways, fortunate. This way, Gervais had gotten to talk to Erika privately before his father had a chance at royally screwing the dynamic up.

But it also meant he had to make this call. Which was something he never looked forward to doing. Years of neglect and dysfunction had their way of clinging to their current relationship. Another lesson of how not to treat children brought to you by Theo Reynaud. Dear old dad loved football and his family, but not as much as romancing women.

Before he could think better of it, Gervais pressed Send on the screen. Feeling the pinch of nerves, he poured himself a glass of bourbon from the pool-deck bar, staring at where a few kids messed around with a stand-up paddleboard. Beyond them, the lights of gambling boats winked in the distance and even farther behind those he could see the bridge that spanned the lake.

Gervais wasn't sure why he felt the need to talk to his dad other than doing him the courtesy of making sure he didn't hear via the grapevine. Discretion wasn't Theo's strong suit. But if Gervais spun the news just right, maybe he could keep a lid on it a bit longer. Erika would appreciate that.

And tonight making Erika relaxed and happy felt like the first priority on a quickly shifting list in his life. But knowing that she carried his children had brought things into sharp focus for him today.

"Hello, son." His father's graveled voice shot through the receiver, yanking him from his thoughts.

Might as well cut to the chase.

"Dad, you're going to be a grandfather."

"About damn time. Damn shame Henri is still carrying a grudge and didn't tell me himself. The divorce was a long time ago."

In the background of the call, the sound of violin music and muted chatter combined with the clink of glasses. The sounds of a bar scene.

Gervais ignored the mention of his parents' dysfunctional marriage. "Henri and Fiona aren't expecting. I'm the one about to make you a gramps."

News about the twins could wait. One step at a time. He was still reeling from that news himself.

"With who? You didn't knock up some groupie looking for a big payoff from the family?" His voice crackled through the phone from across the Atlantic.

"Dad, that's your gig. Not mine." And just like that, he was on the defensive. Gervais was not his father. He would never be like his father. And the fact that his father thought he had that in his nature sent him reeling.

"No need to be disrespectful." Bells chimed in the background of the call, an unmistakable sound of a slot machine in payoff mode.

So much for keeping the subject of his parents' divorce off the table. "You destroyed your marriage with your affairs. You ignored your own sons for years. I lost respect for you a long time ago."

"Then why are you here now telling me about this baby?"

Gervais closed his eyes, blotting out the lights from the distant boats on the lake, listening to the sound of the water. With his spare hand, he pressed on his eyes, inhaling deeply. Exhaling hard, he opened his eyes, resolve renewed.

"Because this news is going to go viral soon and I want to make sure you understand I will not tolerate any inappropriate or hurtful comments to the mother of my child." That was something he absolutely would not allow. From anyone. Least of all his father. He would protect Erika from that.

"Understood. And who might this woman be?" An air of interest infused his words.

"Erika Mitras." He sat down, inspecting his ice cubes as he waited for his father to make some sort of off-color remark.

"Mitras? From that royal family full of girls? Well, hell, son. It's tough to find someone not out for our money, but kudos to you. You found a woman who doesn't need a damn thing from you."

The words cut him, even though, for once, his father hadn't meant any harm by them. Erika had said as much about not needing Gervais's help. But he wanted to be there for his children. For her. Seeing those two tiny lives on that monitor today had blown him away.

And knowing that Erika was already taxed from travel and devoting her beautiful body to nurture those children made him want to slay dragons for her. Or, at the very least, put a roof over her head and see to her every need.

"Thanks. That wasn't forefront in my mind at the time."

"When you were in England, I assume?"

"Not your business."

"You always were a mouthy bastard." Smug words from the other end of the receiver.

"Just like my old man." He downed half of his glass of bourbon. "Be nice."

"The team's winning. That always puts me in a good mood."

"Nice to know you care." Not that his father owned a cent of this team. The Hurricanes belonged to Gervais and Gervais alone.

"Congratulations, Papa. Name the little one after me and I'll give—"

"Dad, stop. No need to try so hard to be an ass."

"I'm not trying. Good night, son. Congrats."

The line went dead. So much for father-son bonding time.

Gervais tossed his cell phone on a lounge chair and tipped back the rest of the ten-year-old bourbon, savoring the honey-and-spice finish in an effort to dispel the sour feel left by the phone call. He didn't know what he'd expected from his old man. That he would magically change into…what? A real father? Some kind of reassurance that maybe, just maybe, he himself could be a good father to not just one but two babies?

Foolishness, that. Theo remained as selfish as they came.

Regardless, though, he knew one thing for certain. He was not going to ditch his responsibility the way his father had.

Tucked in the big guest bed in Gervais's house, Erika snuggled deeper beneath the lightweight comforter, hugging the pillow closer as sleep tugged her further under. She was exhausted after the hospital visit and the strain of pregnancy that seemed to drain all her physical resources. She would feel better after she rested, and she couldn't deny taking extra pleasure at sleeping under the same roof as Gervais.

During her waking hours, she did all in her power to keep the strong attraction at bay so she could make smart decisions about her future. Her children's future. But just now, with sleep pulling her under, and her body so perfectly comfortable, she couldn't resist the lure of thinking about Gervais. His touch. His taste…

Her memories and dreams mingling, filling her mind and drugging her senses with seductive images…

The press of Gervais's lips on hers sparked awareness deep in Erika's stomach. He pulled back from the passionate kiss, and she surprised herself when she was disappointed. She wanted his lips on hers. And not just there. Everywhere.

But he led her toward the couch in his den.

His den?

A part of her brain realized this was not a memory. She was in Gervais's house. In Louisiana. She could smell the scent of the lake mingling with the woodsy spice of his aftershave as he drew her down to the leather couch, tossing aside a football before he landed on the cushion while she melted into his lap. And it felt right. Natural. As if she belonged here with him.

Her heart slugged hard in her chest, the strength and warmth of his so incredible she could stay for hours. Longer. She wanted this. Wanted him. She'd never felt so alive as during those days when she'd been in his bed, and she couldn't wait to feel that spark inside her again. The hitch in her breath. The pleasure of sharp orgasms undulating through her body, again and again.

Now he tilted her chin up, searched her eyes for something. A mingle of nerves, anticipation and desire thumped in her chest as he kissed her forehead. Her lips. Her neck. She trembled as he touched her, her whole body poised for the fulfillment he could provide.

Her eyes closed, and the muted noise of a football game on a television behind them began to fade away until only the sound of their mingled breaths remained.

"Erika," he whispered in her ear before kissing her neck again. The heat of his breath on her skin made her toes curl.

"Mmm?" A half question stuck on her lips.

"Stay here with me." His request was spoken in clips between kisses, then a nip on her earlobe.

His hands tugged at the heavy jeweled collar around her neck. He removed it from her, the metal crown charms clanking against the coffee table. How good it felt to set that weight aside.

"Let me take care of you. Of them." Wandering hands found her shoulders, slipped underneath the thin straps of her dress. She burst to life, pressing into him with a new urgency. A want and need so unfamiliar to her.

As he kissed her, he rocked her back and forth. The scent of earthy cologne seemed to grow stronger. Demanded more of her attention...

"Erika?" a deep voice called, a man's voice.

Gervais.

Opening her eyes, she had a moment of panic. This was not the hotel room.

As the suite came into focus, she realized where— and when—she was. This was Gervais's house, his guest bedroom. She wasn't in London, but rather in Louisiana. Still, the memory pounded at her mind and through her veins.

She wanted to go back there now. To her dreamworld in all its brilliant simplicity.

But Gervais himself stood in the doorway of the guest suite.

His square jaw flexed, the muscles in his body tensed, backlit from a glowing sconce in the hall.

"Erika?" He crossed the threshold, deeper into the room, his gaze intense as he studied her. "I heard you cry out. I was worried. Are you okay? The babies?"

The mattress dipped as he sat beside her, stirring heated memories of her dream.

"I am fine. I was, um, just restless." The sensuality of her dream still filled her, making her all the more aware of his hip grazing hers through the lightweight blanket. The electricity between them was not waning. If anything, she felt the space between them grow even more charged. More aware.

"Restless," he repeated, eyes roving her so thoroughly she wondered what she looked like. Her hair teased along her bare shoulder, her silk nightdress suddenly feeling very insubstantial, even though the blanket covered her breasts.

Images from her dream flitted back into her mind,

and she bit her lip as her gaze moved down his face, to his hands reaching up to her exposed shoulders. Looking back at him through her eyelashes, she could tell he sensed the charged atmosphere, too. But his hands didn't move. Not as she'd expected—and wanted—them to. There was something else besides hunger in the way he held her gaze. Something that looked a bit like worry.

"Gervais, I truly am all right. But are *you* all right?"

He ran his hand through the hair on top of his head, eyes turning glossy and unfocused. "I called my dad tonight to tell him about the pregnancy. Not the twin part. Just…that he's going to be a grandfather. I didn't want him to hear it in the news."

She thought of how the day had gone so crazy so fast simply because she passed out. "I wish we could have told your family together."

"You didn't include me when you told your family."

She looked away, guilt stinging her. And didn't that cool the heat that had been singeing her all over?

"You've told your family, haven't you?" he asked, his eyes missing nothing.

"I will. Soon. I know I have to before it hits the news." She wanted to change the subject off her family. Fast. "What did your family have to say? Your brothers were quiet at the emergency room."

"My brothers are all about family. No one judges. We love babies."

Erika raised her eyebrows, unsure how to take the casual tone of what felt like a very serious conversation. She noticed he didn't include his father in that last part.

"That is all?" she asked, knowing she had no right

to quiz him when she hadn't shared much about her own family.

"That's it. Now we need to tell your parents before they find out."

"I realize that."

"I want to be with you, even if it's on the phone in a Skype session." His jaw flexed in a way she was beginning to recognize—a surefire sign of determination. He slid his arms around her and said, "I want to reassure them I plan to marry their daughter."

Seven

"You have forgotten we have *no* plans to get married. I have plans—other plans. Our plans are in flux."

Erika pulled out of Gervais's arms so fast he damn near fell off the bed. He wasn't sure why he'd raised the issue again, other than not wanting to be like his father, and certainly the timing of his proposal hadn't been the smoothest. But the least she could do was consider it, since they hadn't taken time to seriously discuss it that first night.

Time to change that now. He shifted on the bed so they were face-to-face. And promptly remembered how little she must be wearing under that blanket. A bare shoulder peeked above the fabric, calling his hands to rake the barrier down and away.

To slide between those covers with her.

"Why not even consider?" he ground out between clenched teeth, determined to stay on track with this talk. "We have babies on the way. Even if we have a civil ceremony and stay together for the children's first year." From the scowl on her beautiful face he could see he was only making this worse. "Erika?"

"I came here to tell you about being pregnant, see if you want to be an active father, and then make plans from there. I didn't come for a yearlong repeat of our impulsive weekend together."

He swallowed. Had his carnal thoughts been that obvious? No sense denying that he wanted her.

"And what would be so wrong with that?"

"I have a life in another country."

"You're out of the military now. So work here. You have more job flexibility than I do."

Red flushed into her cheeks, making her look more like a shield maiden and less like a delicate princess in need of saving. "You are serious?"

The more he thought about it, the more it felt right. A marriage of convenience for a couple of years. He stroked her hair back and tucked it behind her ear, the silky strands gliding along his fingers. "We have amazing chemistry. We have children on the way. You're already staying in my home—"

"For two weeks," she said, finality edging her voice.

"Why not longer? Things have changed now with the twins. Two babies at once would be a lot for anyone to care for."

He needed to be involved. A part of his children's lives.

"I have plans for this fall. A commitment to my career. You are thinking too far into the future." She shook her head, a toss of silvery-blond hair in the moonlight. "Please slow down."

She angled an elbow against a bolster pillow, reclining even as she remained seated. And damn, but he wanted to be the one she leaned against, the one who supported her incredible body through the upcoming months while she carried this burden for them.

"We don't have that option for long. And you yourself said you were concerned about the babies being boys and being caught up in the family monarchy as next in line. If they're born here and we're married here in the States…" He wasn't exactly sure what that would mean for the monarchy, but it certainly would slow things down. Give them time to become a family. And to figure out how everything would work together.

She clapped a hand over his mouth. "Stop. Please. I cannot make this kind of decision now."

The magnolia scent of her lotion caught him off guard. He breathed in the scent, enjoying the cool press of her skin on his lips. Would have said as much if he hadn't noticed the glimmer of tears in her eyes.

A raggedy breath before speaking. "Can we please think about our future rationally? When I am rested and more prepared?" Though she did her best to look past him, every inch a regal monarch in that moment, he could see the strain in her cheeks.

She'd had a helluva long day. Fainted. Found out she was pregnant with twins. And she still had not gotten her damn chili dog.

There was a lot going on.

He could cut her some slack, give her space to collect herself. It was no use pushing so hard while she was emotional. And she had every right to be. Hell, he'd been upset tonight, too, uncharacteristically irritated with his father.

So he would revise his approach until cooler heads prevailed. This tactic to get her to stay was not the right one. She'd dismissed it out of hand.

Who could blame her, though? He'd given her no real reason to stay. And, as much as he hated to admit it, Erika Mitras was a woman who did not need him for anything. She could afford the best care and doctors for her pregnancy the same as he could. She would have highly qualified help with day-to-day care in her homeland.

But what she hadn't realized yet was that they were so damn good together. There was something between them, a small spark that could be more. And they had the children to consider.

Rather than insist she stay, he'd convince her. Which meant she was in for some grade A romancing. That was something he could give her that she couldn't just find in a store.

He would win her the old-fashioned way. Because like hell if he was losing his children. Missing out on the lives of his offspring simply wasn't an option. He'd make sure of that.

The next evening Erika still could not make sense of what had happened the night before. But no matter which way she spun Gervais's actions in her bed last night, nothing made sense. She'd been so sure that he wanted her. That he felt that same sharp tug of attraction between them, but his decision to simply walk away and let her go to bed alone had left her surprised. Confused. Aching. Wanting.

He hadn't mentioned the baby issue at all the whole day, then he surprised her with this dinner date, a night out in the city they called the Big Easy.

Draping an arm along the white-painted wrought-iron railing of the patio, her hand kept time to the peppy jazz music playing. She hadn't realized her head nodded along to the trumpet until Gervais flashed her a smile.

Heat flushed her cheeks as she turned her attention away from the very attractive man in front of her. She pushed around the last bite of her shrimp and andouille sausage, a spicy blend of flavors she'd quizzed their waiter about at length. Every course of her meal had been delicious.

Attention snapping to the present, she caught a whiff of something that smelled a lot like baked chocolate and some kind of fruit. Maybe cherries, but she couldn't be sure. All she knew was that her senses were heightened lately.

As were her emotions.

What was Gervais up to with this perfect evening? Was he trying to charm her into changing her mind without discussing the logistical fact that he still moved too fast?

Setting her fork down, she inclined her head to the meal. "Dinner was lovely. Thank you."

His dark eyes slid over her. One forearm lay on the crisp white linen tablecloth, his tanned hand close to where hers rested. He made her breath catch, and she felt sure she was not the only woman in the vicinity who was affected. She liked that he didn't notice. That his gaze was only for her.

"I'm glad you enjoyed yourself. But the evening doesn't have to end now." His hand slid closer to hers on the table.

Her tummy flipped. Did he mean—

Standing, he folded her palm in his. "Let's dance."

She was relieved, right?

Oh, heavens, she was a mess.

She took his hand, the warmth of his touch steadying her as he guided her over to the small teak dance floor. Briefly they were waylaid by an older couple who congratulated Gervais on the Hurricanes' win the day before. But while he was gracious and polite, he didn't linger, keeping his attention on her.

On their date and this fairy-tale evening that Gervais had created for her.

Beneath the tiny, gem-colored pendants, he pulled her into him as the slow, sultry jazz saxophone bayed. With ease, his right hand found the small of her back, and his left hand closed around her hand. As they began to sway, he tucked her against him, chest to chest underneath the din of the music and the lights.

The scents and sounds were just a colorful blur, though, her senses attuned to Gervais. The warm heat of his body through his soft silk suit. His fingers flexing lightly on her back, his thumb grazing bare skin where a cutout in her dress left her exposed.

She swallowed. Each fast breath of air she dragged in pressed her breasts to the hard wall of his chest, reminding her how well her body knew his. What would it be like to be with him now, with her senses so heightened? It had been incredible two and a half months ago.

She couldn't hold back a soft purr. She covered by saying, "The music is beautiful."

"It's the heartbeat of our city. The rhythm the whole place moves to."

He whirled her past the bass player, where the deep vibrations hummed right through her feet.

"There's so much more about my hometown to show you beyond our sports. So much history and culture here. And of course, some amazing food."

Which she could still smell drifting on the breeze. The scent of spices thickened the air, making the heat of the evening seem more exotic than any of the places she'd ever been to during her stint in the military.

"I cannot deny this Big Easy fascinates me." She could lose herself in these brick-and-wrought-iron-laced streets, the scent of flowers heavy in the air. "But I want to be clear, as much as I enjoyed the food tonight, or how much I might like the sound of jazz, that is not going to make me automatically change my mind about your proposal. We have nothing in common."

His voice tickled in her ear, a murmur accompanying the jazz quartet. "Sure we do. We both come from big families with lots of siblings."

A shiver trembled along her skin, and she reminded

herself it was just the pregnancy making her so suscep-
tible to him. It had to be. No man could mesmerize a
woman so thoroughly otherwise. Her hormones simply
conspired against her.

"I guess your family does qualify as American royalty." She held up her end of the conversation, hoping
he could not see the effect he had on her. "So that is
one thing we have in common. Just minus the crowns."

"True. No tiaras here." His head dipped closer to
speak in her ear again. "Although thinking of you in
a tiara and nothing more—that's an image to die for."

She knew he joked. That did not stop her from imag-
ining being naked with him.

"An image that will have to remain in your mind
only, since I do not pose for pictures. After what happened to my sister because of the sex tape with the
prime minister," she said, shuddering, "not a chance."

Gervais almost missed a step, though he recovered
quickly enough.

"Your sister was in a sex tape?"

"You must be the only person in the world who did
not see it." That snippet of footage had almost ruined
her family. The publicity was all the more difficult to
deflect, since their monarchy was both defunct and not
particularly wealthy. They'd had precious few resources
to fight with.

"Never mind." Gervais shook his head, dismiss-
ing that conversation. "That's beside the point. First, I
wasn't speaking literally. And second, I would never,
never let you be at risk that way."

Her neck craned to look at him, eyes scanning his

face. There was no amusement in her eyes. "Perhaps more to the point, I will not put myself at risk."

"You're an independent princess. I like that."

"Technically, I am a princess in name only. The monarchy doesn't have ruling power any longer."

"Fair enough."

Gervais spun her away from him. There was a moment before she returned to the heat of his body that left her with anticipation. She wanted him to keep touching her, to keep pressing his body against hers.

After they resumed their rhythmic swaying, he said softly into her ear, "You are pretty well-adjusted for someone who grew up in a medieval castle surrounded by servants and nannies."

"What makes you think we had servants and nannies?"

A smile played with his sexy mouth. "That princess title."

She rolled her eyes. "The castle was pretty crumbly and we had some maintenance help, since we opened part of the palace to the public, and tutors volunteered just to have it on their résumé that they'd taught royalty. But definitely no nannies."

"Your parents were the involved types." Somehow they had gotten closer, lips barely a breadth away from each other. The thought of how close he was made it hard for Erika to concentrate. So she pulled back a bit, adjusting her head to look out over the crowd, toward the band.

"Not really. After class we had freedom to roam. We were quite a wild pack of kids. Can you imagine having your own real-life castle as a playground? We had everything but the unicorn."

"You make it sound fun."

"Some days it was fun. Some it was lonely when I saw the kids on tour with their parents." She hesitated. The last thing she wanted from Gervais was sympathy. She'd accepted what her family was and was not a long time ago. So she continued, "And some days were downright dangerous."

"What do you mean?"

"My sisters and I wanted a trampoline for Christmas." Which sounded perfectly normal. Except for the Mitras clan, there was no such thing as normal.

"Okay. And?"

"You do not get those on royal grounds. It does not fit the historical image, and without the tours we didn't have money. So, we made our own."

"Oh, God." A look of horror and intrigue passed over his face.

"We pulled a couple of mattresses down the stairs, stacked them under a window... And we jumped."

Gervais's eyes widened. "From how high?"

She shrugged. "Third story. And the ceilings were high."

"You're making me ill."

"It was only scary the first time when one of my sisters pushed me." And, later, when another sister broke an arm and the game ended for good.

"Pushed you?" Disbelief filled his voice. Surely his brothers had done equally dangerous things as forms of entertainment when they had been younger.

She'd seen the Reynaud males up close, and there was an air of confidence and arrogance about all of them that didn't exactly coincide with a sheltered upbringing.

"I was the test dummy," she informed him. "As the youngest and the lightest, it was my job to make sure the mattress had been placed correctly and had enough bounce."

"And did it?"

"We had to add some duvets and pillows."

"So it hurt."

"Probably no more than playing football without shoulder pads."

Tucking a loose strand of her hair behind her ear, he whispered, "You're such a badass. I expected a story like that from a family of boys, but not girls."

Not all girls were the descendants of female warriors. And that was usually the justification for their shenanigans as children. "We considered it our gym class. It was more interesting than lacrosse."

"Lacrosse, huh? I didn't expect that." He brushed his lips across her temple, his breath warm, his brief kiss warmer.

Her body even warmer still with want.

Just when she thought she would grip his lapels and melt right into him, he stepped back.

"I should get you home, Princess. It's late."

And just like that, the fairy-tale book was closing. She felt close to him all evening, physical distance aside. And every time it seemed as if there was something more between them, he pulled back.

While part of her was relieved that he'd stopped pushing for more, a larger part of her wanted him. She had to weigh her options. Had to be strong for her unborn children and make the wisest decision possible. It wasn't just her life in the balance.

After a sleepless night dreaming of Gervais's touch, Erika hadn't awoken in the best of moods. And now she had to make the phone call she had been dreading. The one that had sent her on edge all morning long until she found her courage and started dialing.

Erika sat on the chaise longue in the guest room as she hugged the device to her ear and listened to the call ring through on the other side of the world. She needed to speak with her parents and tell them that she was pregnant. With twins. There was no sense in avoiding the inevitable any longer.

Her mother answered the phone. "Hello, my love. What brings about this lovely surprise of a call?"

"Um, does there have to be a special reason for me to call you?"

"There does not have to be, but I hear a tone in your voice that tells me there is a reason. Something important perhaps?"

Her mother's surprise intuition tugged at her already tumultuous emotions.

"I am pregnant. With twins." The words tumbled out of her mouth before she had even had a chance to respond to the pleasantries with her mom.

So much for the long speech Erika had outlined and perfected. Glancing down at the piece of paper in front of her, she noted that her talking points were basically for show. There was no going back now.

Silence fell from the other end of the receiver for what seemed like an eternity.

"Mother?" she asked, uncertainty creeping into her voice.

"Twins, Erika? Are you certain?"

She nodded, as if her mother could see. "Yes, Mother. I'm certain. I went to the doctor two days ago and heard the two distinct heartbeats with my own ears. The tradition of twins lives on in the Mitras family."

"Who is the father?" Her mother's interest pressed into the phone.

"Gervais Reynaud, the American football team owner—" she began, but her mother interrupted.

"A son of the Reynaud shipping empire? And Zephyr Cruise Ships? What an excellent match, Erika. American royalty. The press will love this."

"Right, but, Mother, I wanted to—"

"Oh, darling, have you considered what this could mean for the family? If you have boys, well…the royal line lives on. This is wonderful, my love. Hold on, let me get your father."

Rustling papers and some yelling came through over the phone. Erika's stomach knotted.

"Your father is on speakerphone. Tell him your news, my love." Her mother cooed into the phone, focused on all the wrong things.

"I'm going to have twins, Father. And I'm just—"

"Twins? Do you know what this means? You could have a boy. Maybe two."

Erika nodded dully into the phone, the voices of her parents feeling distant. As if they belonged in someone else's life. The way they had when she was a child. The image of the royal family always seemed more important than the actual well-being of the family itself.

They weren't interested in hearing what she had to say but were already strategizing how to best monetize this opportunity. The press was about to have an all-access pass to her life before she even knew how she was going to proceed.

"Mother, Father," she said, interrupting their chatter, "I've had quite the morning already." They didn't need to know how much it taxed a woman to daydream about Gervais just when he'd decided to pull back. "Do you mind if I call you later, after I've rested?"

Tears burned her eyes for a variety of reasons that shouldn't make her cry. Pregnancy hormones were pure evil.

"Of course not, my love."

"Not at all, my dear," her father said. "You need your rest if you are going to raise the future of the royal line. Sleep well."

And just like that, they were gone, leaving her cell phone quiet as the screen went dark. They had disconnected from the call as abruptly as they often did from her life, leaving her all alone to contend with the biggest challenge she'd ever faced.

"Well, we're surprised to see you so early, that's all," Dempsey said from a weight bench, his leg propped up on a stool. He pressed around his knee, fidgeting with the brace. An old injury that had cost him his college football career. It was flaring up again. Most days, it didn't bother him. But then there were days like today.

Gervais understood Dempsey's position. He'd been sidelined from the field, as well. One too many concussions. But quite frankly, he enjoyed the business side of owning the Hurricanes.

There were new challenges, new ways of looking at the game and new styles of offense to develop as players came up stronger and faster than ever before. And he was still involved in football, which had been his ultimate goal anyway. This had just been another way to get at the same prize.

As an owner, he would not only strategize how to field the best possible team, he would also make the Hurricanes the most profitable team in the league. Corporate sponsorships were on track to meet that goal in three years, but Gervais had plans that could shorten that window to two. Maybe even eighteen months. The franchise thrived and the city along with it.

"I'm not sure what you two find so fascinating about my night out with Erika." Gervais curled the dumbbells, sweat starting to form on his brow as they worked out in a private facility within the team's training building.

The team lifted in a massive room downstairs, but Gervais had added a more streamlined space upstairs near the front offices.

"We just want to know what's going on in your life. With the baby. And you," Henri, their father's favorite, added. Theo had high hopes that Henri would one day wear a Super Bowl ring for the Hurricanes and continue in the old man's footsteps as a hometown hero.

The whole family was here, with the exception of their father and their brother Jean-Pierre, who played for a rival team in New York and didn't get to Louisiana much during the season.

And while Henri technically worked out with the team, he never minded putting in some extra hours in the upstairs training center to try to show up his older brothers in the weight room.

"That offer still stands, by the way, if you want it to," Henri said, his voice low enough so only Gervais could hear. Gervais knew that things had been hard for Henri and his wife since they hadn't been able to conceive. It affected everything in their marriage. But Gervais wasn't about to give them his unborn children. He wanted to raise them, to be an active part of their lives. To be the opposite of their father.

"Hey now, secrets don't make friends," Dempsey snapped, his face hard. Henri rolled his eyes but nodded anyway.

"So, Pops—" Dempsey shot him an amused grin "—have you decided what you are going to do?"

"Yeah, how are you going to handle fatherhood in the public eye with a princess?" Henri teased, huffing out pull-ups on a raised bar.

"I told you both, I'm taking care of my children." And Erika, he added silently. His main goal as they got ready for the game in St. Louis was to show her that they could be together. That they were great together. An unconventional family that could beat the odds. He was prepared to romance her like no other. And he might have shared that with Henri and Dempsey, if not for the man that rounded the corner, stopping in the entrance to the weight room.

From the door frame, a familiar booming drawl. Theo. "I'm here to meet the mother of my first grandchild."

Eight

As the limo driver faded from view, Erika sped into the Hurricanes' office building. She moved as fast as her legs would carry her, feeling less like royalty and more like a woman on a mission.

Twenty minutes ago, Gervais had called her. Urgency flooded his voice. He needed her in the office stat.

Pushing the heavy glass door open, she took a deep breath, feeling ever so slightly winded. The humidity was something she had yet to fully adjust to, and even small stints outside left her vaguely breathless. The rush of the cool air-conditioning filled her lungs as she crossed the threshold, a welcome chill after the New Orleans steam bath. Striding beneath the black-and-gold team banners hanging overhead, she struggled to figure out what was wrong that he needed her here.

Taking the stairs two at a time, she made it to the second floor and hung a right. Headed straight for the glass wall and door with an etched Hurricanes logo.

The secretary smiled warmly at her from her desk. Adjusting her glasses, she stood. "Princess Erika, Mr. Reynaud is expecting you—"

Extending a manicured hand, she gestured to another door and Erika didn't wait for her to finish. Hurrying forward, she reached the polished double doors made of a dark wood. And heavy. She gave one side a shove, practically falling into the huge office of the team owner.

Currently an empty room.

Erika looked around, heart pounding with nerves. And, if she was being honest, disappointment.

Spinning on her heel, she practically ran into the secretary. Grace was not on her side today.

"My apologies, ma'am," the secretary started in a quiet voice. "Mr. Reynaud will be back in a few minutes, but please make yourself comfortable. Can I get you anything while you wait? We have water, soda, tea. And of course enough Gatorade to fill a stadium."

"Thank you." As the words left her lips, she settled down. Slightly. "I'm just fine, though."

"Of course." The secretary smiled, exiting the room and closing the door with a soft click.

So she was here. In his office without him. While not ideal, it did give her a chance to feel out what sort of man he was. At least in the business sense.

A bank of windows overlooked the practice field below, the lush green grass perfectly manicured with the white gridiron standing out in stark contrast. Silver bleachers glimmered all around the open-air facility with a retractable dome. Funny they didn't have the stadium roof on today when it was so beastly hot outside, but perhaps the practice had been earlier in the day as there were no players in sight now.

Turning from the wall of windows, she paced around the office. She noted the orderly files, the perfectly straightened paper stacks on the massive mahogany desk. The rows of sticky notes by the phone. The walls were covered with team photos and awards, framed press clippings and a couple of leather footballs behind glass cases. The place was squared away. Tight.

Not too different from the way she kept her own living quarters, either. Impersonal. Spit-shined for show. They might not have done a lot of talking in London, but clearly they had gravitated toward each other for reasons beyond the obvious. After last night she felt as if they had more in common than they realized.

A tightness worked in her chest. So desperately did she want to trust him now that they found themselves preparing to be parents together. But trust came at a high cost. It wasn't a commodity she candidly bestowed. It was earned—her most guarded asset. Years of being royalty had taught her to be suspicious.

Shoving her past aside, she approached a picture on the farthest corner of his desk. It was different than the rest. It seemed to have nothing to do with the Hurricanes. Or football, for that matter.

The photograph was faded, old—probably real film instead of digital. But she would have recognized him anyway. Gervais. His brothers. A woman. His mother, she assumed. But no Dempsey. Which struck her as odd.

She would have continued to stare at the picture as if it could give her the answers she was after if she didn't hear a man clearing his throat behind her.

She glanced over her shoulder, through the blond strands of her hair. Gervais stood in the doorway. And he looked damn sexy.

He was disheveled. Not nearly as put together as his office. His hair was still wet from a shower, and his shirt was only half buttoned. For the quickest moment she had the urge to finish undoing it. To kiss him—and more.

The urge honestly surprised her. She had promised herself yesterday that after a good night's sleep, she would be levelheaded today. She needed logic to prevail while she figured out if he could be trusted. Only then could she decide what to do next.

Leaning against the desk, and looking at his lips with feigned disinterest, she asked as casually as possible, "What is the emergency? Is something wrong?"

He shook his head, closing the door behind him. "Not really. I just wanted to speak with you privately about—" he hesitated "—a…uh…new development."

Her smile faded. He was leaving. People always did. Her parents, who never remained in town with their kids for long. The vast majority of her friends who hung around only because she was royalty. The dozens of tutors who only helped for long enough to get a good reference before moving on to an easier job than five hell-raising sisters.

Schooling her features to remain impassive, she sat

down in a leather wingback chair. She needed the isolation that chair represented. She didn't need him tempting her by sitting next to her on the sofa or walking up to her to brush against her. Touch her. Weaken her resolve.

"Tell me." She met his gaze. Steeled herself.

"Remember that I told you I called my father a couple of days ago to tell him about the baby?" His dark eyes found hers for a moment before he stalked toward the wall of windows and looked down at the field. "Apparently, he decided to make a surprise visit."

"Your father is here? In the building or in New Orleans?"

The tight feeling in her chest returned, seizing hold of her. Erika was as unsure of how to deal with his family as she was her own. Selfishly, she had hoped they would have alone time together—without family making plays and demands—to figure out how to handle their situation. And to figure out if there was something there between them, after all.

"He was in the building but he's taking his girlfriend out to lunch before coming to the house later. I wanted to warn you in person and couldn't leave work."

More confirmation she didn't want to hear. But she felt compelled to hear it anyway. "Why do I need warning?"

"He's not a good person in spite of being charming as hell when he wants to be. I just want to make sure you're prepared. Feel free to steer clear of him."

"I can take care of myself. If he becomes too much to handle, I will flip him with Krav Maga I learned in the military." The warrior blood boiled beneath her skin. She would not be taken for a fool.

"You're pregnant."

"I am not incapacitated. But if you are concerned, I will simply pretend I do not understand his English." Uncrossing her arms, she gave him a wickedly innocent grin. Eyes wide for full effect. "It worked on almost half the tutors who showed up at the Mitras household prepared to teach the rebellious princesses."

"Good plan. Wish I'd thought of that as a kid."

A laugh escaped him and he turned toward her, a good-natured smile pushing at his cheeks. Funny how that smile slid right past her resolve to let logic prevail. To be levelheaded. That shared laugh stirred a whole wealth of feelings that had been building inside her ever since she'd stepped onto the practice field to face Gervais Reynaud.

Thinking back to the photograph on the desk, she had to admit, she was curious about him. His past. What it was like growing up in New Orleans. She had so many things to learn about him that it could take a lifetime. And wasn't it perfectly *reasonable* of her to learn more about him when her children would share his genes?

Emboldened by the rationalization, she thought she might as well begin her quest to know him better right now. "But you did not need to arm yourself with elaborate schemes to outwit the grown-ups around you as a child. You and your brothers are so close—or the three of you I've met."

The faintest pull of unease touched his lips. "We weren't always. Dempsey didn't come to live with us until he was thirteen. Our dad… Maybe you already know this."

"No, I do not."

"That's right." He shifted away from the windows to move closer to her, taking a seat on the edge of the desk. "You're not a big follower of football and the players."

"I am learning to be. You make me curious about anything that relates to you." Leaning forward, she touched his arm gently.

"I'm glad." A small victory. She could see him struggling with his family history, despite the fact that it was, apparently, public knowledge.

"Why did Dempsey come to live with you later?"

"We have different mothers."

"Your parents got divorced? But—" That certainly did not seem strange.

He met her gaze, his expression tight. "The ages don't match up. I'm the oldest, then Dempsey, followed by Henri and Jean-Pierre. Dad slept around on Mom, a lot."

"Gervais, I am so very sorry." She touched his arm lightly, which was as much sympathy as she dared offer without risking him pulling away or shutting down.

"My father used to go to clubs with his friends. Remember, this was before the internet made it possible to stalk your date before you'd ever met." He took another breath, clearly uncomfortable.

Erika's eyes widened, realizing that he was opening up to her.

"All families have…dead bones in the closet," she said quietly.

A smile pushed against his lips. "You mean skeletons?"

"Is that not the same thing?" She ran her hand over his.

"More or less, I suppose. Anyway, he hooked up with Dempsey's mom, Yvette, at a jazz club. She got pregnant. Worked a lot of jobs to raise Dempsey, but never found my father, since he hadn't even been honest about who he was, apparently. Until his image was blasted all over the sports page and she recognized his face. Yvette thought it was her ticket out of the slums. She arranged a meeting with my father. But he insisted Dempsey become part of the family. And Dempsey's mother agreed. For a price."

How horrible for Dempsey. And, from Gervais's perspective, how horrible it must have been for him to assimilate a new brother almost his own age when they were both young teens. She avoided focusing on him, however, guessing he would only shift gears if she did.

"That had to be strange for your mother," she observed lightly.

He bit back a bark of a laugh. "Strange? She wasn't much of a motherly type. After one more kid got added to the mix, she left."

"That is so much change for children." Her heart swelled with sympathy for him. She had no idea that there was so much struggle in the Reynaud family.

"We didn't handle it well. I was jealous. Henri was my shadow, so he followed my lead. We blamed Dempsey for breaking up our parents, which was ridiculous from an adult perspective. But kids can be cruel."

"What happened?"

He looked at her sidelong. "We were living in Texas then. Staying at our grandfather's ranch while our father chased our mother around, trying to work things out. Anyway, I dared Dempsey to ride a horse. The biggest, meanest horse on the ranch."

"Oh, my."

"You don't sound horrified."

She shrugged her shoulders. "Remember? My sisters threw me out a third-story window. I know how siblings treat each other even when they have grown up together."

"True enough." He nodded. "Of course, he had no idea how to ride—not even a nice horse. So he was... completely unprepared for a high-strung Thoroughbred used to getting her own way."

"That's scary. What happened?"

"She threw him clear off, but he landed awkwardly and broke his leg. We both almost got trampled while Henri and Jean-Pierre ran to get help."

"You did not mean to break his leg." Ah, sibling cruelty was something that existed in all countries.

"Things were difficult between us for a long while, even once we all made up. I don't want my children to live in a fractured family. Not if I can help it. I want them to have a firm sense of belonging, a sense of being a Reynaud."

"And a Mitras," she reminded him.

"Yes. Both." He reached out to take her hands in his and squeezed. "I want your strength in our children. They will need it."

His words warmed her even more than his touch, and that was saying a lot when a thrill danced over her skin.

Too breathless to answer, she bit her lip, unwilling to allow a dreamy sigh to escape.

"Erika, please stay here with me for a while. We need more time to get to know each other." He drew her to her feet, his eyes pleading with hers at a time when her resolve was at an all-time low.

Her heart beat wildly, her lips parted. Anticipating the press of his mouth to hers.

He rubbed her arms, sliding them up until his hands tangled in her hair. They kissed deeply, with open mouths and passion. Tendrils of desire pulsed through her as he explored her mouth with his tongue, tasting her as she tasted him right back. She had not been passive in their lovemaking before, and she could already feel the urge to seize control driving her to the brink now.

It could have gone on like that for hours, for days even, if not for the sound of the door opening. She pushed back. Looked down. Away. At anything else but him.

While Gervais spoke in a low voice to his secretary, Erika used the time to collect herself. Straighten her dress. Find her purse. She had to figure this out soon. It was apparent there was chemistry simmering hot just beneath the surface. But now there was also a tenderness of feeling. An emotional connection. How would she ever forget that look in Gervais's eyes when he told her about the guilt of seeing Dempsey hurt? Of course she understood why he wanted to keep his own family intact. His children connected.

That was admirable, and a deeper draw for her than the sensual spell he cast around her without even trying. It had been difficult enough resisting just one.

How would she ever keep her wits about her with both those persuasive tools at his disposal?

On the private plane to St. Louis later that week, Erika replayed the kiss in Gervais's office over and over again. Of course, she had already relived that moment in her mind more than once, awake and asleep. Every look between them was filled with so much steam she could barely think, much less trust herself to make logical decisions around him.

At least they were on different planes today, so she could avoid temptation for a few hours. All the wives and girlfriends traveled first-class, while the team went on a chartered craft. Gervais had a meeting in Chicago first, something to do with corporate sponsorship for the Hurricanes. But he would arrive in St. Louis at the same time she did.

With any luck, she could use this flight to get her bearings straight.

But even as she tried to focus on being objective, her mind wandered back to the kiss in the office. A kiss that hadn't been repeated despite the fact that they'd spent time together over the past few days. It felt as though he was always on the clock, managing something for the team or overseeing business for one of the other Reynaud family concerns. So he was a bit of a workaholic; not a flaw in her opinion. In fact, she respected how seriously he took his work. He expected nothing to be handed to him in life.

And when they were together, he was fully present. Attentive. Thoughtful. He'd even helped deflect

an awkward run-in with his father and his father's girlfriend because she hadn't felt ready to face Theo after
what she'd learned about him. And knowing how little
his own son trusted him.

Erika's instincts had seldom failed her. In London,
there had been something between them. Something she
hadn't imagined. And the more she thought about the
past few days, the more excited she was to be with him
again. To have another kiss. To throw away caution as
quickly as clothes peeled away in the heat of passion.

To make love again and discover if the fire burned
as hot between them as she remembered.

Erika clutched a long silver necklace in her hand,
running the charm back and forth. Just as she did as
a child.

Fiona, Henri's wife, gently touched her arm. "You
know, we have a book club to help pass the time when
we're on the road with the guys."

"A book club?" She glanced at the row across from
her, to where Gervais's father's girlfriend stared intently
at a fashion magazine.

Fiona scrunched her nose. "I should have asked. Do
you like to read?"

"Which language?"

Fiona laughed lightly. "No need to get all princess-sy
on me."

"I apologize. That was meant to be a joke. Sometimes
nuances, even though I speak all those languages, get
lost. Tell me more about the book club."

"We choose books to read during all those flights

and then we have one helluva party while we discuss them."

"Party?"

Fiona nodded. "Spa or five-star restaurant or even the best room service we can buy."

"Did Gervais ask you to sit here and use the time to convince me it is fun to be on the road?" Try as she might, Erika couldn't keep the dry sarcasm out of her voice.

"I am simply helping you make an informed decision. It's not just about partying. We have homeschooling groups for families with children, as well." Shadows passed briefly through her eyes before Fiona cleared her throat. "It's amazing what you can teach a child when your field trips involve traveling around the country. Even overseas sometimes for the preseason. Our kids have bonds, too. There are ways to make this kind of family work. Family is important."

Damn. That struck a chord with her. Maybe Fiona had a point. She had just dismissed the women of the group without bothering to really get to know them. And that certainly was not fair.

Maybe she could strengthen her ties to Gervais's world this way. She already knew she wanted to explore their relationship more thoroughly—to take that first step of trust with him and see where indulging their sensual chemistry would lead. But in the meantime, why not work on forging bonds within his world? If things between them didn't work and they ended up co-parenting on opposite sides of the world, she would need allies in the Reynaud clan and in the Hurricanes organization. Growing closer to Fiona would be a good thing for her children.

All perfectly logical.

Except that a growing part of Erika acknowledged she wasn't just thinking about a rational plan B anymore. With each day that passed, with every moment that she craved Gervais, Erika wanted plan A to work. And that meant this trip was going to bring her much closer to the powerful father of her children.

There was nothing Gervais hated more than a loss. It rubbed him the wrong way, sending him into a dark place, even though he knew that a preseason loss didn't matter. The preseason was about training. Testing formations. Trying out new personnel. The final tally on the score sheet didn't count toward anything meaningful.

Opening the door to his suite, he was taken aback by what he saw on the bed. Erika in a Hurricanes jersey. On her, it doubled as a dress, hitting her midthigh. Exposing her toned legs.

His mind eased off the loss, focused on what was in front of him. "I wanted to catch you before you went to bed."

She closed the book she'd been reading and uncurled her legs, stretching them out on the bed. "I am sorry about the game."

"I won't lie. I'm disappointed we lost this one. But I'm realistic enough to know we can't win every time, especially in the preseason when we don't play all of our starters or utilize our best offensive strategies. The whole point of the preseason is like a testing ground.

We can create realistic scenarios and see what happens when we experiment." He told himself as much, but it didn't soothe him when he saw a rookie make poor decisions on the field or watched a risky play go up in flames.

"You have a cool head. That is admirable."

Her head tilted sympathetically.

Gervais was floored. Unsure of what to make about Erika's behavior. For the first time since her arrival in the United States, it felt as if she was opening up to him. But could that be?

She'd been so adamant on keeping distance between them, urging logic over passion. She was probably just being polite to him. After all, they would have to be civil to each other for the sake of the children. She had said as much more than once.

Still, damn it, he knew what he saw in her eyes, and she wanted him every bit as much as he wanted her. Back in his arms.

In his bed.

"Thank you. I'm sorry I've been so busy the past few days." He had taken a red-eye to Chicago to be there this morning for a meeting to secure a new corporate sponsor for the team. He was exhausted, but the extra hours had paid off, and he was one step closer to making the Hurricanes the wealthiest team in the league.

"You have been very thoughtful." She leaned forward, her posture open, words unclipped.

Her gaze was soft on him. And appreciative, he noticed. So maybe he hadn't been so off base. "I was concerned you would feel neglected having to fly in a separate plane."

"I understand you have other commitments. And I had a lovely conversation with Fiona—in case you were wondering, since you made sure we had seats beside each other." Erika raised her eyebrows as if daring him to deny it.

"Are you angry?" He couldn't help that he wanted to give her reasons to stay in New Orleans. But he knew she did not appreciate being manipulated.

He'd never met a more independent woman.

"Actually, no. She was helpful in explaining the logistics of how wives blend in to the lifestyle of this team you own."

He hadn't expected that.

"She answered all of your questions?"

"Most…" Shifting on the bed, she crawled toward him. "I had cats when I grew up."

All of his exhaustion disappeared.

His eyes couldn't help but watch her lithe form, the way her breasts pushed against the jersey he'd given her. An unforgettable vision.

And the sensory overload left him dumbly saying, "Okay."

"We had dogs, too, but the cats were mine."

Trying his damnedest to pull his eyes up from the length of her exposed legs, he stumbled over the next sentence, too. Focusing on words was hard. And he had thought that tonight's loss had left him speechless. That was nothing compared to the sight in front of him. "Um, what were their names?"

Erika's lips plumped into a smile as she knelt on the bed in front of him. "You do not need to work this hard or pretend to woo me."

"I'm not pretending. I am interested in everything about you." And he was. Mind, spirit…and body. He tried to keep his mind focused on the conversation. On whatever she wanted to talk about.

"Then you will want to know the real reason why I mentioned the cats. I loved my cats. And yet my children—our children—will not be able to have pets when they are traveling all over the country to follow this team that is part of their legacy." She gave him a playful shove, her smile still coy.

"Actually, I have a baseball buddy whose wife travels with her dog." He deserved a medal for making this much conversation when she looked like that. "I think the guy renegotiated his contract to make sure she got to have her dog with her."

"Oh," Erika whispered breathily. Moved closer to him, hands resting on his arms. Sending his body reeling from her touch.

"Yes, oh. So what other questions went unanswered today? Bring it. Because I'm ready."

"I do have one more question I did not dare to ask your sister-in-law." Her hands slid up to his neck. Pulled him close. Whispered with warm breath into his ear. "Will it mess up your season mojo if we have sex?"

Nine

Erika's heart hammered, threatening to fall right out of her chest as she stared at Gervais. All the time on the plane and waiting for him tonight had led her here. To this moment. And while the direction of her life may have been still uncertain, she knew this was right.

This was exactly where she needed to be. There was a closeness between them, one she had been actively fighting against.

Gervais's eyebrows shot upward. "What brought on this change?"

"I desire you. You want me, too, if I am not mistaken." Direct. Cool. She could do this.

"You are not mistaken. I have always wanted you. From the moment I first saw you. Even more now."

"Then we should stop denying ourselves the one

thing that is uncomplicated between us." And it was the truth. Everything was happening so fast, but it was undeniable that there was an attraction between them. In her gut, she knew that he would be there to support their babies. But it was more than that.

It was a deeper connection between them. When she had boarded the plane for New Orleans, she hadn't expected much from him. People had a nasty habit of leaving her, using her for the minimal privileges her royal status awarded her. She'd never expected to be welcomed and treated so well. In the past, her friends were dazzled by the idea of her world, rarely seeing beyond the outer trappings to the person beneath.

She also hadn't thought his family would be so accepting. It had scared her a bit, how many people were in the Reynaud clan. The number of people suddenly fussing over her and trying to get to know her had been overwhelming.

But they had also been kind. And maybe, just maybe, she'd be able to see past her preconceived notions about family. She had no real idea how to make a family anyway. But with Gervais…

"You're sure?" His forehead furrowed as he scrutinized her face. The look said everything. This was as far as he'd go without confirmation from her.

"Completely certain." She wanted to take a chance on him. On them. To give them an opportunity to be a couple.

And now that she'd made the decision after careful reasoning, she could finally allow her emotions to surface. She felt all her restraints melting away in the heat of the passion she'd been denying.

Even as she felt those walls disintegrate, she could sense a shift in Gervais. Like shedding a jacket and tie, he seemed to set aside his controlled exterior as a look of pure male desire flashed through his gaze. He closed the distance between them, his brown eyes dark and hungry while he raked his gaze over her.

He peeled the jersey up and over her head. She shook her hair free in waves that fanned behind her, leaving her rounded breasts bared to his devouring gaze. Heat pulsed through her veins—and relief. She had missed him since their incredible time together two and a half months ago, and she'd worked so hard to keep her desire for him in check for the sake of her babies so that she could make a smart decision where he was concerned. Now it felt so amazing to let go of those fears and simply fall into him.

She'd wondered what he would think of the subtle changes pregnancy had brought to her body. Her full breasts had fit in his palms before; now she knew they would overflow a hint more.

But Gervais's eyes were greedier for her than ever, and he stared at her with need he didn't bother to hide. Lowering her to rest on her back, he followed her down to the bed, his touch gentle but firm. His woodsy scent familiar and making her ache for him.

He hooked his thumbs in the sides of her pale blue panties, tugging gently until she raised her hips to accommodate. He slipped the scrap of satin down and off, flinging it aside to rest on top of the discarded Hurricanes jersey. His throat moved in a slow gulp. "That incredible image will be seared in my brain for all time."

He rocked back for a moment, his eyes roving over her.

Then his gaze fell to rest on the ever so slight curve of her stomach. The pregnancy was still early, but now she realized that the twins had been the reason her pants had grown a little snug faster than she would have expected.

A glint of protectiveness lit his eyes. "Are you sure this is safe? You passed out just last week. I don't want to do anything that could risk your health."

She thought she might die if he did not touch her, actually. But she kept that thought locked away.

"The doctor said I am healthy and cleared for all activities, including sex. Well, as long as we do not indulge in acrobatics." A wicked memory flashed through her brain. "Perhaps we should not re-create that interlude on the kitchen table in your London hotel room."

His heart slugged hard against his chest. Against hers. She wanted to arch into his warmth like a cat seeking the sun.

"No acrobatics. Understood." He trailed kisses beneath her ear and down her neck. "I look forward to treating you like spun glass."

A shiver tripped down her spine, her skin tingling with awareness. Tingles of heat gathered between her legs, making her long for more. For everything.

"I will not break," she promised, needing the pleasure only he could bring her.

He skimmed a fingertip down the length of her neck.

"Oh, careful, light touches can be every bit as arousing as our more aggressive weekend together."

She licked her lips. Swallowed over her suddenly dry throat.

"I look forward to your persuasion—once you take those clothes off." She ran her hands down his chest and back up his shoulders. "Because, Gervais…" She savored the feel of his name on her tongue. "You are seriously overdressed for the occasion. Undress for me."

His brown eyes went molten black with heat at her invitation, and his hands went to work on his tie, loosening the knot and tugging the length free, slowly, then draping the silver length over the chaise at the end of the bed. And oh my, how she enjoyed the way he took his time. One fastening at a time, he opened his white button-down until it flapped loose, revealing his broad, muscled chest in a T-shirt. In a deliberate motion he swept both aside and laid them carefully over his tie.

Her mouth went moist and she bit her bottom lip. She recalled exactly why she hadn't bothered with light, teasing touches the last time they were together. His body was so powerful, his every muscle honed. She hadn't been able to hold herself back the last time.

He winked at her with a playfulness that she didn't see in this intense man often.

She could not stop a wriggle of impatience, the Egyptian cotton sheets slick against her rapidly heating flesh.

Then all playfulness left his eyes as swiftly as he took off his shoes and pants, leaving his toned body naked and all for her.

The thick length of him strained upward against his

stomach. Unable to hold back, she sat up to run her hands up his chest, then down his sides, his hips, forward to clasp his steely strength in his hands. To stroke, again and again, teasing her thumb along the tip.

With a growl of approval and impatience, he stretched over her while keeping his full weight off her. He braced on his elbows, cupping her face and slanting his mouth along hers. His tongue filled her mouth and she knew soon, not soon enough, he would fill her body again.

His hands molded to her curves, exploring each of her erogenous zones with a perfection that told her he remembered every moment of their time together as much as she did. His hard thigh parted her legs, the firm pressure against her core sending her arching closer, wriggling against him, growing moist and needy. She clutched at his shoulders, breathy whispers sliding free as she urged him to take her. Now. No more waiting. He'd tormented her dreams long enough.

Then the blunt thickness of him pushed into her, inch by delicious inch. He was so gentle and strong at the same time. She knew she would have to be the one to demand more. Harder. Faster. And she did. With her words and body, rocking against him, her fingers digging into his taut ass to bring them both the completion they sought.

Her fingers crawled up his spine again and she pushed at his shoulders, nudging until he rolled to his back, taking her with him in flawless athleticism. His power, his strength, thrilled her. She straddled him, her sleek blond hair draped over her breasts, her nipples just peeking through and tightening. Gervais swept aside her hair and took one pink peak in his mouth. He circled with his tongue, sending bolts of pleasure radiating through her. Sighs of bliss slipped from between her lips. She rolled her hips faster, riding him to her completion. Wave after wave of her orgasm pulsed through her.

She heard his own hoarse shout of completion, the deep sounds sending a fresh wash of pleasure through her until she melted forward onto his chest. Sated. Every nerve tingling with awareness in the aftermath.

The swish of the ceiling fan sent goose bumps along her skin. The fine thread count of the sheets soothed her.

But most of all, the firm muscled length of him felt so good; the swirls of his body hair tempted her to writhe along him again.

If she could move.

And just like that, Erika realized how utterly complicated being with him was. Because like it or not, she had feelings for him. Feelings that were threatening to cloud her judgment.

And while this may have felt right for her, she needed to be sure it was right for him, too.

Gervais poured the flowery-scented shampoo into his hand. Her magnolia scent filled the steam and teased his senses as they stood under the shower spray in a vintage claw-foot tub. The sheer plastic curtain gave both privacy and a view of the room filled with fresh flowers he'd ordered sent up especially for her.

There was so very much he wanted to do for—and to—this incredible woman.

Drawing Erika close to him, he kissed her neck, nuzzled behind her ear, savored the wet satin of her skin against his bare flesh. Already he could feel the urge building inside him to lift her legs around his waist and surge inside her. To bring them both to completion again, but he was determined to take his time, to build the moment.

And yes, draw out the pleasure.

He lathered her hair, the bubbles and her hair slick between his fingers as he massaged her scalp. Her light moan of bliss encouraged him on, filling him with a sense of power over fulfilling all her needs. He continued to rub along her head, then gently along her neck, down to her shoulders in a slight massage. He wanted to pamper her, to show her he was serious about her and the babies.

She leaned into his touch but stayed silent. Feeling her let out a deep sigh, he decided he wanted to really get to know this beautiful, incredible woman. Sure, they'd spent some time together…but there was still so much he could learn about her. That he wanted to learn about *her*. Everything, not just about her beautiful body, but also about that magnificently brilliant mind of hers.

Such as why she had chosen a career in the military after growing up as royalty.

"So tell me about your time in the service. What did you really do?"

"Just what I told you that day we met."

"Truly? Nothing more? Not some secret spy role? Or dark ops career no one can ever know about?"

"How does the saying go in your country? I could tell you but then I would have to kill you."

He laughed softly against her mouth. "As long as we go while naked together, I'll die a happy man."

She swatted his butt playfully, then her smile faded. "Truthfully, there is nothing more to tell. I was a translator and handled some diplomacy meetings."

"I admire that about you." It had been a brave move. A noble, selfless act.

Shrugging, she tipped her shampooed head back into the water. Erika closed her eyes, clearly enjoying the feel of the steamy water. The suds caught on her curves, drawing his gaze. She was damn sexy.

"Why are you so dismissive of your service to your country?"

Eyes flashed open, defensive. He could tell it in the way she chewed on her lip before she answered, "I wanted to be a field medic and go into combat zones. But I was not allowed."

He nodded, trying to be sympathetic. To understand the complication of letting a princess, even from defunct royalty, into an active war zone.

"I can see how your presence could pose a security risk for those around you. You would be quite a high-value captive."

Her half smile carried a hint of cynicism. "While that is true, that was not the reason. My parents interfered. They did not want me to work or join at all. They wanted me to marry someone rich and influential, like I was some pawn in a royal chess game from a thousand years ago."

"Still, you made your own way. That's commendable. Why a field nurse and not in a military hospital?" He respected her drive. And her selfless career choices. She wanted to help people. Something told him she would have been a good field medic. Strong, knowledgeable, fearless.

"I did not want special treatment or protection because of my family's position. And still, I ended up as a translator not even allowed anywhere near a combat zone." Her voice took on a new determination. A tenacity he found incredibly attractive.

"So you made plans to continue your education after your service was finished." He knew she'd registered for coursework that would begin next month in the UK but had assumed she would ask for her spot to be held until after the children were born.

"I will not be deterred from my plans because of my family's interference." Eyes narrowed at him. Every bit a princess with that haughty stare. "I can support myself."

"Of course you can." He brought his negotiating skills to the conversation, hoping to make her see reason. "This is about more than money, though. You have a lot on your plate. Let me help you and the babies while you return to school."

"That makes it sound like I am incapable of taking care of myself the way my parents always said." Bitterness edged back into her voice. And something that sounded like dulled resignation.

"This isn't just about you. Or me. We have children to think of. You know I want you to marry me. I've made that clear. But if your answer is still no, at least move in with me. Make this easier for all—"

She pressed her mouth to his, silencing him until she leaned back, water dripping between them again.

"Gervais, please, this time is for us to get to know one another better. This kind of pressure from you about the future is counterproductive."

One thing was for sure—she had been opening up. Maybe asking her to marry him again was too much too soon. But he could feel the connection between them growing. So he would back off. But not forever. He just had to figure out a way to show her how good they were together. "Then how about we find food?"

Her smile was so gorgeous the water damn near steamed off his skin. "Food? Now that is music to this pregnant woman's ears."

The strands of Erika's hair fell damp against the cloth of the jersey. They sat in the suite's kitchen. She was on the countertop, cross-legged, peering over at Gervais's back.

He'd retrieved an assortment of ripe fruit—pitted cherries, chocolate-dipped strawberries, pineapple slices and peach slices. At the center of the platter was a bowl of indulgent-looking cream.

Stomach growling, she looked on in anticipation. He brought it next to her and pulled up a bar stool so that they were eye level.

Extending her hand to grab a cherry, he stopped her.

"Let me, Princess." With a playful smile, he lifted

a cherry to her lips. Inside, she felt that now-familiar heat pulse. He was tender, charming.

A threat to her plan of objectivity, too.

She popped a chocolate-dipped strawberry into his mouth. He licked the slightly melted chocolate off her fingertips, sending her mind back to the shower. Back to when she had thought this was uncomplicated.

Needing to take control of the situation, Erika cleared her throat. Her goal was the same as before. To get to know him. "What did you want to be as a little boy growing up?"

Finishing chewing, he tilted his head to the side. "Interesting question."

"How so?" It had seemed like a perfectly reasonable question. One she had been meaning to ask for a while now.

"Everyone assumes I wanted to be a pro football player."

To Erika, Gervais had seemed like the kind of man who wasn't nearly as cut-and-dried as that. He might live and breathe football, but it didn't seem as if it was the only dimension to him. Childhood dreams said a lot, after all. She'd wanted to be a shield maiden from long ago. To protect and shelter people. Her adult dream was still along those lines.

A nurse did such things. "And you did not want to be a football player like the rest of your family?"

"I enjoy the game. Clearly. I played all through elementary school into high school because I wanted to. I didn't have to accept the offer to play at the college level. I could afford any education I wanted."

"But your childhood dream?" She pressed on, before taking the cream-covered peach slice he'd offered her. She savored the taste of the sweetness of the peach against the salty flavor of his fingers.

Looking down at his feet, then back at her, he smiled sheepishly. "As a kid, I wanted to drive a garbage truck."

Her jaw dropped. Closed. Then opened again as she said, "Am I missing something in translation? You wished to drive a truck that picks up trash?"

"I did. When my parents argued, I would go outside to hide from the noise. Sometimes it got so loud I had to leave. So I rode my bike to follow the garbage truck. I would watch how that crusher took everyone's trash and crushed it down to almost nothing. As a kid that sounded very appealing."

Thinking of him pedaling full-tilt down the roads as a child put an ache in her heart she couldn't deny. "I am sorry your parents hurt you that way."

"I just want you to understand I take marriage and our children's happiness seriously."

His brown eyes met hers. They were heated with a ferocity she hadn't seen before.

This offer of a life together was real to him. His offer was genuine, determined. And from a very driven man. She needed to make up her mind, and soon, or she could fast lose all objectivity around Gervais.

Ten

It had only been three days since he'd gotten home from the loss in St. Louis. He needed time to think of his next strategy. And not just for the Hurricanes. With Erika, too.

Which was exactly why he'd pulled on his running shorts and shirt. Laced up his shoes and hit the pavement, footsteps keeping him steady.

Focused.

Sweat curled off his upper lip, the taste of salt heavy in his mouth. The humid Louisiana twilight hummed with the songs of the summer bugs and birds.

This always set his mind right. The sound of foot to pavement. Inhale. Exhale. The feel of sweat on his back.

He'd been quite the runner growing up. Always could

best his brothers in distance and speed. Especially Jean-Pierre, his youngest brother.

Jean-Pierre had to work harder than all his older brothers to keep up with them as they ran. Running had been something of a Reynaud rite of passage. Or so Gervais had made it out to be. He'd always pushed his brothers for a run. It was an escape from the yelling and fighting that went on at their home. Whether the family was at the ranch in Texas, on the expansive property on Lake Pontchartrain or on the other side of the globe, there was always room to run, and Gervais had made use of those secured lands to give them all some breathing space from the parental drama.

Slowing his pace, he stopped to tighten his shoelace. Looking at the sparkling water of the lake, he realized it had been too long since he talked to Jean-Pierre. Months.

Gervais knew he needed to call him…but things hadn't been the same since Jean-Pierre left Louisiana Tech to play for the Gladiators in New York. Sure, Jean-Pierre maintained a presence on the family compound, sharing upkeep of one of the homes where he stayed when he flew into town. But how often had that been over the past few years? Even in the off-season, Jean-Pierre tended to stick close to New York and his teammates on the Gladiators. When he did show up in New Orleans, it was to take his offensive line out on his boat or for a raucous party that was more for friends than family.

How Jean-Pierre managed to stay away from this quirky, lively city was beyond Gervais. When they were younger, the family had spent a lot of time in Texas. Which, make no mistake, Gervais loved, but there was a charm to New Orleans, a quality that left the place rarified.

He wanted to share those things with Erika. The cultural scene was unbeatable, and the food. Well, he'd yet to take her to his favorite dessert and dancing place. He pictured taking her out for another night on the Big Easy with him. She'd love it if she'd give him a chance to show her.

And though they'd fallen into a pattern over the past few days, he felt as distant as ever and all because she wouldn't commit even though they had children on the way. Sure, they made love nightly now. And he relished the way her body writhed beneath his touch. But it wasn't enough. He bit his tongue about the future and she didn't say anything about leaving.

Or staying.

And he wanted her to stay. Starting to run again, he picked up the intensity. Ran harder, faster.

He didn't want her to leave. He didn't want a repeat of London. Before he'd even woken up, she'd packed her things and let herself out of the hotel suite. Though it had been only one weekend, he had fallen for her. Now they'd spent days together.

Rather blissful days. Mind wandering, he thought to the last night in St. Louis when they'd explored the rooftop garden that was attached to their hotel suite. There'd been a slight chill in the air, but things between them had been on fire. In his memory, he traced the curves on her body.

Though she might be pumping the brakes on the future, he was getting to know her. To see past her no-nonsense facade to the woman who was a little sarcastic, kindhearted and generous.

The thought of her just leaving again like in London... it made his gut sink.

Rounding the last corner on his run, he didn't hold back. He sprinted all out, as if that would allow him to hold on to Erika.

This was damn awful timing, too. He knew he needed to focus on his career. To turn the Hurricanes into a financial dynasty to back the championship team Dempsey assured them they had in place. And this thing with Erika—whatever it might be—was not helping him. Sure, he'd nabbed that sponsor in Chicago. But every day he spent with her was a day that he wasn't securing another sponsor that would make the Hurricanes invincible as a business and not just a team. They'd been teetering on the brink of folding when he'd purchased them, and he'd reinvigorated every facet since then, but his work was far from done to keep them in the black.

But damn. He could not. No. He *would* not just let her leave as she had before. This wasn't just about the fact they were having a family, or that they were amazing together in bed.

Quickening his pace, he saw the Reynaud compound come into sight. The light was on in Erika's bedroom.

His grandfather had taught him a few things when he was a kid. Two of the most important: *build your dream* and *family is everything.* Two simple statements. And he wanted Erika to be a part of that. To create the kind of home that his own kids would never want to run from.

Sitting cross-legged on a cushioned chair in the massive dining room, Erika absently spread raspberry jam on her puffy biscuit. Try as she might, she couldn't force her mind to be present. To be in the moment.

Instead, her thoughts drifted back to Gervais and last night. He'd knocked on her door after his run. She'd opened the door, let him in. And he'd showered her in determined, passion-filled kisses. There was an urgency, a sincerity in their lovemaking last night. A new dimension to sex she had never thought possible.

Last night had made it even harder for her to be objective about their situation. She wanted Gervais. But she also wanted what was best for them both. Balancing that need seemed almost impossible.

A motion in the corner of her eye brought her back to the present. She found Gervais's grandfather filling his plate at the buffet with pork grillades and grits, a buttered biscuit on the side.

Gracious, she could barely wait for the morning to wane so the queasy feeling would subside and she could indulge in more of the amazing food of this region. Everything tasted so good, or perhaps that was her pregnancy hormones on overload. Regardless, she was hungry but didn't dare try more for a couple more hours yet.

She looked back at Gervais's grandfather, keeping her eyes off the plate of food. Leon hadn't gone with them to St. Louis, but Gervais had explained how travel anywhere other than from his homes in New Orleans and Texas left the old man disoriented.

He took his place at the head of the table, just to the left of her, and poured himself a cup of thick black coffee from the silver carafe. "So you're carrying my first great-grandchild—" He tapped his temple near his gray hair. "Grandchildren. You're having twins. I remember that. Some days my memory's not so good, but that's sticking in my brain and making me happy. A legacy. And if you won't find it disrespectful of me to say so, I believe it's going to be a brilliant, good-looking legacy." He toasted her with his china coffee cup.

"Thank you, sir. No disrespect taken at all. That's a delightful thing to say, especially the smart part." She gave him a wink as she picked at her biscuit. Praise of her intelligence was important. Erika had worked hard to be more than a pretty princess. Wanted her worth and merit to be attached to her mind's tenacity. To realize her dreams of setting up a nurse-practitioner practice of her own someday, one with an entire section devoted to homeopathic medicines and mood-leveling aromatherapy.

"That's important." He sipped more of his coffee before digging into his breakfast. "We have a large family empire to pass along, and I want it to go into good hands. I didn't do so well with my own children. But my grandkids, I'm damn proud of them."

"Gervais will make a good father." Of that she had no doubt. He was already so attentive.

"He works too much and takes on too much responsibility to prove he's not like his old man, but yes, he will take parenthood seriously. He may need some books, though. To study up, since he didn't have much of a role model. He sure knows what not to do, though." A laugh rasped from the man's cracked lips and he finished more of his coffee.

"I believe you played a strong part in bringing up your grandchildren." She reached for the carafe and offered to refill his cup, even though she wasn't drinking coffee. She stuck to juice and water these days.

He nodded at her, eyes turning inward as if he was reading something she couldn't see. "I tried to step in where I could. Didn't want to bring up spoiled, silver-spoon-entitled brats again." His focus returned to her. "I like that you went into the military. That speaks well of your parents."

Her mother and father had pitched an unholy fit over that decision, but she would not need to say as much. "It was an honor to serve my country."

"Good girl. What do you plan to do now that your studies are on hold?"

Technically, they weren't. She would be back in university in autumn.

"When I return to school, I will undertake the program to become a nurse-practitioner, even as a single mother." And she would. No matter how long it took.

"Really? I didn't expect you to, um—"

"Work for a living? Few do, even after my military service." Her voice went softer than she would have liked.

"You'll take good care of my grandson when I'm

gone?" His question pierced her tender heart on a morning when her emotions were already close to the surface.

"Sir, you appear quite spry to me."

"That's not what I mean and if you're wanting to be a nurse-practitioner, you probably know that." He tapped his temple again. "It's here that I worry about giving out too soon. The doctors aren't sure how fast. Sometimes I prefer the days I don't remember talking to those experts."

"I am so very sorry." She hadn't spent a lot of time with Leon Reynaud. But she could tell he was a good man who cared a lot about his family. And the stories Gervais told her only confirmed that.

"Thank you. Meanwhile, I want to get to know you and spend time with you so you can tell my great-grans all about me." He pointed with his biscuit for emphasis and she couldn't help but smile.

"That sounds delightful," she said to Gramps, but her eyes trailed over his head. To Gervais, who strode into the dining hall.

Sexy. That was the only word that pulsed in her mind as she looked at him. Dressed in a blue button-down shirt, he looked powerful.

"Don't mind me," he mumbled, smiling at her. "Just grabbing some breakfast before heading to the office. You can go back to telling embarrassing stories about me, Gramps."

Gramps chuckled. "I was just getting ready to tell my favorite."

Gervais gave him a faux-injured grin, swiping a muffin and apple from the table.

He stopped next to her. Gave her a hug and a kiss. Not a deep kiss or even lingering. Instead, he gave her one of those familiar kisses. A kiss that spoke of how they'd been together before. That they knew each other's bodies and taste well. She bit her bottom lip where the taste of him lingered, minty, like his toothpaste.

As he walked away, everything felt…right. Being with him seemed so natural, as if they had been doing this for years. It'd be so easy—too easy—to slide right into this life with him.

And that scared her clean through to her toes.

It had been a long day at the office, one of the longest since their return from St. Louis. Gervais had tried his best to secure a new technology sponsor for the Hurricanes, a west coast company with deep pockets that was currently expanding their presence in New Orleans. The fit was perfect, but the corporate red tape was nightmarish, and the CEO at the helm hadn't been as forward thinking as the CFO, whom Gervais had met on another deal the year before. Not everyone understood the tremendous advertising power of connecting with an NFL team, and the CEO of the tech company had been reluctant. Stubborn. It had been a hellish day, but at least the guy hadn't balked at the deal. Yet.

Gervais had left work midday to talk with some of Gramps's doctors. They were discussing treatment plans and some of the effects of his new medicines. All he wanted to do was give the best he could to his family.

Family. Gramps. Hurricanes. Jean-Pierre. Work and Reynaud business had swirled in his mind all day. The only thing he wanted to do this evening was see Erika. The thought of her, waiting at home for him, had kept him fighting all day. Besides, he had a gift for her and he couldn't wait to present it to her.

Walking into her room, he felt better just seeing her. She was sitting on the chaise longue, staring blankly at her suitcase.

Her unzipped suitcase.

That fleeting moment of good feeling vanished. Was she leaving? If he had come home later, would she have already been gone, just like London?

Taking a deep breath, he set aside his gift for her and surveyed the room. The two arrangements of hydrangeas and magnolias were on her dresser alongside an edible bouquet of fruit. He'd had them sent to her today while he was at work. For her to think about their time in St. Louis together.

As he continued to look around the room, he didn't see any clothes pulled out. So they were all either in the drawers or in her bag.

He hoped they were still in the drawers. Gervais didn't want her to go. Instead, he wanted her to stay here. With him. Be part of his family.

Tapping the suitcase, he stared at Erika "That's not full, is it?"

He tried to sound light. Casual. The opposite of his current mental state.

She looked up quickly, her eyes such a startling shade of blue. "No, of course not. Why would you think that?"

"You left once before without a word." He wanted to

take her in his arms and coax her into bed for the day, not think about her leaving.

"I promised you I would stay for two weeks and I meant it. After that, though, I have to make a decision."

He tensed.

"Why? Why the push?"

"I need to move forward with my life at some point." Chewing her lip, she gestured at the suitcase.

"I've asked you to marry me and move in with me, yet still you hold back. Let me help support you while you make a decision, with time if not money, wherever you are." He would do that for her and more.

She looked at him with a steady, level gaze. "Seriously? Haven't we had this discussion already? We have time to make these decisions."

"The sooner we plan, the sooner we can put things into place."

"Do not rush, damn it. That is not the way I am. My parents learned that when they tried to push me into their way of life, their plans for me." Her gaze was level, icy.

"So you plan to leave, just not now?"

"I do not know what I am planning." Her voice came out in a whisper, a slight crack, as well. "I am methodical. I need to think through all of the options and consequences."

"Is that what you did the morning you left me? Stayed up and thought about why we needed to turn our backs on the best sex ever?" Dropping onto the edge of the bed across from her, he caught her gaze. Looked at the intensity of her blue eyes. She was damn sexy.

Beautiful. And he wasn't going to let her walk away as if this was nothing.

"Best sex ever? I like the sound of that." She licked her lips seductively, leaned toward him, her breasts pressing against her glittery tank top.

So tempting. And definitely not the direction he needed to take with her.

He raised his brow at her. "You're trying to distract me with your beautiful body."

"And you are using flattery. We need more than that." Crossing her arms, she scrutinized his face.

"I've made it clear I understand that. That's what our time together has been about. But I am willing to use everything I have at my disposal. I am not giving up."

"Everything?" She gestured to the flowers, the candy and a small jewelry box.

He'd forgotten about the gift he'd brought for her.

Pushing off the bed, he approached her, leaned on the arms of the chaise longue. He kissed her forehead, one arm around her, the other still cradling the box. "Flattery, which is easy because you are so very lovely. Charming words are tougher for me because I am a businessman, but for you, I will work so very hard with the words. And, yes, with gifts, too. Will you at least open it?"

She took the box from his hands, eyes fixed on his. Her fingers found the small bow. Gently, she slowly pulled the white bow off. The Tiffany box was bare, undressed now.

Erika lifted the lid, let out a small gasp. Two heart earrings encrusted in diamonds glinted back at her.

Gervais's voice dropped half an octave. "It made me think of our children. Two beautiful hearts."

He tucked a knuckle under her chin and raised it to see her face. Tears welled in her eyes.

Pulse pounding, he put his arms around her, held her tight to his chest. "I didn't mean to make you cry."

She shook her head, her silky blond hair tickling his nose. "It is sweet, truly. Thoughtful. A wonderful gift."

Kneeling in front of her, he wiped the tears off her pale cheeks. He'd wanted to get her something meaningful. Drawing her hands in his, he kissed the back of each one, then the insides of her wrists in the way he knew sent her pulse leaping. He could feel it even now as he rubbed his thumbs against her silky skin. "I want this to work. Tell me what I can do to make that happen. It is yours."

Her eyes flooded with conflicting feelings. It was as if he could see into her thought process where she worked so hard to weigh the pros and cons of a future. Somehow he knew she was at the precipice of the answer she'd been looking for. One he was scared as hell to receive.

And, cursing himself for his weakness, he couldn't resist this one last chance to sway the outcome. To make her want to stay. So he kissed her deeply, ebbing away the pressure of speech to make room for the pleasure they both needed.

Eleven

Gervais had Erika in his arms and he wanted that to go on for… He couldn't think of a time he wouldn't want her. Every cell inside him ached to have her. So much so his senses homed in to her. Almost to the exclusion of all else. Almost to the point where he lost sight of the fact he'd left the door ajar.

And now someone was knocking lightly on that door.

With more than a little regret, he set her away from him and struggled to regulate his breathing before turning to the door to find…a security guard?

Hell. How could he have forgotten for even a second that his family's wealth and power carried risk? They needed to stay on watch at all times.

Security guard James Smithson stood on the other side of the half-open door, his chiseled face grave.

Gervais had always liked James—a young guy, athletic and focused. James had almost made the cut for the team. The poor kid was in an interesting position; he'd declined a college football scholarship when his high school girlfriend became pregnant. James attended an online school while helping raise their son, but he'd shown up at a couple of Hurricanes training camps with impressive drive, even though his stats weren't quite strong enough.

So before Dempsey could send him home, Gervais had taken him aside and found out he had skills off the field, too. He'd offered him help forming his own security company, making him a part of the Hurricanes family.

"Sorry to disturb you, sir, but we have some unexpected company."

"I don't accept unexpected guests. You know that." Gervais stared at the guard. Who, to be fair, was doing a damn good job at not looking at Erika in her tight-fitting sparkly tank top that revealed her killer curves. Even so, he found himself wanting to wrap her up in a sheet. Just to be safe.

"I understand that, sir," James assured him. "But…"

Erika looked back and forth between the guard and Gervais. "I'll leave the two of you to talk." She closed the jewelry box and clutched it to her chest. "If you'll excuse me."

James held up a hand. "Ma'am, I believe you'll want to stay."

Ericka's face twisted in confusion. "I'm not sure how I can be of help—"

James scrubbed his jaw awkwardly. "It's your family. Their limos are just now coming through the front gate."

Gervais blinked slowly. "Limos?" Plural?

"My family?" Erika stammered, color draining from her skin. "*All* of my family?"

James gave a swift nod, his gun just visible in a shoulder harness under his sports jacket. "It appears so, ma'am. Both of your parents, four sisters, three of them married and some children, I believe?"

Gervais scratched the back of his head right about where an ache began. Talk about a baptism of fire meeting all the in-laws at once. So many. "I think we're going to need to air out the guesthouse."

The pressure of a headache billowed between Erika's temples. As she stood in the grand living room, attention drawn outside, past the confines of this room, she felt everything hit her at once. First, her conflicting feelings for Gervais, and now this.

Her entire family, down to her nieces, was here. Now. Her eyes trailed past the bay windows to where Gervais, her father, Gervais's brothers and his grandfather stood on the patio. Having drinks as if this was the most casual affair ever. As if this was something they had done together for years. Gervais had a gift with that, taking charge of a situation and putting everyone at ease.

She'd spent so much time focusing on the reasons to hold back, she forgot to look for the reasons they should. There was a lot to admire about this man. His obvious love of his family. His honorability in his standing up to care for his children. And the way he handled his business affairs with a mix of savvy and compassion. Her heart was softening toward him daily, and her resolve was all but gone.

And of course there was the passionate, thorough way he made love to her. A delicious memory tingled through her. She tore her eyes from him before she lost the ability to think reasonably at all.

Her father, Bjorn Mitras, slapped his knee enthusiastically at something Gervais had said. So they were getting along.

The mood inside the living room was decidedly less jovial. She could feel her sisters and mother sizing her up. Determining what Erika ought to do. And if she had to bet, getting her Master's in Nursing wasn't even on the table anymore. They'd never supported her ambitions. And if she was carrying a male child…well, they'd certainly have a lot of opinions to throw at her.

For the first time since learning she was pregnant, Erika felt alone.

She had hoped for an ally in Fiona, but Fiona hadn't come to meet everyone. She wasn't feeling well. Erika was not feeling all that great herself right now. Her family overwhelmed her in force.

Turning reluctantly from the bay windows, she studied her mother. Arnora Mitras had always been a slight, slim woman. Unlike other royals, she recycled outfits. But Arnora was a friend of many fashion designers. She was always draped in finery, things quite literally off the runway.

Her four sisters—Liv, Astrid, Helga and Hilda— stood in the far corner, discussing things in hushed tones. The twins, Helga and Hilda, both had the same nervous tic, tracing the outline of their bracelets. It was something that they had both done since they were little girls. Erika squinted at them, trying to figure out what had them on edge.

But it was Astrid who caught her gaze. Blue eyes of equal intensity shone back at her. Astrid gave a curt nod, her honey-blond bob falling into her face.

It was a brief moment of recognition, but then Astrid turned back to the conversation. Back to whispering.

Three of her sisters had married into comfort, but not luxury. Not like what the Reynauds offered. And they lived across Europe, leading quieter lives. No male heirs, no extravagance. A part of Erika envied that anonymity, especially now.

Of course, Gervais had seen to every detail. And in record time. He called in all the staff and security. Arranged what looked like a small state dinner in record time. He even had nannies brought in for her nieces.

Beignets, fruit and pralines were decadently arranged into shapes and designed. It looked almost too beautiful to eat. Erika watched as her sisters loaded their plates with the pastries and fruit, but they eyed the pralines with distrust. They weren't an open-minded bunch. They preferred to stick to what they knew. Which was also probably why they skipped over the iced tea and went straight for the coffee. That was familiar.

"Mother—" the word tumbled out of Erika's mouth "—some advance notice of your visit would have been nice."

"And give you the opportunity to make excuses to put us off? I think not."

Sighing unabashedly, Erika trudged on. "I was not putting you off, Mother. I was simply..."

"Avoiding us all," Helga finished for her as she approached. The rest of the Mitras women a step behind her.

"Hardly. I wanted time to prepare for your visit and to ensure that every detail was properly attended to."

Helga gave a wave to the spread of food and raised her brow. She clearly didn't believe Erika's protest. "This place is amazing. You landed well, sister."

"I am only visiting and getting things in order for our babies' sake." Erika's words were clipped, her emotions much more of a tangle.

"Well, you most certainly have something in common. Relationships have been built on less. I say go for it. Chase that man down until he proposes." The last word felt like nails on a chalkboard in Erika's ears. She schooled her features neutral, just as she had done when she was a translator. No emotions walked across her face.

Erika stayed diplomatically quiet.

Her mother's delicately arched eyebrow lifted, and she set her bone china coffee cup down with a slow and careful air. "He has already proposed? You two are getting married?"

"No, I did not say we are getting married."

"But he *has* proposed," Hilda pressed gently.

"Stop. This is why I would have preferred you wait to meet him. Give Gervais and me a chance to work out the details of our lives without family interference, and then we will share our plan."

Liv waggled her fingers toward the French doors leading to the vast patio. "*His* family is here."

"And they are not pushy," Erika retorted with conviction. She wasn't backing down from this. Not a chance.

"We are not pushy, either. We just want what is best for you." Hilda's porcelain complexion turned ruddy, eyes widening with hurt and frustration like during their childhood whenever people laughed at her lisp. She always had been the most sensitive of the lot.

Smoothing her green dress, Liv—always the prettiest, and the most rebellious, the infamous sex tape being the least of her escapades—took a deep breath and touched her hair. "I think all of this travel has made me a bit weary. I shall rest and we will talk later."

And with that her mother, Liv, Helga and Hilda all left the grand living room, heels clacking against the ground.

But Astrid didn't leave. She hung back, eyes fixed on Erika.

Anger burned in Erika's belly. Astrid was her oldest sister. The one who always told her what to do. She had been the sister to lecture her as a child. Erika fully anticipated some version of that pseudo-parental "advice" to spill out of Astrid's lips.

"Keep standing up for yourself. You are doing the right thing."

Gaping, Erika steadied herself on the back of the tapestry sofa. "Seriously? I appreciate the support but

I have to say it would be nice to have with Mother present."

Astrid shrugged. "She is frightening and strong willed. We all know that. But you do understand, you are strong, too. That is why we pushed you off the balcony first."

"Wow, thanks," Erika grumbled, recalling the terrifying drop from balcony to homemade trampoline.

"You are welcome." Astrid closed her in a tight embrace. In a half whisper, she added, "I love you, sister."

"I love you, too." That much of life was simple.

If only the other relationships—her relationship with Gervais—could be as easily understood. Or maybe they could. Perhaps the time had come to stop fighting her emotions and to embrace them.

Starting with embracing Gervais.

With the arrival of Erika's family, work for the Hurricanes had taken a backseat. Not that he would have had it any other way. They were his children's aunts and grandparents. They were important to him. He had to win them over—particularly her father, the king, not that King Bjorn had shown any sign of disapproval.

But important or not, they were the reason he was just now getting to his charts and proposals in the wee small hours of the morning.

Gervais pressed Play on the remote. He was holed up in the mini theater. He had a few hours of preseason games from around the league to catch up on. This was where he'd been slacking the most. Hadn't spent much time previewing the talent on the other teams yet. Because while Dempsey would fine-tune a solid fifty-three-man roster from the talent currently working out with the team, Gervais needed to culti- vate a backup plan for injuries and for talent that didn't pan out. That meant he needed to familiarize himself with what else was out there, which underrated play- ers might need a new home with the Hurricanes before the October trade deadline.

A creak from the door behind him caused him to turn around in his seat. Erika was there, in the doorway. A bag of popcorn in one hand, with two sodas in the other.

She certainly was a sight for his tired eyes. He drank her in appreciatively, noting the way her bright pink sundress fit her curves, the gauzy fabric swishing when she walked. The halter neck was the sort of thing he could untie with a flick of fabric, and he was seized with the urge to do just that.

As soon as possible. Damn.

"I thought this could be like a date." She gave him a sly smile, bringing her magnolia scent with her as she neared him, a lock of blond hair grazing his arm.

He took the sodas from her and set them in the cup holders on either side of the leather chairs in the media room.

"Well, then, best date ever."

"That seems untrue." Worry and exhaustion lined her voice. "I am sorry about my family arriving unex- pectedly. And for how much time they are taking out of your workday."

"It's no trouble at all. They are my children's grand- parents. That's huge." Pausing the game, he gave her a genuine smile, conceding that he wouldn't be giving the footage his full attention now. But he had notes on the talent across the league, of course. As an owner, he didn't run the team alone.

And right now nothing was more important to him than Erika and his children.

Settling deeper into the chair beside him, Erika flipped her long hair in front of one shoulder and centered the bag of popcorn between them.

"I also appreciate how patient you have been. And my sisters loved the tours through New Orleans." Erika leaned on his shoulder, the scent of her shampoo flooding his mind with memories of London. St. Louis. And last night. Making love, their bodies and scents and need mingling, taking them both to a higher level of satisfaction than he'd ever experienced.

Damn. He loved that. Loved that this smell made her present in his mind.

"Of course." He breathed, kissed her head, inhaled the scent of her hair and thought of their shower together.

Her breath puffed a little faster from her mouth. She nibbled her bottom lip and gestured to the screen. "May I ask what you are doing?"

Gervais hit Play, a game springing to life. "Well, I have to get a feel for who is out there. I have a team to build. So I may have to replace my current rookies with some of these guys."

Erika nodded. "And why is this so important to you? Why do you spend so much time on football when, according to the press, they are worth only a fraction of your overall portfolio?"

"Someone's been doing her research," he noted. Impressed.

"I was not joking when I told you that I am trying to figure out where to go from here. I am thinking through all possible paths." Her blue gaze locked on him. "Including the one you have proposed."

His chest ached with the need to convince her that was the best. But he restrained himself. Focused on her question.

"Why the focus on football?" he repeated, reaching into the popcorn bag for a piece to feed her. "My family is a lot like yours. They come with expectations. But I have my own expectations, and I've always wanted to carve out something that was all mine within the vast Reynaud holdings. Some success that I made myself, that was not handed to me. Does that make any sense?"

He presented her with the popcorn and she opened her lips. His touch lingered a bit longer than necessary against her soft mouth.

She chewed before she answered. "You want to stand on your own two legs?"

Gervais smiled inwardly. Her idiom use was so close. "Something like that. If I can stand on my own two feet, make this team into something…" His mind searched for the correct words.

"Then no one can take that away from you. It is yours alone."

Gervais nodded, stroking her arm. "Exactly. I imagine that's why you want your Master's in Nursing so badly. So that is holistically yours."

"Mmm," she said, tracing light lines on his chest.

"Very wise of you. You have been listening to me, I see."

Her touch stirred him. Heat rushed through his veins as he set aside the remote.

"We are more alike than you think." He curled an arm around her shoulders and drew her closer, his fingers skimming through her silky hair to the impossibly soft skin of her upper arm.

"Because we are both stubborn and independent?" She slid her finger into the knot of his tie and loosened the material.

"It's more than that." He wrenched the tie off, consigning the expensive Italian silk to the floor.

"We are both struggling to meet the expectations of too much helpful family?" She arched a pale brow at him, all the while fingering open buttons on his shirt.

The hell with waiting.

He slid an arm under her knees and lifted her up and onto his lap, straddling him. Her long sundress spilled over her thighs, covering her while exposing just the smallest hint of satin panties where she sat on his thighs.

"And we both need to lose ourselves in each other right now." His fingers sifted through her hair, seeking the ribbon that secured the halter top of her sundress.

"You are correct," she assured him, edging down his thighs so that their hips met.

Her breasts flattened to his chest.

A hungry groan tore from his throat.

He kissed her hard, his control fractured after so many days of thinking through every move with her, of strategizing this relationship like the most important deal of his life. Because while it was all that and more, Erika was also the hottest, most incredible woman he'd ever met, and he wanted her so badly he ached.

She met each hungry swipe of his tongue with soft sighs and teasing moans that threatened to send him right over the edge. Already, her fingers worked the fastening of his belt, her thighs squeezing his hips.

"This day has been too much," she admitted, her whispered confession one of the few times she'd confided her feelings. "I need you. This."

And he wanted to give it to her. Now and forever.

But he knew better than to rattle her with talk of forever. Understood she was still coming to terms with a future together. So he forced himself to be everything she needed right now.

Flicking free the tie at her neck, he edged away from the kiss just enough to admire the fall of the gauzy top away from her beautiful breasts. Her skin was so pale she almost glowed in the darkened theater, his tanned hands a dark shadow against her as he cupped the full weight of one breast.

Molding her to his palm, he teased his thumb across the pebbled tip, liking the way her hips thrust harder against his as he did. She was more sensitive than ever, the least little touch making her breath come faster. Making her release quicker.

Just thinking about that forced him to move faster, one hand skimming down her calf to slip beneath the hem of her long dress. He stroked her bare knee. Smoothed up her slender thigh. Skimmed the satin of panties already damp for him.

She cried out his name as he worked her through the thin fabric, coaxing an orgasm from her with just a few strokes. Her back arched as the tension pulsed through her in waves, her knees hugging him until the spasms slowed.

He didn't waste time searching out a condom, since they no longer needed one. He let her go just long enough to shove aside the placket of his pants and free his erection.

She took over then, her fingers curling the hard length and stroking up to the tip until his heart damn near beat its way out of his chest. He kissed her deeply, distracting her from her erotic mission, leaving him free to enter her.

And oh, damn.

The slick heat of her squeezed him, the scent of her skin and taste of her lips like a drug for his senses. He gripped her hips, guiding her where he wanted. Where he needed. And looking up at her in the half-light reflected from the dim screen, he could see that she was as lost as him. Her plump lips were moist and open, her eyes closed as she rode him, finding her pleasure with as much focus and intensity as him.

He must have said her name, because her eyes opened then. Her blue gaze locked on his.

And that did it.

More than any touch. Any kiss. Any sexy maneuver in the dark. Just having Erika right there with him drove him over the edge. The pleasure flared over his skin and up his spine, rocking him. He held on tight to her, surprised to realize she had found her own peak again right along with him, their bodies in perfect sync.

After the waves of pleasure began to fade and the sweat on their bodies cooled, he stroked her spine through that long veil of her hair, savoring the feel of her in his arms, her warm weight so welcome in his lap. He wanted her every night. Wanted to be the one to take care of her and ease her. Pleasure her.

But even as his feelings surged, he could tell she was pulling back. Throwing up a seemingly impenetrable wall of ice as she edged back and tugged her dress into place. Her family's arrival had shaken her. Awakened an instinct to define herself in opposition to their expectations.

A part of him understood that. And was damn proud of her, too. But that same urge that motivated her to stand her ground, meet her parents and family dead-on, might also be the reason he felt frozen out.

The more he thought about it, the more real seemed the idea of losing not just his children, but her, too.

And as if she sensed his thoughts, she got to her feet. "Gervais, my family's here, so I would appreciate it if we didn't sleep together with them nearby."

"Seriously?" He propped himself up on his elbows.

"I know it may seem silly with the babies on the way, but…them being here? I need space."

He studied her face, her platinum-blond hair tumbling around her shoulders. "Damn it, Erika, all I've done is honor your need for space, taking cues off you."

"A few short days. Less than a month. And you call that space? Time?" Her throat moved. "Clearly we have very different ideas about taking our time. Maybe we don't understand each other nearly as well as you think."

Frustration fired inside him as he felt victory slip away word by word. He tugged on his pants, all the while searching for the right words and coming up short.

Not that it mattered, since before he could speak, she'd left the room. The click of that door made it clear.

She was running scared and he wasn't welcome to join her now.

If ever.

Twelve

The excitement of the fans at the home Hurricanes game was dwarfed in comparison to the buzz going on in the owners' box.

Erika sat against the leather chair, taking it all in, her heart in her throat after the way she'd left things with Gervais last night. But the way he made her feel scared her down to her toes. He made her want too much at a time when she had to be more careful than ever about protecting her heart and her future.

Gramps Leon called out to the Mitras clan. "Did Erika tell you how the Reynauds came into their fortune?"

"No, Leon, she hasn't shared much of anything with us. We'd love to know. American origin stories are so fascinating," Hilda said darkly, shooting her a daggered look across the spread of shrimp gumbo and decadent brownies. Erika rolled her eyes, moving closer to the glass to get a look at the field. Somehow, this game she had disliked so much was starting to make sense to her.

"Grampa Leon, we all know that story," Fiona said with a light laugh, her hands wringing together. She was nervous but Erika couldn't tell why.

"Yes, but the beautiful princesses and queen haven't. And they want to. Who am I to deny them that?" he said with a wink at Hilda, whose face was already turning into a toothy grin.

"It was a high-stakes poker game. My surly old Cajun ancestor was sweating as he stared at his hand of cards. The stakes were incredibly high, you see," Gramps Leon began, leaning on his knees.

"What were the stakes, Leon?" Queen Arnora asked, on her best behavior, since Erika had been emphatic with her mother that histrionics would not be tolerated. The babies were Erika and Gervais's, not potential little royal pawns.

Arnora had vowed she simply wanted to bond with their expanding family and was thrilled over impending grandparenthood.

"If my riverboat grandpa won, he would get a ship out of the deal. But if he lost, he would have to sign a non-compete. And stay working for the tyrant captain who kept him away from home for months on end. Needless to say, the cards laid out right for him and he won the first ship in the fleet. The Reynaud family empire was born. Just like that." He snapped his fingers, eyes alight with a new audience to entertain. "The rest is history. The family has been successful ever since. Especially my grandboys."

King Bjorn inclined his head. "You feel responsible for your grandchildren's success?"

"Yessir, King Bjorn. I'm proud of all of those boys. Feel like I practically raised them myself. Though I kind of did," Gramps Leon wheezed, eyes drifting to Theo, who shrank in the back corner, "My son almost made it big…eh. No matter. My grandboys did. That's what matters in the end."

Erika watched as Theo fidgeted with his drink, balling up a cocktail napkin in his right fist. She knew he hadn't been the best father, but a small part of her felt sympathy for him.

"And what did all your grandchildren do?" Arnora asked lightly, swirling the champagne in her glass.

Erika had often wondered how her mother had such ease with others but not as much with her children. Her mom took her role as a royal, a liaison to the world, seriously. Erika looked around at the Reynaud family and saw their bond, but not only that. She saw their relaxed air. The way they kept life…real. Connected. She wanted that for her children, as well.

And yet she'd pushed her babies' father away the night before out of fear of living like her parents.

Gramps Leon's dark eyes gleamed with pride and affection. "Well, you know Gervais bought his own team. I figure they'll make it big soon the way that boy works. And Dempsey is the youngest coach in the league's history. Henri is already a franchise quarterback looking for his first championship ring. Even Jean-Pierre is doing good things as a quarterback for that northern Yankee team. Where is he again?"

Theo cleared his throat. "New York. Jean-Pierre is the starting quarterback for the New York Gladiators." Pride pierced his words, and he lifted his eyes to meet Leon's. So he did care, Erika thought. It was just masked.

She wished it was that easy to tell what was going on with Gervais. Nothing he'd said so far betrayed any level of an emotional depth. Just sex. But that wasn't enough for her. And that was the reason she hadn't been able to help but pull away the night before.

Last night when she'd gone to him, she'd believed he might really care for her. Sure, the sex was great and he wanted to provide for their children. But she'd started to think that he also genuinely liked her, sex and children aside.

Before then, she'd been so sure of him. Of the decision she was close to making.

As she sat in the owners' box again, she realized she couldn't stop replaying seeing the bed empty when she woke up, knowing it was her fault for pushing him away but not knowing what she could have done differently. Erika would have continued to analyze the situation if it wasn't for the approach of Liv, her sister. The one that had been through the sex tape fiasco.

The scandal had almost cost Liv everything.

Liv narrowed her gunmetal eyes at Erika, pinning her. She sat next to Erika, hands firmly grasping the wineglass's stem. The smell of alcohol assaulted Erika's sense of smell, turning her stomach sour.

"Sister," she said lazily, "this family…"

Erika straightened, finishing the sentence for her. "Is filled with wonderful, loving people."

Liv nodded solemnly. "Yes. And how do you say—American royalty?"

Erika's eyes remained out toward the field, toward where Gervais stood with a reporter giving an interview, players and photographers around them. She would not be dignifying her sister's comment with a response.

"All I am trying to say, dear sister, is that you need to be here. You could be royalty for real if you did." Liv's words, spoken in a hushed tone, had a bit of a slur to them.

"That's not what matters to me. What matters is—" But the words caught in her throat as she watched Gervais get hit by two men locked in a tackle. Gervais was on the sidelines, knocked to his feet, his bare skull slamming back into the ground. Hard. Tackled on the sidelines with no equipment.

She barely registered what the Mitrases or the Reynauds were doing. In an instant, the panic that stayed her breath and speech was replaced by a need to move. A need for action. The damn need to get to his side.

Pushing her way to the door that led down to the stands, she ran smack into James, the security guard who had first alerted them that the whole Mitras clan was arriving. He stood at the door to the tunnels leading through the bowels of the stadium and out onto the field. His credentials were clipped to his jacket, a communication piece in his ear. "Princess, I am afraid I can't allow you onto the field. Please wait here. I promise to keep you updated about Mr. Reynaud."

James put a hand on her shoulder. Consoling? Or to restrain? Either way, it didn't matter to her because this man kept her from Gervais.

Years of practice drills during her time in the military pressed her muscles into action. Without sparing a second thought, she grabbed his hand and bent back his pinkie. A minor move but one that could quickly drive a man to his knees if she pushed farther. "James, I am a nurse, but I am also former military. I can flip you onto your back in a heartbeat and you cannot—will not—fight me because I am pregnant. Now, we can do this simply or we can make this difficult, but one way or another, I am going to Gervais."

James's eyes narrowed, then he exhaled through gritted teeth. "I could lose my job for this." He shook his head, rolling his eyes. "But come with me. You'll need my credentials to get through to the field."

She bit her lip hard in relief. "Thank you."

"Um, ma'am, could you let go of my pinkie?"

"Oh." She blinked fast, having forgotten she'd even still held him pinned. She released his hand and stepped back.

Wincing, he shook his hand. "Follow me."

She followed him through the corridors, urging him to go faster and barely allowing herself to breathe until she saw Gervais with her own eyes. He waved off his personal security team as soon as she came into sight, his face twisted in pain as the team doctor shone a small flashlight in front of his eyes, checking his pupils.

Her medical training came to the fore and took in his pale face. He sat on the ground, upright, and was not swaying. His respiration was even, steady. Reassuring signs. Her heart slowed from a gallop. He would need a more thorough exam, certainly, but at least he was conscious. Cognizant.

"Gervais? Are you okay?" Erika knelt beside him, then turned to the team's doctor, her voice calm and collected now. "Is he all right?"

On the field beside him, the game continued, the fans cheering over a play while Erika's focus remained on Gervais and all that mattered to her.

"I'm fine," Gervais growled, then winced, pressing his hand to the back of his head.

The doctor tucked away his flashlight into his bag. "He's injured, no question, given the size of that goose egg coming up. Probably a concussion. He should go to the emergency room to be checked over."

"Then let us go." She barked the command at the doctor. Meanwhile, the game had resumed playing, and she trailed behind him.

As she stepped out of the arena with Gervais, leaving her family behind, reality crashed into her. Her heart was in her throat for this man. He was the father of her children. But she barely knew him and already he'd turned her world upside down. She felt as if she, too, had taken a blow to the head and her judgment was scrambled. How could she care so much so soon?

What was she doing here? She had started to love him, but maybe she just loved the surface image. Maybe she'd done what her family had done—just looked at the surface. After all, he'd offered no feelings, no emotions to her. Just convenient arrangements for their children and sex. His marriage proposal had never included mention of love.

And she couldn't settle for less than everything from him, just as she wanted to give him her all.

What if in spite of all logic, she had fallen in love with him and he could never offer her his full heart?

There were only a few times in his life that Gervais had felt extreme elation and intense concern all at the same time. This was certainly being added to that tally.

Later that night as he stretched out in his own bed, Erika hovering, he was still replaying that moment Erika had rushed out to him. His head throbbed but his memories were crystal clear.

Watching Erika care enough about him to rush to his side filled him with a renewed purpose. He'd been blown away and more than a little unnerved watching her rush to his side, somehow having persuaded James to let her through security and out onto the field.

Make no mistake, he always wanted her there. By his side. But he didn't want any harm to come to her or their children, either. The thought of harm befalling her or their children by her own rash actions gnawed at him. The security was there for a reason. God, she was everything to him. Everything. And he wasn't sure how he could have missed out on realizing the depth of that.

They could be so good together, but it also seemed as if the risk of her pulling back was at an all-time high. All of her interactions with him since the CT scan came back had been rigid. Formalized. As if she was a nurse doing a job, not a woman tending to her lover.

That reaction clapped him upside the head harder than the wall of a football player that had crashed into him. Her reactions didn't add up. She had been so upset on the sidelines, so freaked out about what was happening to him. And now she was answering in snippets of sentences. He didn't want to upset her more, or keep her awake all night. But his family had been in and out of the room for hours. It was nearing morning before he finally had a moment alone with her.

His head throbbed far more from this situation than his minor concussion.

Propped up on the bed, he quietly said, "How did you get James to let you join me on the field?"

She flushed the most lovely shade of pink, her hand fidgeting with her blond hair draped over her shoulder. "I used some of my military skills to persuade him. Nothing extreme, given my condition, of course, just a small but painful maneuver."

"Seriously? Apparently, I need to have you train my security."

"And give away my secrets?" She gave him a princess-like annoyed scoff. "I think not. Besides, he should not have tried to keep me from you."

"While I find that sexy on one level, you have to be careful and think about the babies. What if you had been hurt?"

She shrugged, looking him square in the eye. "I was careful. You are the injured one. Now, relax. You may not be stressed but you have to stay awake. Do as the doctor instructed or I am taking you back to the hospital."

He felt the prickles of her emotions. Had to change the direction. Bring it back to breezy. Shooting her a sly smile, he said, "We could have sex. That would keep me awake."

"You're supposed to rest." Eyes narrowing with annoyance, Erika crossed her arms.

"Then take advantage of me. I'll just lie back and be very still." He closed his eyes, then half opened one of them to look at her. Hoping to elicit some sort of response out of her. Hoping to see that radiant smile spread across her face. Damn. He loved that smile.

"Oh, you think you are funny. But I am not laughing right now. You are injured and I am here to make sure you take care of yourself."

"You could tie me up so I don't get too…boisterous."

"Boisterous? Now, that's an interesting word choice and a challenge. But sadly, for your own health, I will have to hold strong against your boisterous charms. Let us play cards." There was no jest in her voice.

"Cards? Strip poker, maybe."

"No, thank you."

"Then I'll pass on the cards. I gotta confess, my vision is a little blurry." He held up his hand, trying to focus on his fingers. A dull ache pulled at him.

Turning, practically out the door to the room, Erika said, "I should get the doctor."

"The doctor has checked me. I've had an X-ray and MRI and CT scan. I'm fine. Concussed, but nothing the players don't face all the time. I'm not going to be a wimp in front of my team."

"They wear helmets."

"I have a thick head. Just ask anyone I work with. Or those I don't work with." He tried his best to crack that smile wide-open, but Erika's face was as solemn as ever. She was shutting him out and he didn't understand why.

"I'm not laughing."

"You want to be serious? Then let's be serious. Erika, I want you to move in with me. Hell, to be honest, I want you to marry me, but I will settle for you moving in here. Go to school here. Let's be together. Life is complicated enough. Let's enjoy more popcorn dates and sex in the screen room and every other room in this place. And in my cars. I have many, you know." The declaration was earnest. He wanted her. For now. Forever. And not just because they were having children together.

Erika slammed her hand on the desk, a quiet rage burning in her fine, regal features. "I am still not laughing, Gervais. We cannot build a relationship on sex. I need something meaningful. I have fought so hard to build a life for myself, to be seen as someone more than ornamental. A royal jewel in the crown meant to bear an heir to the line, defunct or not."

"Erika. It's not like that. I don't think of you as a crown jewel." Gervais searched her face, trying to understand her.

"All you have done since I told you I was pregnant is press for marriage. I have worked hard to gain my independence, my happiness, and I will fight for my children, as well. They deserve something more."

"Erika, I—" Gervais, the man who always had a plan, stammered, fighting for words.

Tears glistened in her eyes, but she stood tall, her shoulders braced as she backed away. "I will wake one of your brothers. It is morning anyway." Erika turned, was already to the threshold and then gone before he could even think of words to delay her.

He had botched this chance to win her over. And what a helluva time to realize just how much he loved her, this proud, strong woman. He loved her intelligence, her passion, even her stubbornness. He adored every hair on her head.

He loved her so deeply he knew any fear of repeating his father's mistakes would not happen. Gervais loved Erika. Real love. The kind that he knew damn well was rare in this world.

And in rushing her, he may have ruined his chance to have her.

As Erika let her feet dangle over the edge of the dock, she focused her attention out on the lake's waters. The late-afternoon sun cast golden shimmers on the surface of the water.

She felt as if the whole day had been a training exercise. Nothing had felt real to her. Since she stormed out of Gervais's room last night, Erika had felt disoriented.

The problem was simple. Despite logic and reason, she was madly in love with Gervais. These past few days had proved how easy it would be to fall into a routine together.

But they had also shown her how difficult it would be for them to become more than…well, whatever this was.

A breeze stirred her loose blond hair, pushing strands in front of her eyes. Though it was humid, and the bugs played a loud symphony, she was comforted by the noises, smells and sights of this foreign land. It was starting to feel a bit like home. Another confusing feeling to muddle through.

The wind gusted stronger, stirring the marsh grass into a beautiful shudder. Boats zipped a ways off from the dock, and she watched the wakes crest and crash into each other.

It was practically silent, except for the boats and bugs. Everyone had gone. She'd packed her family into their limos, watched from the dock until the landscape of New Orleans swallowed them up.

The Reynauds were gone on a day trip. Theo's idea, actually. He'd even taken Gramps with them. All the Reynaud men, save for Jean-Pierre, on one trip in one spot. Probably something that didn't happen too often.

Inching backward on the dock, she pulled her knees to her chest. Erika was at a complete loss of what to do.

If only it could be as simple as the word *love*. She loved her children. She loved their father. But she still didn't know if he loved her back. On the one hand they hadn't known each other long, yet she was certain of her feelings. She needed him to be just as sure.

Her head spun with it all.

And her heart twisted.

She knew what she wanted, but it didn't make sense. She wanted to say to hell with logic and stay here with Gervais. To move in. To love him. To build their family together and pray it would all work out.

Footsteps echoed along the dock, startling her an instant before she heard Gervais's deep voice.

"You did not leave with your family."

Whipping her head up, she took him in. Fully. And a lump formed in the back of her throat.

"Did you think that I would do that without saying goodbye to you?" She would never have done something so cruel. Not after what she felt for him and all they'd been through together.

His chin tipped, the moonlight beaming around him. "Is this your farewell, then?"

"I am not going home with them."

He pressed further, drawing near to her. "And to school in the UK?"

Decision upon decision. Layer upon layer. "Do you think I should?"

"I want you to stay here but I cannot make this decision for you. I don't want to rush you."

His answer surprised her. "I expected you to try to persuade me."

"I've made my wishes clear. I want you to stay. I want us to build a life. But I can see you're afraid. I'll wait as long as you need." He knelt to her level, touched her face with his steady hand.

She bristled. "I am not afraid. I am wary. There is a difference."

"Is there?"

She churned over his words. "If you want to mince words in translation, then all right. I am afraid of making the wrong choice and having our children suffer because of it."

"And you think we are the wrong choice?"

"I think that I love you." There. It was out there. This was how she'd make her decision. Let him know exactly where she stood.

"I know that I love you."

She swallowed hard and blinked back tears, barely daring to believe what she was hearing. "You do?"

"I absolutely do. No question in my mind." His voice wrapped around her heart like a blanket, soothing and private and intimate all at once. He was...everything.

"I believe you and I want so very much to believe that will be enough."

"Then be willing to challenge that warrior spirit of yours and fight for what we feel for each other."

Fight? Erika had been used to fighting for the things that mattered to her. Maybe this battleground wasn't so foreign, after all. "Fight."

"Yes, stay here. Get to know me. Let me get to know you. And every day for the rest of our lives we'll get to know more and more about each other. That's how it works."

"I will move in with you?" The idea was tantalizing this time and she wondered why she had dismissed it so readily before. Out of pride? The thought of losing herself in her family again reminded her how hard she had fought for her freedom to live her life. And truth be told, she wanted to live here, in this fascinating town with this even more fascinating man. She wanted to give her children a family life like the Reynauds.

She wanted Gervais.

Looking over his shoulder, her eyes took in the mansion.

"Yes. If that is what you wish."

"I can go to school here?" She hadn't even looked into programs around here, but she could. There were ways to make this work. Now that she knew, beyond a shadow of a doubt, that he loved her.

"Yes. If that is what you wish," he said again, those final words making it clear he understood her need for control over her life.

"We bring up our children here?"

"Yes, and in your country, too, whenever possible, if you wish. And most of all I hope that you'll do all of that as my wife." He squeezed her hand, brought her to a standing position.

Erika looked up at him, reading his eyes. "As simple as that?"

Pulling her into him, he shook his head. "Not simple at all. But very logical."

"Love as a logical emotion?" The idea tickled her.

"The love I feel for you defies any logic it's so incredible. It fills every corner of me. But I do know that my plan to work harder than I've ever worked at anything in my life to make you happy? Yes, that will be a plan I'm not leaving to chance. I will make that a conscious choice. But if you need time to decide—"

She cupped his face in her hands. "I do not need any more time at all. Yes."

"Yes?" Lines of excitement and relief tugged at his face.

She breathed in the scent of him, feeling balanced and renewed. Sure, for the first time in weeks, that this was where she was supposed to be.

"Yes, I love you and I will move in with you. I will go to school here. I will have our children here. And most of all, yes, I will marry you."

He gathered her closer, a sigh of relief racking his big, strong body. "Thank God."

"How did I ever get so lucky to meet and fall for such a wonderfully stubborn man?"

"We knew that day we met."

"In spite of logic."

"Instincts. With instincts like ours, we will make a winning team—" he rested his mouth on hers "—for life."

* * * * *

MILLS & BOON®

Desire

PASSIONATE AND DRAMATIC LOVE STORIES

A sneak peek at next month's titles...

In stores from 11th February 2016:

- **The CEO's Unexpected Child** – Andrea Laurence
  and **Snowbound with the Boss** – Maureen Child

- **The SEAL's Secret Heirs** – Kat Cantrell *and*
  His Secretary's Surprise Fiancé – Joanne Rock

- **The Rancher's Marriage Pact** – Kristi Gold *and*
  One Secret Night, One Secret Baby – Charlene Sands

Available at WHSmith, Tesco, Asda, Eason, Amazon and Apple

Just can't wait?
Buy our books online a month before they hit the shops!
visit www.millsandboon.co.uk

These books are also available in eBook format!

0216/51

MILLS & BOON®

Let us take you back in time with our Medieval Brides...

The Novice Bride – Carol Townend

The Dumont Bride – Terri Brisbin

The Lord's Forced Bride – Anne Herries

The Warrior's Princess Bride – Meriel Fuller

The Overlord's Bride – Margaret Moore

Templar Knight, Forbidden Bride – Lynna Banning

Order yours at
www.millsandboon.co.uk/medievalbrides